CARRIER

These are the stories of the Carrier Battle Group Fourteen—
a force including a supercarrier, amphibious unit, guided
missile cruiser, and destroyer. And these are the novels that
capture the blistering reality of international combat. Excit-
ing. Authentic. Explosive.

CARRIER . . . The smash debut thriller about the ultimate
military nightmare: the takeover of a U.S. Intelligence ship.

VIPER STRIKE . . . A renegade Chinese fighter group
penetrates Thai airspace—and launches a full-scale invasion.

ARMAGEDDON MODE . . . With India and Pakistan on
the verge of nuclear destruction, the Carrier Battle Group
Fourteen must prevent a final showdown.

FLAME-OUT . . . The Soviet Union is reborn in a military
takeover—and their strike force shows no mercy.

MAELSTROM . . . The Soviet occupation of Scandinavia
leads the Carrier Battle Group Fourteen into conventional
weapons combat—and possible all-out war.

COUNTDOWN . . . Carrier Battle Group Fourteen must
prevent the deployment of Russian submarines. The problem
is: They have nukes.

AFTERBURN . . . Carrier Battle Group Fourteen receives
orders to enter the Black Sea—in the middle of a Russian
civil war.

continued on next page . . .

ALPHA STRIKE . . . When American and Chinese interests collide in the South China Sea, the superpowers risk waging a Third World War.

ARCTIC FIRE . . . A Russian splinter group have occupied the Aleutian Islands off the coast of Alaska—in the ultimate invasion of U.S. soil.

ARSENAL . . . Magruder and his crew are trapped between Cuban revolutionaries . . . and a U.S. power play that's spun wildly out of control.

NUKE ZONE . . . When a nuclear missile is launched against the U.S. Sixth fleet, Magruder must face a frightening question: In an age of computer warfare, how do you tell friends from enemies?

CHAIN OF COMMAND . . . Magruder enters the jungles of Vietnam, looking for answers about his missing father. Little does he know that another bloody war is about to be unleashed—with his fleet caught in the crosshairs!

BRINK OF WAR . . . Friendly war games with the Russians take a deadly turn, and Carrier Battle Group Fourteen must prevent war from erupting in the skies. Little do they know—that's just what someone wants!

TYPHOON SEASON . . . An American yacht is attacked by a Chinese helicopter in international waters, and Carrier Battle Group Fourteen is called to the front lines of what may be the start of a war between the superpowers . . .

book fifteen

CARRIER
Enemies

KEITH DOUGLASS

JOVE BOOKS, NEW YORK

If you purchased this book without a cover, you should be aware that this book is stolen property. It was reported as "unsold and destroyed" to the publisher and neither the author nor the publisher has received any payment for this "stripped book."

This is a work of fiction. Names, characters, places, and incidents are either the product of the author's imagination or are used fictitiously, and any resemblance to actual persons, living or dead, business establishments, events, or locales is entirely coincidental.

CARRIER: ENEMIES

A Jove Book / published by arrangement with
the author

PRINTING HISTORY
Jove edition / August 2000

All rights reserved.
Copyright © 2000 by Penguin Putnam Inc.
This book may not be reproduced in whole or part,
by mimeograph or any other means, without permission.
For information address: The Berkley Publishing Group,
a division of Penguin Putnam Inc.,
375 Hudson Street, New York, New York 10014.

The Penguin Putnam Inc. World Wide Web site address is
http://www.penguinputnam.com

ISBN: 0-515-12869-4

A JOVE BOOK®
Jove Books are published by The Berkley Publishing Group,
a division of Penguin Putnam Inc.,
375 Hudson Street, New York, New York 10014.
JOVE and the "J" design
are trademarks belonging to Penguin Putnam Inc.

PRINTED IN THE UNITED STATES OF AMERICA

10 9 8 7 6 5 4 3 2 1

ONE

Wednesday, 3 May

Tomcat 101
The Greece/Macedonia border
21000 feet
2300 local (GMT −2)

Greek Captain Antipodes Spiros flipped his American-built Tomcat into a tight barrel roll. He tilted his head back, braced against the ejection seat and stared up through the canopy above—no, below—no, above—hell, it was outside, that was all that mattered. Swaths of green earth that ran between ancient ruins and brown craggy low hills swapped places with a sky so blue it hurt his eyes. Spiros squinted his eyes until the colors ran together, until everything outside his cockpit dissolved into streamers of color and light.

"Enough!" his backseater howled.

Spiros ignored him, concentrating on the delightfully befuddled feeling creeping into his inner ear. A few more rolls and he'd be . . . *there*. It hit him all at once, the dizzying disorientation as the fluid in his ears roiled and bubbled against the delicate aural bones. He switched his gaze to the instruments, thoroughly disoriented, and eased the aircraft back into level flight.

Rolling, rolling, his mind insisted. *Still turning, banking now, descending, ascending.* A series of confused and inconsistent messages, each one increasingly urgent, each one dead wrong. Spiros watched the artificial horizon, the altimeter and accelerometer, and let his instruments convince him that he was in level flight.

"Why do you do this?" his backseater demanded. "Every time, every flight. If I vomit, you will clean it. Not me."

Spiros chuckled. Irritating his backseater was just an added bonus. He could have explained, he supposed. It wouldn't have hurt him to do so, nor would it have kept him from rolling himself sick at some point during every flight. Little did his backseater know that it was as much to keep his whining guy-in-back safe as it was to amuse a bored pilot.

Barreling his brains out came under the heading of preventive training. It was a habit he'd adopted during Tomcat pipeline at an American air base when a close friend of his had inadvertently stalled out, lost control of his aircraft in a flat spin, and been unable to recover. Spiros had listened over tactical as Kapi had screamed out his corrective actions, sobbing and wailing, damning the horizon that rotated around him and defied his Kapi's best efforts to stabilize his aircraft. Finally, the backseater had punched them out, but they'd been too close to the ground. Neither had survived.

During the solemn debrief that'd followed, the IP—instructor-pilot—had been brutal in his conclusions.

"He got fixed on the horizon. His instruments were telling him the truth, but once you get disoriented, you can convince yourself real easily that the instruments are wrong. You start going with what you see instead of what the aircraft is telling you. Then you lose the bubble. Then you make an uncontrolled descent to the ground." The IP had hammered out the narrative in a hard Texas twang, his voice a monotone. He'd stopped then, stared at the deadly quiet class.

"Every man in here believes it won't happen to him.

Well, it will. At some point, you're going to get disoriented. You might have a head cold, an inner ear infection, or you might just be doing your damnedest to get away from some MiG on your ass. Whatever the cause, you're going to lose it. If you're not prepared for it, if you don't believe what your instruments are telling you, you're going to die just as surely as if you'd gotten a Sidewinder up your ass."

In the days after that, the IPs had hit them particularly hard with in-flight emergencies, spins, loss of power, everything they'd been over in the preceding fourteen weeks. Haunted by the memories of Kapi's last transmission, Spiros had sworn that he'd never, ever forget the lesson.

Hence the barrel rolls, the spins, constant aerobatics. By now he'd learned how to recognize when he was disoriented, how to rely on the instruments. And he'd come to believe that whatever else might happened to him while he was a pilot, he wouldn't kill himself and his backseater by losing the bubble.

Mercifully, the RIO was too busy trying not to puke to continue berating him. If Spiros ignored the gagging sound, he could almost believe he was in a single-seater aircraft, alone in the sky, unencumbered by a wingman or lumbering transport to escort, with a straightforward mission to execute, one that required little more than what he loved to do best—flying.

Even the surveillance center was leaving him alone tonight. While the ground radar site was Greece's first line of defense in the ongoing conflict with Macedonia, it could be a real pain in the ass for a pilot, particularly if the ground control intercept officer got nervous over a few barrel rolls. From the way they complained, you'd think that there was no need for airborne patrols.

But while the GCI's long-range radar covered more sky

than the radar mounted in this export model F-14 Tomcat, it had one major disadvantage. Contacts showed up as green-painted lozenges on scope, accompanied by an IFF identification if they were carrying the proper transponder. It might even break with a mode four IFF code, indicating that it was a friendly aircraft, a military one at that.

But even the finest radar could not put eyes on target, could not check the status of a wing loadout nor verify that a mode four aircraft was not actually an enemy fighter. While mode four was supposedly an infallible method of telling friends from foe, there were still instances in which daily crypto codes had been stolen and given to the other side.

Nowhere was the problem of fraternal treason more difficult than between Greece and Macedonia. The two countries were brothers, bound by blood ties stretching back thousands of centuries, into the mists of time before even Alexander the Great. In 1991, a misguided United Nations had recognized a small landlocked area the size of Belgium as the Republic of Macedonia. Spiros snorted in disgust. Macedonia *was* part of Greece, no matter how she manipulated the sentiments of foreign nations into thinking otherwise, no matter how the land had been apportioned following the world war. Even the name—Macedonia—belonged to *Greece*, not to some part of the artificial state that had been called Yugoslavia.

Why couldn't they at least call it Skopja, the correct ancient name for the region? Or some name that incorporated Macedonia? That had been the Greek government's latest capitulation in the face of overwhelming international pressure.

Personally, Spiros found that as much of an insult as calling it the Republic of Macedonia. No, it should go by its proper name, Skopje.

"Fifteen minutes," his backseater called out, evidently

now sufficiently recovered to resume his tiresome reminders. As if the fuel gauge were not mounted right in front of Spiros, as if the pilot could not see the seven-day clock ticking off the minutes. He knew they had fifteen minutes—fourteen now—before they commenced their return to base. He'd given himself just enough time to completely recover from the barrel rolls before he'd be on final approach. Spiros clicked his mike twice in acknowledgment and returned to his train of thought.

Not that it was entitled to independence anyway. Aside from the fact that it was historically wrong, it set a dangerous precedent. A large portion of the Greek coast on the Aegean was referred to as Greek Macedonia. This upstart mongrel country would soon make a move on that as well—indeed, they'd started already, claiming that Greece was abusing its ethnic Macedonian citizens.

The whole conflict had exploded when the smaller nations of the UN, each with its own independent agenda aimed at ensuring the rights of smaller countries, had began funneling weapons and aircraft into Macedonia. A few fighter aircraft, some anti-air batteries, and within a few months the renegades had staged a threatening presence on the border along Greek Macedonia. Access to the Aegean Sea, that's what they wanted. And these patrols along the border were designed to ensure that the rebels didn't get it.

As if a pilot ought to have to care about history. All Spiros wanted to do was fly, strap this sweet aircraft onto his ass once or twice a day and slip the surly bonds of earth. There were other people whose job it was to worry about history.

The general, for instance.

Spiros slid the Tomcat into a tight, hard turn, watching the stars pirouette above him. Yes, the general understood history. But in fact, if the truth be known, Spiros suspected that the general was more interested in making history than understanding it.

"Tomcat 101, requests a status report." The voice of the ground intercept controller interrupted Spiros's train of thought. He sighed and toggled the microphone on. Always, there was someone who wanted to interrupt his moments of communing with the open sky.

"Ground, 101. All systems normal. No contacts." Spiros waited, knowing that the inquiry had been merely a preliminary to a request from the controller.

"Roger, 101. Request you vector 230 at best speed to intercept contact designated possible hostile," the controller said. "Ground control radar to the north holds contact and will provide locating data."

Spiros perked up. Actual work to do—now that would be a change of pace. After weeks of chasing radar ghosts or some flight of fancy on the part of the ground controller, a real contact, even if it only proved to be a commercial air contact off course, would be worthwhile.

He shoved the throttles forward to full military power and put the Tomcat into a gentle climb. Altitude was always a good thing to have plenty of, and in this case, it would increase his radar range. "How far away is it?" he asked, studying his own radar scope. No sign of anything so far, but that didn't mean it wasn't there. This particular Tomcat's radar set was notoriously unreliable, as bad as the rag tag airframes the Macedonians flew.

"Sixty miles," Ground replied. "Contact is on heading 050 making 80 knots over ground."

Eighty knots. Not a fighter aircraft, then. Probably a helicopter, maybe a corporate or news camera team that had decided there was no need to file a flight plan ahead of time. Or maybe a Macedonian combat helo, making one of its rare nighttime forays into Greece, dropping off provocateurs and spies. Not that they flew that often at night . . . no, probably a news helo. ACN had established a particularly visible presence along the border, and seemed to feel that it had the right to fly anywhere and anytime it chose, with no regard for proper flight plans.

Well, they would learn differently tonight. The entire span of airspace along the border between Skopje and Greece was tightly controlled, ostensibly as a matter of safety of flight. In reality, everyone knew that the air corridor control measures were designed to prevent freedom fighters from reinforcing and to stifle the little economic activity that there was in Macedonia. Everything had to be routed through official Greek channels, absolutely everything.

"Roger, ground. 101, vectoring to intercept now." Spiro toggled his radar control selector to the widest range possible, waiting for his first glimpse of the helicopter.

Tavista Air Base, northern Greece
2310 local (GMT −2)

Two hundred miles away, at the ground facility in Greece, General Dimitri Arkady was weighing the possibilities. In all probability, the helicopter contact—and that's what it appeared to be, based on its speed—was either an international news team or part of UN forces in the area. Both sets of intruders were as unwelcome as the plague.

Why was it so difficult for other countries in the world to understand the nature of the problem with Macedonia? Surely many others of them had ethnic enclaves within their own nations, small communities of zealots that were at odds with most of the people? It was an internal matter, purely internal. A Greek problem that could be solved by

Greeks without outside intervention. No edict from the UN could change that.

He sighed, contemplating the problem of busybodies on the international scene. No sooner had the first news photos hit the wires than the United Nations had begun passing resolutions. Each one was aimed at creating the illusion that the UN had power to force the parties to a settlement, that the collective wisdom of the states of the world could solve this problem of nationalism.

No matter that many of them were experiencing similar problems within their own borders. In fact, that was all the more incentive for other nations to advocate a UN presence in Greece. With the meager UN forces tied up meddling in Greek affairs, there was less chance that they'd be dispatched to deal with other problems. Like the Kurds in Toronto. Like the Indians and Mexico. Like Taiwan and China.

No, instead they were in Greece, ranged along the border between Macedonia and the rest of the country, spending the UN member–nation contributions on a problem they couldn't solve.

And wasn't that the problem that most often faced the UN these days? There were no global threats, not unless you counted China, still the sleeping giant, barely flexing her muscles in the Pacific Rim now. Or the United States, although the latter was often shocked to discover that the rest of the world regarded her as a threat on par with the former Soviet Union.

No, there were truly no world threats. Thus, to justify their own existence, the world's militaries tried to insert themselves in places that they didn't belong. Yes, there was a place for the United Nations, when world powers such as Germany or the Soviet Union threatened with overwhelming force to destabilize the rest of the world, or when states disintegrated into warring nations and factions. Then, perhaps, an outside adjudicator of the claims and merits of each side might be needed.

But not for a matter such as this. Not for internal matters, no.

And particularly not for Greece.

"Make certain the pilot obtains a visual identification on this contact," General Arkady said. "In fact, have him execute a close pass on the contact. A very close pass. It's time we made our displeasure evident to these intruders." He glanced over at the ground controller to make sure he understood what the general intended.

The ground controller nodded. He picked up the microphone and called 101.

Tomcat 101
The Greece/Macedonia border
21000 feet
2315 local (GMT −2)

Now this was more like it. Not only VID, but a fly-by as well. Ah yes, the general's intent was perfectly clear, at least to Spiros. Time to shake things up a little bit with something besides aerobatics. At least this would give his backseater something to do besides whine and complain.

Spiros clicked the mike twice to acknowledge the orders. He could see the helicopter now, a faint blur on the horizon. Ungainly, a collection of flying parts that had no business being airborne together.

Well, he'd show that pilot just what it meant to be an aviator. He made a slight correction in the course, flying by visual rather than radar now, and nudged the Tomcat into afterburner.

ACN Helo 7
642 feet
2318 local (GMT −2)

ACN correspondent Pamela Drake listened to the argument raging within the helicopter. Everyone was shouting, not because emotions were running high, but because it was the only way to be heard over the distinctive sound of the helicopter blades. So far, she'd heard the argument cycle through four familiar arguments, and she was waiting for the fifth one to surface on schedule.

It wasn't that she had no interest in the argument, not at all. It was just that she'd been through it so many times, had heard both sides of each question repeatedly thrashed out, and was tired of it. In the end, she had no real opinion on the conflict or the merits of the arguments between Macedonia and Greece. There were merits to both sides, and problems with each position as well.

In the end, it didn't matter. Her job was to report the news, not make it.

Although, she had to admit there'd been times in the not-so-distant past when it seemed that she was part of the story rather than her network's most aggressive, on-the-spot international reporter. Like in Cuba, where she'd been taken hostage by the military in revolt. And Turkey, were she'd been the one to spot the first signs of the subterfuge by Russia. And other times as well, too many to count.

She sighed, shifted in her seat, and listened to the other two correspondents move on to the next point. They were glancing at her occasionally, as though wondering why she did not join one side or the other. Hell, even the camera guy had an opinion on the conflict, for what it was worth.

"Creating a state requires the consent of the people,"

Brett Fallon said. He stabbed his finger at Mike Carne, the French reporter along with them. "You study political science—you at least ought to understand that."

Mike shook his head. "It's not so simple as that. Geography drives a lot of it, you know. What works in the United States, with the U.S. being so isolated from the rest of the world by two oceans, doesn't work in Europe. Here, nations overlap, history blurs the boundaries. You'll never get the consent you need to make a state out of a nation here, because the nations are too overlapped. And in the end, being a state is about a nation controlling it's own land. You people think the two terms, nation and state, are synonymous."

Brett's voice cycled a notch higher. "Nationalism. Nothing more than leftover tribal instincts."

"It runs deeper than that. Study your cultural anthropology for a change instead of just current events," Mike argued. "People have always formed into clans, groups, based on things that they have in common. They are fundamental things, beliefs that run so deep that no externally imposed concept of statehood can overcome them. Look at Northern Ireland and England."

"My point exactly," Brett shot back. "So you're saying the answer is to simply give up in Northern Ireland?"

Mike shook his head again, now clearly irritated at the others obtuseness. "Not at all. But England's tactics won't work, not in the long run. You can't force statehood on a country that doesn't want it. Even a country where half of the population doesn't want it."

"So we just give up?" Brett asked.

Mike nodded. "And that's the fundamental things that people like you don't understand. Sometimes there are no answers, at least no answers that work. There are only degrees of bad."

Frustrated, Brett turned to Pamela. "So whose side are you on?"

Before she could start to frame her answer, the pilot broke in over the ICS. "Looks like we've got company, people. If you're not strapped in, do it now. Sometimes these Greek fighters play rough."

Pamela was the only one with her seat belt still in place. She learned through hard experience that it always paid to be prepared for turbulence. Mike and the cameraman reached for their belts. Brett ignored the suggestion and continued the argument. "I mean, you're the one who's supposed to be the expert, Pamela." There was something ugly and suggestive in his voice.

Pamela debated whether or not to recognize what he was insinuating, then decided against it. Brett's ambition was a well-known fact within ACN. To answer what he was implying would simply lower her to his level, and there was no need for that.

She twisted around in her seat until she could see forward to the gap between the pilot and the copilot. The other aircraft was visible now, a Tomcat by the looks of it. The canted vertical stabilizers and swept-wing silhouette were a dead giveaway. After covering so many military conflicts, Pamela could recognize most of the major airframes on sight from any angle.

Must be one of the Greek fighters dispatched on regular intervals to patrol the border. Part of Greece's solution to Macedonia's independence had been to close trade routes and crack down on air space violations, in an attempt to cut off the landlocked nation's international commerce.

Standard border war tactics—or at least what the rest of the world called the border. Greece itself refused to admit that there was any border between Macedonia—or Skopje, as they called it—and Greece.

"Any indications of a radar lock?" she asked the pilot,

ignoring the rest of the news team. A deep, sick feeling was starting in her gut. Too many times she'd had to rely on her instincts to survive when reporting combat situations, and she'd come to trust that feeling that told her that something was about to go terribly, terribly wrong.

"How should I know?" the pilot answered. "It's not like I have a threat receiver in this cockpit. He doesn't look too friendly, though, does he?"

Pamela shook her head. "No, he doesn't." The Tomcat was closing on them at top speed, and Pamela could see the fire gouting out of its tail from the afterburners. How fast was he going? Max speed of the Tomcat was well over Mach two. She squinted, trying to see if the forward edge glove vanes were extended, but couldn't make out the details. At speeds above Mach one, the glove vanes moved the aerodynamic center of the aircraft forward and reduced the load on the tail.

But surely he wouldn't conduct a fly-by at those speeds? The wake turbulence of his wake could be deadly to lighter aircraft and helos, and the Tomcat pilot had to know that. It would be pure insanity, dangerous conduct of the most egregious kind, particular when aimed at a neutral party.

But was the press ever really a neutral party these days? *So fast, approaching so fast.* She could see the outlines of the canopy now, see the two figures seated inside. "I think we'd better—"

Just as she started to make a suggestion, the helicopter pilot decided on his own that they were in a very unhealthy bit of airspace. He shoved the collective forward and headed for the deck.

The nose of the helicopter pitch down at a hard angle, throwing her forward against her seat belt and harness. Loose gear in the cabin rolled forward, creating a cloud of debris.

The cameraman screamed. "What the hell is—?"

The Tomcat's wake smack into the light helicopter with the force of the tsunami. The helicopter rolled immediately, and kept rolling, unable to bite into the air with its rotors inverted half the time. Pamela grasped the side of her seat, felt her mouth open to scream as she watched the world spinning through the window to her side, blue sky replaced by a tree canopy, blue sky again, then more trees. The uneasy feeling she'd been experiencing turned into serious nausea. She bit down hard with her back teeth, forcing herself not to vomit.

Brett had other things to worry about. He hadn't manage to get his seat belt fastened, and the first roll threw him violently against the overhead. He slid down it as the aircraft careened onto its side, and smashed into the other side. Blood streaked the Plexiglas. His mouth was open but his screams were drowned out by the noise of the rotors and the shriek of disintegrating airframe.

The pilot was screaming now too, shouting orders to the copilot as they desperately tried to regain control of the helicopter tumbling through the air.

It wasn't going to work. In the first few seconds of the roll, Pamela knew that was a certainty.

Is this how it ends? Not with a bullet, not with a missile shot in Cuba, but in a stupid, stupid accident? No, I won't let it. It's not going to happen like this.

The helicopter was falling now, the roll dampened out by the downward motion. She felt it wrench hard to the left, counter to the motion of the roll as the pilot applied maximum rudder in an effort to stabilize the airframe. Amazingly, the engines were still screaming, although the sound had a sick, unhealthy undertone to it. Then the engines sputtered, coughed twice, and died.

The silence was deafening. She could hear the wind now as it sought out the cracks and crevices in the once-

solid airframe, feel it spinning through the passenger compartment and cockpit. At least they were upright, and she
could hear the pilot and copilot frantically trying to restart
the engines, trying anything to slow their downward descent.

"Auto rotate," the pilot screamed. "If we can just get a
little bit of power, we can . . ."

Auto rotate. Not a chance. While at least in theory the
ground effect and rotation of the helicopter blades might
soften the impact, this helicopter was too far out of control
to even consider it as a possibility. At least the roll had
stopped as gravity took control. They were nose down,
maintaining some forward speed as they plummeted
through the night air.

Pamela grasped frantically at straws. They were upright. That gave them a chance, since the helicopter was
built to take impact on its undercarriage. There was a
chance, at least a chance, that they could survive.

"Into that bare spot," the copilot shouted, gesturing off
to his right. "Not very big, but if we can just clear the
treetops, we might make it."

The helicopter jerked hard to the right as the pilot
forced it into a shuddering turn. The front windscreen was
gone and wind tornadoed through the cockpit, battering
her with loose gear. She could see blood trickling down
the side of the pilot's face. A grim, determined expression
was on his face. The noise was unholy, atmosphere
shrieking mixed with the screams of metal shattering under forces it was never designed to bear.

"Brace yourselves," the pilot shouted. Brett lay moaning on the floor of the helicopter, barely conscious. Pamela leaned forward to try to pull him up into his seat, then
stopped. Depending on how badly he was hurt, moving
him could simply make matters worse. After the battering
he'd taken inside the compartment, there was no telling

whether or not he could survive the crash at all. Or if any of them could. Better to let him die where he lay rather than torture him by moving him to the illusion of safety in his seat.

The cameraman and Mike were holding on to their armrests, stark white faces gleaming dimly in the moonlight. Had she been given a choice, this was not the company she would've chosen to die with. No, if she had a choice, she would have died with . . .

Tombstone. For a moment she tasted the name in her mouth, heavy with memory and regret. What they had had, what had mattered then . . . she would never know now, would she? She had screwed up, screwed up badly, and there would never, ever be a chance to make it right.

The helicopter approached the clearing in the forest, its rate of descent increasing. It passed over the first line of trees, then the front skid caught on the tip of a pine tree. It wasn't a large tree, but given the helicopter's instability, the impact was enough to flip it tail over nose in an airborne summersault. Pamela's last vestige of hope vanished, just as the face she saw in her mind was beginning to seem so real.

Tombstone. Oh, Stony. What have I done? Then the world disintegrated into noise and blackness.

Tavista Air Base, northern Greece
2325 local (GMT −2)

General Arkady slammed his hand down on top of the radar set. The picture wavered, went blank, then reappeared, the contacts slightly offset from their previous locations. Clearly a transmitter alignment problem, one that the operator would have to correct later. But for the moment, in the face of General Arkady's rage, no one dared move. Not the watch officer in charge of the ground control center, not his supervisor, not the officer of the day, not even General Arkady's chief of staff, Colonel Zentos.

"I gave an order," Arkady howled. "A simple, direct order. 'Conduct a fly-by.' You all heard that, didn't you?" He glared at the assembled men and women. A chorus of nods answered him.

"You," he said, pointing at the officer of the day. "What went wrong?"

The officer of the day tried to stammer out an answer, aware that by selecting him as the scapegoat for the entire incident, General Arkady had just terminated the OOD's career in the Army, unless he could find a way to reverse the situation. The OOD thought frantically.

Finally, it dawned on him. An old military adage, one as true today as it had been in the days of the Pelleponesian wars. Shit rolls downhill. If ever there were a time when he needed that to work, it was now.

"The pilot," the OOD began uncertainly. He saw General Arkady's eyes shift slightly, and felt more confident. "Yes, General, the pilot. He disobeyed your orders. I distinctly heard you give the order, sir. It is clearly the pilot's fault. An almost treasonous act, I would call it." By now the OOD's voice was strong, and he felt the mood of the crowd begin to shift.

It seemed an eternity, but General Arkady's expression finally thawed slightly. "Yes, of course," the general said. "Have him return to base immediately. And bring him to me. I will deal with this matter personally."

Tavista Air Base, northern Greece
2350 local (GMT −2)

The airfield stretched out before him like a giant game of tic-tac-toe. Spiros banked the Tomcat gently, slowly bleeding off air speed and altitude. Touching down on a land-based airfield was child's play compared to his experiences as an exchange student with the United States Navy. The carrier landings . . . he shuddered at the memory, the black, clawing sea, the shifting deck and uncertain winds. How they manage to do it every day, every night, he would never know. He still had nightmares about his last night trap.

This, however, was simple—maybe too simple. He made a slight correction in the course, lining up on the runway now. Anyone could do this. For a moment, just a moment, he realized he missed the challenge of trying to wrestle tons of aircraft onto the deck of an aircraft carrier.

The touchdown then, light and gentle. He rolled out smoothly, taking up more runway than he actually needed. He used his nose wheel steering gear to turn the jet toward the flight line. A yellow "follow-me" truck appeared.

After he had completed his post-flight shutdown checklist, Spiros unstrapped from his ejection harness and swung out over the side of the aircraft. His feet sought out the familiar pattern of the boarding ladder, and he jumped lightly to ground. His backseater was still in the aircraft, stuffing charts and kneeboards into his flight suit.

Colonel Zentos was waiting for him, much to his surprise. Spiros snapped off a hasty salute, stammered out a greeting.

"Sir?" Spiro stammered. "Did you want to see me?" *Of course he does, you idiot. That business with the helo—it's your fault, you know. You'll be lucky if you're still flying after this.* He felt a wave of regret, a rush of sympathy for the helo pilot. He hadn't intended to swat them out of the air like an insect, but it had happened.

"The general wants to see you," the colonel said finally. "You will come with me immediately." He turned and led the way back to his vehicle. The driver had kept the engine running.

"But my aircraft," Spiros began. "My RIO."

Without turning back, the colonel said, "You alone. The flight line crew will take care of the aircraft. Come immediately."

Spiros glanced back at the plane captains who had taken charge of his aircraft. The senior-most nodded reassuringly, giving him a thumbs-up. They probably thought that the general was going to honor him in some way, Spiros thought. None of them knew what had happened.

Spiros managed a jaunty wave, and strode off after the colonel, who was already seated in the back of the vehicle.

General Arkady's office
Tavista Air Base, northern Greece
0030 local (GMT −2)

"What did I tell you?" the general demanded. "What were you thinking, in the name of all that is holy?"

Spiros stood braced at attention, his hand shaking alongside his legs. This was bad, worse than he'd ever thought possible. The possibility that he might somehow keep his wings had now completely vanished, and Spiros was now wondering whether or not he would be in the army by the time the day was over.

"General, I . . . it was unintentional, sir," Spiros finally choked out. "I didn't mean to get so close."

"Intentions don't matter. I hold you responsible for your conduct," the general said. "About-face, soldier. I cannot stand to look at your stupid, cowlike face."

Spiros executed a shaky about-face by sheer reflex, and stood at attention with his back to the general. The shaking had spread from his hands down the spine now, and he could feel his leg muscles dancing as though he'd just run ten kilometers. A court-martial, perhaps. Time in military prison, disgrace to his family. Spiros heard a soft, slithering sound behind him. His panicking brain tried to make sense of it. Then cold metal touched the back of his neck, just at the spot where his spine met his skull.

"I do not tolerate excuses," Arkady said calmly. The general pulled the trigger.

The bullet shattered Spiros's spinal cord, then tore out most of his neck, severing his head from the body. Before the head had a chance to fall away from the torso, the bullet cracked through his brain, ricocheted off the interior of his skull, and reduced the remaining flesh to bloody pulp. Spiros was dead long before his head bounced on the hardwood floor of the general's office.

For moment, no one moved. The general held his pose, arm outstretched in front of him, staring down at the decapitated body of the pilot. Finally, he let his arm fall to his side. He replaced the gun in his holster and gazed at the rest of the officers. No words were necessary. They all heard his unspoken comment: Let this be a lesson to all of you.

The general walked back around his desk and took his seat again. He started riffling through the papers centered on the highly polished wood in front of him. Without looking up, he said, "Have someone clean that up." He reached into his desk drawer, took out a pen, and began signing his name to the papers.

Colonel Zentos was the first to react. He stepped forward, picked up Spiros's bloody, staring head, and glanced at the officer of the day. "You heard the general." Zentos placed the head on top of the body. "Get the cleanup crew in here. *Now*."

The room exploded into a flurry of activity. No one wanted to be the next target of the general's temper.

TWO
Thursday, 4 May

Vice Admiral Matthew "Tombstone" Magruder stared at the minute hand on the clock on the wall across from him. If he squinted his eyes just a little bit—not that he'd ever admit needing to do so—he could actually see it move. It crept with glacial slowness around the face of the clock. He looked away, hoping to encourage it to go faster. At sea, that sometimes worked during long hours of pulling alert five in the cockpit of his Tomcat. Back then, the seven-day clocks seemed to know when you were looking at them and slowed down.

Tombstone hadn't spent enough time ashore to be absolutely certain of it, but he'd been under the impression that time passed more quickly here. Certainly, it was easier to get up and move around when you weren't confined to the flight deck waiting to launch. You could leave the building, you weren't stuck on the carrier. There were even magazines—a few months old, but newer than most of the stuff found in any ready room at sea. And a collection of Navy professional publications, some of them little more than publicity rags for various warfare communities, a copy of the *Navy Times*, and a few back issues of *Proceedings*. Maybe this was some kind of test. He surreptitiously glanced at the chief petty officer serving as receptionist. Was anyone taking notes, waiting to see which magazine he picked up to read?

The *Navy Times*, he decided. The Broadside cartoons printed on the editorial pages were always worth reading.

The office of the chief of naval operations was one of the few places that a three-star admiral might be expected to cool his heels for a while, along with some parts of the joint chiefs of staff. But even in JCS, a three-star out-ranked ninety-nine percent of the men and women as-signed to the most prestigious joint command in the world. Here, in the inner sanctum of his own service, he was just another flag officer.

The chief looked over at him, then up at the clock. "Can I get you some more coffee, Admiral?"

Tombstone shook his head. "No thanks, Chief. I'm fine."

The chief stood. "Well, let me see what's keeping him, sir. He's usually not this far behind schedule." The chief slipped quietly into the inner office, shutting the door firmly behind him. Moments later, he reappeared. "Ad-miral, the CNO is ready for you now, sir." He held the door open and stepped to one side.

Tombstone stood, relieved to be moving again. Maybe there were alert-five stretches of time in every job, not just in the squadron. If so, the admiral version of it was at least air-conditioned. He walked past the chief into the CNO's office.

"Matthew." The chief of naval operations stood and came around from behind his desk to greet him. He held out his hand, and clasped Tombstone's in both of his. "It's good to see you again, Stony. Sorry you had to wait—a little crisis over in the Med."

"Good to see you again too, sir." Tombstone shook the man's hand warmly. The term of respect came automati-cally to his lips. Admiral Thomas Magruder might be his uncle, brother to Tombstone's father, but he was still the chief of naval operations. They had worked out their own ways over the years of knowing when they were interacting as family and when they wore their hats as senior officers in the service they both loved. It had become increasingly difficult as Tombstone had become more senior, and their relationship had been stretched almost to the breaking point a year ago when Tombstone had decided to find out what had really happened to his father. His uncle, by then the CNO, had been firmly opposed to the mission. It had been his brother, he argued, and the family connection between the two of them was just as strong as it was between father and son. His brother was dead, had died years ago on a mission over Vietnam.

But when Tombstone uncovered evidence that his father had indeed survived the ejection and had been taken as a prisoner of war, his uncle had been surprised. Then later, when a chain of events proved that father and brother Magruder had been taken from Vietnam to Russia for further interrogation, Uncle Thomas had come over to his side completely. It had been difficult for both of them, realizing that their government had not only lied to the civilian population at large, but to its most trusted senior officers as well.

"Have a seat, Stony," the CNO said, pointing to the couch. "I've got a problem—two problems actually—and you may be the solution to both."

Tombstone sat down and waited. He was getting mixed signals from his uncle. Usually you could tell immediately whether Uncle Thomas wanted to talk about family or Navy. The use of his nickname and his tone of voice were key indicators.

This time, he couldn't decide. Uncle Thomas . . . or was he the CNO right now? . . . looked grave. He sat in a chair facing Tombstone on the couch, apparently struggling with how to begin. Finally, he said, "Oh, hell. I never was any good at being tactful with you, Tombstone. So I'll just say it." He took a deep breath. "Your mission to Vietnam—it's causing problems." He held up one hand to forestall comment. "I know, I know. You would do it all again if you had to. And just the same way, I imagine. But that doesn't mean there aren't consequences to it, Stony. Big consequences."

"I knew that when I went after him, sir," Tombstone said. "But the government lied to us—lied to you and me." He shook his head, remembering how he had to go through an underground network of POW families to find the first clues. "If they just told us what they knew, told the families the truth, it would have been over a lot faster."

The senior Magruder nodded. "No argument from me on that. But the fact remains that you have embarrassed a number of high-ranking people in the Navy by proving that your father was taken to Russia. I don't have to tell you that it doesn't matter how right you were about it. It should, but it doesn't."

Tombstone shrugged. "I'll be as blunt as you are, Uncle. This isn't news. So what's your point?"

"It has to do with your next assignment, Stony," his uncle said. "At one time, there was some talk that you might be in line for my job." He made a gesture, encompassing his office, the vast spaces beyond, and whole Pentagon. "I don't think you would have liked it, but now it's pretty clear you won't have a chance to find out." He paused for a moment, giving Tombstone time to absorb it. "So the question is, what do we do with you now?"

"I'll stay on active duty as long as they let me, Uncle," Tombstone said immediately. "Unless I'm grounded." He held his breath for a moment, hoping that was not the case. But they couldn't simply yank his flight qualifications without his knowing about it. And he'd have heard long before through the rumor mill, even before any official notification. Besides, there'd have to be a naval flight board of some sort. No, they couldn't do that.

Or could they? The rules might contain some loophole exception for an admiral who'd stepped too far out of line.

"I'm not, am I? Grounded, I mean?" Tombstone asked.

His uncle shook his head. "Not as far as I know. No, it's not about flying. I wish to hell it were."

"Then what?" Tombstone asked. As long as he could fly, anything else would be bearable.

"Since you're not headed for CNO, there are some that think that the available operational three-star billets should be reserved for those who are. As much as I hate to say it, that makes sense to me, too," his uncle said. "We have too many admirals and too few billets."

Tombstone was aghast. "They're not going to make me retire, are they?" He felt a strange sensation of fear combined with relief at the thought. What would it be like to be a civilian? He couldn't remember—it had been too many years, since the time he was eighteen. After high school, he'd entered the Naval Academy, and ever since then had been on active duty. At the same time, he felt strangely curious about what it would be like to be a civilian.

And what would Tomboy think? His wife, now Commander Joyce Magruder, was commanding officer of VF-95. Of course he would not expect her to retire if he did. No, that wouldn't be fair at all. He'd had his shot at it, and now it was her turn.

"I'm one of the ones that thinks there's still a place for you in the Navy," his uncle said. "Tombstone, the places you've been, the conflicts you've seen—I'm willing to bet that you've had more actual combat time than any other admiral in the navy. Myself included. I've spent too many years flying a desk."

"Somebody had to do it. I'd rather have been there than here."

His uncle made an impatient gesture. "I know, I know. Still, there are times I wish that it could have been different. For both of us. Maybe I should have encouraged you to spend more time in DC, build up a power base. If you had more friends here, it might lessen the impact of this whole mess."

Tombstone didn't know what to say. Privately, he knew he would never have survived his uncle's career path. Sure, there were plenty of officers who did, including his oldest friend. Batman—Admiral Everette Wayne now— had seen his share of combat, but had also spent the required tours at the Pentagon. If anyone was headed for the CNO job, it was Batman.

"What would you think about coming onboard my staff as a troubleshooter?" his uncle asked. "And I don't mean administrative matters—I mean actual conflict."

"What do you mean?"

His uncle smiled. "You're a great straight man, Stony. That brings me directly to my second problem. Are you following what's happening in Greece and Macedonia?"

Tombstone nodded. "Mostly through CNN, but I've seen some of the classified traffic as well. The Republic of Macedonia may be independent, but Greece isn't acknowledging the fact. Not as long as they've got the word Macedonia in the name. I know they're worried about Greek Macedonia and the coast, too. From what I heard, it sounds like it's getting bloody."

"You don't know the half of it. Two hours ago, the Greeks knocked a news helicopter out of the sky."

"They shot it? Was it ACN?" Tombstone asked. His mind started racing to the inevitable possibility.

His uncle met his eyes. "No missiles. Evidently some Greek Tomcat pilot caught them in a jet wash. But you're right about the rest of it. It was ACN. Pamela Drake was onboard."

Tombstone was stunned. Was it possible, after all these years? The seemingly invincible Pamela Drake, killed in a helicopter crash? It was, he thought, the way she would have wanted to go. On the trail of a hot story, in the middle of the action. Although Pamela had grown older gracefully, he suspected that she never would have been really comfortable as she aged. Her industry was peculiarly brutal to women, and he suspected Pamela Drake would be no exception.

"Is there any word on survivors?" he asked quietly, already offering up a private prayer for Pamela Drake's soul.

His uncle shook his head. "Rescue efforts are under way, but it looks like they went down in a pretty rocky area. I have to say, Stony, I don't think there's much hope she survived. There have been no emergency beacons, nothing like that."

Tombstone let out a long, slow breath, one that felt like he'd been holding for years. "I appreciate your telling me yourself, Uncle. You could have let me hear it on the news."

His uncle made a dismissive gesture. "Don't start thinking I'm getting soft, nephew." He leaned forward, now evidently at the heart of the issue. "We've got problems in Greece, big problems. You know what happens when a member of the news media gets killed. Every other one jumps into the feeding frenzy, and a conflict gets blown all out of proportion." He shook his head gravely. "The one thing all these people never seem to understand is that war is a constant. It's always been with us, and I'm afraid it always will be."

Tombstone nodded. "So what's going to happen? There's already a UN peacekeeping force in place. Not that they've been able to exercise much control over the Greek nationalist, I hear."

"It's not that simple. Sometime tomorrow, the UN will pass a resolution calling for peace and a negotiated cease-fire in Macedonia. There's thought in some quarters that the Greeks aren't going to be any too happy about that. They may even back down from the few compromises they've been willing to live with up until now."

"But Greece is a member of the United Nations," Tombstone said. "They've had members on every peace-keeping mission so far. They always support the UN."

"Sure, but it's different when it's applied to your own country. You know how touchy they are. They don't like having a peacekeeping force in their own country one little bit. And Macedonia is going to be even less willing to cooperate with anything that might possibly infringe on their new independence."

"I can see how it's going to be a problem," Tombstone said thoughtfully. "But this doesn't sound like a Navy problem. Macedonia is landlocked."

"For now. That's apparently part of the problem. Greece is claiming that there's a camp of rebel insurgent nationalists conducting guerilla operations along the Aegean coast inside Greece itself. So they're thinking that they'll need more of a naval presence than originally planned. Besides, nothing's as flexible as an aircraft carrier—and it's a good deal more diplomatic to have an airfield outside the twelve-mile limit than aircraft on the ground inside Greece."

"Makes sense," Tombstone admitted. "So where do I come in?"

"How would you like to be a special advisor to the commander of the UN peacekeeping force that's ordered into Greece?" his uncle asked. "Think about it for a moment before you answer. For one thing, it would be composed primarily of ground troops, although *Jefferson* would be on scene off the coast providing air support, logistics, that sort of thing. And you'd have a whole host of resources to draw on from the Med. But the primary action would be on the ground. Frankly, I think that will make assigning a naval officer even more attractive to the Greeks. They'll think you won't understand the ground actions, that maybe they can baffle you with bullshit."

Tombstone nodded. "After my little forays into Vietnam and Russia, I understand more about that aspect of war. They might not expect that. On the other hand, I might miss some subtleties a ground-pounder would pick up. An army or marine officer might be a better choice."

"There's one other factor involved. Remember who we're talking about. This is Greece, the most ancient seagoing nation in the world. They were building combat fleets when our ancestors were still throwing sticks at each other. If there's a conflict there, even with an inland country like Macedonia, naval warfare will play a big part. For one thing, there are islands scattered up and down throughout the Med and the Aegean. Perfect for remote supply bases and reinforcements. Any peacekeeping force in the area is going to have to do some island hopping just to keep things quiet."

Tombstone nodded. "But still, the primary thrust of the battle is going to be on land."

"Yes, it is. But like I said, this is a naval warfare country. Their land tactics are invariably influenced by their tactics at sea. You've seen that yourself at the Naval War College. It's a way of thinking, an approach to operational art that's different from our own. That's why I thought you might be able to bring a unique perspective to the situation. You understand naval tactics and operational art

better than any other officer I know. If anyone can out-
guess the Macedonians and puzzle out any hidden Greek
agendas, it will be you."

"What makes you think the other nations would buy
into it?" Tombstone asked. Already the possibility of going to Greece was starting to appeal to him.

*But not in command. You'd be one of those staff offi-
cers, those special advisors, that you've spent half your
life bitching about.*

"That's my end of the ball game, Stony. Trust me, I
know how to handle the politics involved. But before I
could go to bat for this—and I'm not doing it as a favor,
mind you, I really think you're the best man for the job—I
have to know whether or not you want it. Because believe
me, being on the inside when there's ethnic warfare involved can eat at you. Brothers fighting brothers—it will
be like the Civil War in the States was. Only uglier. And
you'd have no real power to do anything other than report
back to the States when something starts stinking to high
heaven. The upside is that you can make a difference in
the world. The UN's got to work as it was intended, as a
force for world peace, and Greece has got to go along
with that."

"Oh, I want it, make no mistake about that," Tombstone
said. "Tomboy's onboard *Jefferson* right now anyway, so
it's not like I have a home life."

His uncle stood. "Well, then." He held out his hand.
"Pack your bags, Nephew."

THREE

Friday, 5 May

USS Jefferson
The Aegean Sea, off the coast of Greece
0800 local (GMT −2)

Airman Greg Smith stared out at the brilliant blue waters of the Aegean Sea. From his vantage point on the sponson, an open air compartment immediately below the flight deck, it seemed as though he were looking out from a cave. Clear sky merged with slightly darker water in an endless wash of blue from horizon to horizon.

Airman Smith was attached to VF-95 and worked as a plane captain. As a member of the line department, he was responsible for the overall care and well-being of his Tomcat when it was on the deck. He washed it, checked it for corrosion, made sure it was chocked and chained even during good weather, because out here you never could tell when a storm would blow in. You leave a bird unwashed, forget for a few days to check the delicate junctures between metals, and the next thing you know, bimetallic corrosion has set in.

Other plane captains might not be as meticulous about maintaining their birds, but there was no way Airman Smith was letting any pilot climb into his particular Tomcat if it wasn't in perfect condition. After all, what if something happened to one of them? Something he could have prevented? He knew most of the pilots by sight now, at least well enough to speak a few respectful words to them as they signed out his bird in the flight logbook. They seemed like good fellows, all right guys. Of course, they had to be, didn't they? Not just anyone got to fly Tomcats.

Right now, though, it wasn't the condition of his aircraft that Airman Smith had on his mind. It was the upcoming mission, the one off the coast of Greece. He sighed, stared at the water, and wondered why the hell he was worrying about it. After all, he was just a lowly airman, Paygrade E-3. There were a lot of people a lot more senior that were getting paid to think about things like this, weren't there? There had to be.

His grandfather had been thinking about it. Smith touched his breast pocket and felt the outline of the letter he kept stashed as a talisman. Not that he was superstitious or anything. No, nothing like that.

But Gramps—his father's father—had been in the Navy, had been an enlisted pilot back during the Korean War. He'd flown lots of missions off carriers back before there were even steam catapults to blast them off the deck. Back then, as Gramps told it, they just started from the stern of the ship, gunned their engines, and prayed after they popped the brakes that they'd have enough airspeed to make it.

And Dad had flown off carriers, too. But a soft cat shot off the *Saratoga* on a North Sea patrol had ended his navy career only two weeks after he'd reported on board. Smith had been six years old when the two black sedans had pulled up in front of their home in navy housing. But even at that age, he knew what a chaplain coming up the sidewalk meant.

"He's with Grandma," Gramps had explained. "They're watching out for us all the time."

"I don't want him to be with Grandma!" Smith had howled. "I want him here!" Gramps had pulled him close, let him cry himself out, and that was how it had started. The twelve years of constant moves, living with Mom and Gramps, watching Mom fade away into a dull, drab woman working two, sometimes three jobs just to keep food on the table. Gramps had explained that, too, had gone to the parent-teacher conferences, watched him play Little League, told him stories about the Navy and his time in Korea fighting the war.

One day after Little League, when Smith had sat on the bench almost the entire game, Gramps had seen the unshed tears shining in his grandson's eyes. "It's not fair," Smith had whined, kicking up the dirt as they'd trudged off to the bus stop. "Coach isn't fair."

"Life's not fair, Greg," Gramps had said. When they got to the bus stop, Gramps sat down on the chilly wooden bench and took his grandson's small hand in his and placed it gently over his left knee. Smith could still remember how the flesh curved away so abruptly under his hand, the cold metal artificial leg that cupped the stump. "Stop thinking that it ever will be. But in America, what matters is how the team does. Not whether you play or score. Not whether you lose a leg and another man loses his life. It's about the team, about how the unit does. You know how I've told you about the war, about why it mattered that we were there, right?"

Smith had nodded. "We had to stop the North Koreans from killing people."

Gramps nodded. "That's right. And America was the only country in the world that was willing to step up to the plate and put an end to it. And I told you why we won, too. Do you remember?"

The young child had sighed. "Because we were on the right side. Because God wanted us to."

"That's right." Gramps fell silent for a moment, then sighed heavily. "Someday you'll see what that has to do with warming the bench. Maybe not now, but some day."

Later on, there'd been more lessons, most of them drawing on Gramp's military background and his grounding in traditional American values. Without even realizing it, his grandson had absorbed those things that Gramps said were American ideals. And when Smith had turned eighteen, shortly after his graduation from high school, he'd gone with Gramps down to the Navy Recruiting Station and enlisted. Later, when he'd told his mother, she'd cried. Gramps had explained things once again, but for some reason his mother hadn't agreed. Smith, however, did.

So why weren't they explaining to him what it all meant, the way Gramps would have? Why was *Jefferson* here? Where was the team spirit, the unit integrity that Gramps had always talked about?

He touched the pocket again. This whole UN business—Gramps was right about that, too. They shouldn't be fighting for someone else like this.

"Hey, asshole," a voice called down from overhead. He looked up and saw Airman Quincy Trudeau, his running mate, staring down at him. "Better get your ass up here. The chief is looking for you."

Smith sighed and took one last longing look at the water. A few minutes of peace and quiet between launch and recovery cycles, that was all he wanted. Maybe one night to sleep all the way through and not get woken up for a watch, some problem with his aircraft, or just because the other guys in the compartment were making too much noise. A little sleep, a little time off—was that too much to ask for?

"Okay, okay. I'm coming." Smith turned his back on the ocean and started up the ladder. It led to the catwalk that ran immediately below the level of the flight deck.

Trudeau was waiting for him there, pointing out at the ocean on the other side of the ship.

"What?" Smith asked.

Trudeau smirked. "Made you look . . ."

Smith punched him, letting his fist fall a few inches short of its target. Trudeau dodged out of the way and they spent a few minutes sparring, hidden from the handler's view by a couple of Tomcats parked side-by-side. Screwing around on the flight deck wasn't allowed, not even for the guys who knew it better than they knew their own berthing compartment.

"So what's really going on?" Smith asked, finally collapsing. "I thought you were asleep down in the chain locker."

Trudeau groaned. "Don't even talk to me about chains, asshole. Not after yesterday."

The two of them had spent twelve hours hauling sets of tie-down chains up to the flight deck, on the rumor from the meteorologist that heavy weather would be setting in. Each aircraft had to be tied down with eight chains for foul weather, and each chain weighed twenty pounds. The airmen hauled them up in sets of ten, up four ladders and down three passageways just to get them to the flight deck.

The storm hadn't materialized, but both men could feel the strain in their backs and legs. One more day with eight-point tie-downs, and then they'd be humping the chains back down to the locker. Why the hell couldn't they store the chains somewhere closer to the flight deck, anyway?

"I had to get back up here anyway," Smith said. "We're on the flight schedule this afternoon."

Trudeau yawned. "Me, too. Hey, did you hear the latest? We may be going to Greece with our birds. The squadron is sending a detachment ashore."

"No shit? Man, I could go for that. Join the Navy and see the world—so far all I've seen of it is Great Lakes, Illinois, and *Jefferson*. One day ashore in Italy doesn't count. Greece—now, that would be a good deal."

Trudeau punched him on the arm. Even the light contact stung his overworked muscles. "Be okay with me, too. Guess we better not get caught at anything for a couple of days if we want to go, you know. They don't send liberty risks on good deals."

Smith nodded. Both of the young sailors had been classified as liberty risks at their last port call, based solely on an innocent misunderstanding with an Italian police officer. Of course, the possibility that it had been their fault and that they'd been drunk out of their minds had occurred to the chief petty officer they worked for. They ended up with an ass chewing and an early curfew.

"Flight quarters, flight quarters. All hands man flight quarters to recover aircraft," the 1MC bleated.

"Whose bird?" Trudeau asked.

"Rogers."

"He getting any better?"

Smith shook his head. "Still one dangerous son of the bitch on the flight deck. He's got no common sense, no matter how many times you tell him. He's going to get someone killed someday."

Trudeau got to his feet. "Well, it's not going to be me. If it's Rogers's bird, I'm staying out of the way." He started off toward the island.

Smith watch him go. That was probably the smart thing to do, although he found himself reluctant to leave the flight deck. Rogers and his bird were part of the squadron, part of the team.

Maybe he'd go over the procedures one more time with Rogers, see if he could knock some sense into him. At least he could keep an eye on the other airman while the engines were still turning, make sure he didn't walk into the jet intake. Rogers was an accident waiting to happen, and everybody knew it.

Greece. Let me go to Greece. I swear to God, I won't screw up. Just give me a few days away from the ship, and I'll be good for the rest of the cruise.

Smith trudged aft, toward where Rogers would be waiting for his bird, careful to stay outside the green lines to avoid fouling the flight line. Halfway there, he felt a familiar elbow in his ribs.

"Guess we're in this together," Trudeau said as he fell into step next to Smith. "My luck, you'd get yourself killed and I'd have to haul twice as many chains alone."

FOUR

Friday, 5 May

Macedonian transport helo 3
1000 local (GMT +2)

Pain was her entire world, all-encompassing and demanding. It ate at the edges of her consciousness, blocking out everything beyond shattered nerve endings and damaged flesh. Time ceased to exist except as a continuum of the agony pounding in her body.

She heard words, could not make them out. One small portion of her brain insisted that she pay attention, that this was very important. She dismissed the thought, too consumed by the agony ripping through her. Nothing mattered but the pain.

But gradually, she became accustomed to it. Pain became a part of her, and faded, if not to the background, at least to a level that might—just might—be endurable

Now she could hear the words, the individual sounds. Someone touched her shoulder lightly, and she groaned.

"The morphine, it is working now?" the voice spoke English, although with a heavy accent running through it. She catalogued it immediately—Greek, probably from the northern area. It was not a conscious analysis, this instantaneous compulsion to peg accents and voices to nationality was just a reflex born of years spent overseas.

"You're still in pain?" the voice asked. She tried to force an answer out between battered lips but could only manage another groan. There was a light prick on her thigh, barely distinguishable from the rest of the pain, and she felt coolness float up her body. "There. That should help."

It did. She found she was at least able to open her eyes without screaming. "Yes, I can see it's helping. It is, isn't it?" the voice said, the words soothing.

"What . . . ?" She heard the word come out, and was unable to recognize the harsh croak as her own voice. She tried again. "What happened?"

Evidently the man leaning over her was accustomed to listening to injured people try to talk. He nodded reassuringly. "There was an accident with your helicopter. Do you remember?"

She tried to think. Had she been in a helicopter? Lord, she seemed to spend half her life in the air, so it was entirely possible. But a crash? How? And why?

"Your helicopter went down," the voice continued. "A mechanical malfunction, perhaps. We don't know what happened."

"How bad?" she asked, forcing the words out.

The voice was serious, though not unkind. "You are the only survivor."

Mike. Brett. And the cameraman . . . she had never even gotten to know his name.

"You're still in pain," the voice said.

Pamela squinted, trying to bring his face into focus, but he remained a blur. She moved as though to touch the face and gentle pressure restrained her.

"Do not move," the voice continued. It bothered her more than she could say that she couldn't see his face. She made her living judging people by their body language and expressions, the way they looked away when they lied to her, the unflinching stare that was even more damning evidence of falsehoods.

"I can't see," she said.

"You're badly hurt," the voice said. "Please, do not try to move. We're taking you to doctors, to the hospital."

"Who are you?" Her curiosity gnawed at her, competing with the pain. A few details from the crash were starting to come back. They'd been coming back from taking some stock footage of the camp inside Greece where the rebels were supposedly headquartered. It had been an easy flight, no sign of trouble. No one was worried about the trip. As in many international conflicts, the news media seemed to have an unspoken guarantee of safety.

"You must not move," the voice said, more sharply now. "There may be serious injuries. Please, you cannot—here." There was another pinch on her thigh, then massive waves of cool blue relief spread throughout her body from that location. She could still feel the pain as a pressure, knew it was there, but it no longer matter. Nothing mattered except the velvet midnight blue darkness that drew her down.

"What . . . ?" She tried to frame a question, but could no longer make her lips move. Nor could she remember exactly what she had wanted to ask. It wasn't important, anyway. Nothing was.

A flash of strong denial inside of her. No, there were some things that were important. Tombstone Magruder. The face materialized in her mind again, a reassuring source of strength.

Tombstone would come after her, she knew. He always had. He always would. She slipped back down into darkness, comforted by that certainty.

Macedonian HQ camp
Five miles inside the Greek border
1035 local (GMT +2)

Colonel Takia Xerxes, the commander of the Macedonian insurgents inside Greece, stared down at the still form on the stretcher. He was lean, with wiry muscles corded on a tall frame. His dark hair was clipped short but still curled into tight half-circles over a high forehead burned dark from hours in the sun. Brilliant green eyes peered out from beneath shaggy eyebrows.

"Why did you bring her here?" Xerxes asked. "Don't you know how many people will be looking for her?"

The medic shrugged. "She was on her way here, wasn't she?"

"Not to this location. To the other one, the one we let leak as our headquarters. No one is supposed know about this camp—no one except those who have to."

"She'd been out there for almost two days. Another couple of hours and she would have died," the medic said. He knelt down by her body, stroked a stray lock of hair back from the battered face. "Is that your idea of good relations with the international press? Letting Pamela Drake die when you could save her?"

Xerxes shook his head impatiently. "No, of course not. But there were other options. If you'd radioed ahead, even asked for instructions, I would have—"

"You would have chewed me out for breaking radio silence," the pilot chimed in. "Admit it. Besides, as long as she doesn't know where she is, she can't tell anyone, can she?"

"It won't work," Xerxes snapped back. "During the Cuban crisis, she was taken hostage by the guerrillas there. They held her as a human shield at their missile site. Everyone will think we're doing the same thing."

Xerxes sighed. How was he to have known of the range of problems he would have to deal with? It had all been so simple when they started out, a question of national pride and their honor as Macedonians. But the details, ah, the details. The devil was in the details.

They'd made plans for logistic support, chosen their allies carefully. Somehow, they'd managed to assemble a credible fighting force out of the disparate aircraft, weapons, and equipment that they'd been able to beg from other countries.

But when had he had time to decide what to do about a pregnant freedom fighter? Or about conflict between his troops, the need for some form of military discipline in this People's Army of equals? Or about a SAR mission that brought an international reporter to his secret headquarters inside enemy territory? All these things and more had never even crossed his mind.

It had been so simple, back when it was just a matter of national honor.

"How is she?" Xerxes asked finally. "Do *not* tell me she's going to die in my camp."

"She's badly hurt," the medic kneeling beside her said. "I need X rays, access to diagnostic procedures we don't have in the field here. She needs a hospital." He looked up at Xerxes, concern evidence in his face.

Xerxes shook his head. "We can't take the chance. It's dangerous enough flying the surveillance missions. I can't risk the men or the equipment to get her into town."

The medic sighed and looked down. "She might be all right," he said. "If there are no internal injuries, no bleeding. I can't tell that now. At the very least, she's got a concussion, and it could be a lot worse." He pointed at her right leg. "Broken. I set it." He pointed at her right shoulder. "Dislocated. And the cuts and bruises are simply too numerous to catalog. But at least she's hydrated now.

It's a miracle that a pack of wild dogs didn't find her while she was unconscious."

"How did she survive?" Xerxes asked. "And more importantly . . . why?"

Tavista Air Base, northern Greece
1040 local (GMT −2)

"What do you mean, they're not there?" General Arkady snapped. "Where could they have gone?"

The helicopter crew stood ranged before him in a rough semicircle. Clearly, word of Spiros's fate had traveled quickly among the ranks of the aviators. These looked to be the juniormost officers and enlisted flight technicians to be found in their squadrons.

Arkady turned to Colonel Zentos. "Do my orders still mean so little?" he asked. He pointed at the men. "Finding this reporter was our top priority. I made it clear, did I not? And yet we send these . . . men who can't even locate the downed helicopter in two days. An explanation. Now, if you please." His tone of voice made clear that this was not a request.

His chief of staff swallowed hard, uneasy. Nor was it the first time since he had joined Arkady's staff.

Colonel Zentos was a career army man, with all that that implied. He believed in order, discipline, a regulated way of life that made it possible for a nation to deploy its military power on a moment's notice. The question of Macedonia and Greece was not one that he thought much about. He had his orders—detect, track and destroy Macedonian forces inside Greece, interdict supplies flowing into Macedonia, and maintain air superiority using primarily army assets. This assignment to General Arkady's staff had been a vote of confidence, and he'd looked forward to serving under the command of the brilliant tactician whose rise through the ranks was virtually legendary. Colonel Zentos was well aware that he was regarded as a strong, methodical officer, the perfect chief of staff. By serving with General Arkady, he'd hoped to expand his reputation as a tactician and planner.

Zentos had thought in the beginning that the rumors about General Arkady's brutality were simply discontented murmurings from staff officers not accustomed to working for a demanding flag officer. He had dismissed the worst of the accounts as too clearly implausible to possibly be true.

But in the past weeks and months, Zentos had started to experience doubts. With the execution—and there was really nothing else that it could be called, could it?—he'd had his worst fears confirmed. General Arkady might possess an awesome intellect, and might be just the person to control the Macedonian problem, but he was a brutal, atrocious human being.

"I will look into this, General," Zentos said carefully, all too aware that his own life hung in the balance. Yet he was unwilling to take the coward's way out and try to shift the blame to the squadron commanding officer, or even to these pilots. The essence of command was the trust and confidence one's subordinates felt in their commanders, their conviction, however unwarranted by the facts, that the commander knew what was best. "I apologize for wasting your time with this. Give me a chance to get to the bottom of this before I have you briefed."

Arkady turned his basilisk glare on Zentos. For a moment, the chief of staff expected the worst. He repressed the shudder that ran through his body. The incident with Spiros yesterday . . . no, it was unthinkable.

But he's capable of it. You know. You were there.

Zentos had directed the removal of the body and the cleanup of General Arkady's office afterward. A team of enlisted men had scoured the room for bits of bloody tissue and spots of bodily fluids then almost silently cleaned the wooden floors and walls. Zentos had stood over them the entire time, trying to keep his body between the men and the general, wincing every time one of them made the slightest bit of unavoidable noise. General Arkady had remained at his desk, ostensibly engrossed in wading through paperwork but attentive as a hawk. It was the most profoundly humiliating episode in Zentos's career thus far.

A court-martial would have been the right thing to do and would have brought the full force of military justice to bear on the foolish pilot. Greece had a long history of democracy, had developed a military culture that rivaled any in the world and extended back to the earliest recorded times. There was much to be proud of, ancient history and traditions to uphold.

Unfortunately, a court-martial would have also revealed the one fact that Arkady did not want made public: that the general himself had ordered the fatal maneuvers, fully conscious of the danger to the helicopter. That was why Spiros had died. Not as punishment for making a critical mistake in the air, but because the pilot had obeyed his orders.

Private executions on the whim of a madman. Am I next? With that thought, as he'd shielded the cleaning crew with his own body, Zentos had turned a corner that not even he fully recognized yet.

Zentos stared at a spot just under Arkady's chin, carefully avoiding direct eye contact and holding his breath, wondering whether he'd bought them all some time. With any luck, events might distract the general from insisting someone pay for the failure to locate the downed helo.

Finally, Arkady appeared to lose interest in him. He turned away, fixing his glare back on the aviators again. "Find out why these men were assigned to fly this mission. After you do, I wish to see their commanding officer."

Zentos nodded, relieved for the men arrayed before him, but now facing a growing fear for the captain of the squadron. He was an old friend, one with whom Zentos had served for many years. Would he meet Spiros's fate in a few hours?

"You heard the general—return to your duty stations at once," Zentos said harshly, aware that every second they spent in Arkady's presence increased the danger that he'd change his mind and make another example out of them. He shepherded the men out of Arkady's office, then closed the door behind them. He turned to face the general alone.

Was there any point in discussing the execution with Arkady? Surely he understood what monstrous misconduct it had been? Could he achieve any real purpose—besides increasing the odds of losing his own life—in offering criticism to the flag officer?

And yet, wasn't that the role of the chief of staff? To serve as a sounding board for ideas, build the staff into a cohesive unit that the general could take into war? Of all the generals that Zentos had ever served under, he had never met one that did not value a chief of staff willing to speak his mind.

Until now. Is it worth my own life? And perhaps even the life of the RIO that the general has forgotten about. If I even bring the incident up, there is every possibility that he will remember that there were two men in that aircraft, not just one.

"I will fly the next mission myself, General," he heard

himself say. He waited for some comment from Arkady, but the general simply nodded.

Arkady's window overlooked ancient hillsides, soaked through the centuries in military blood. Battles and campaigns that the entire world now studied had been waged in these hills, not so far from that very location. And even then, the Macedonians and the Greeks had been at odds.

His brother was married to a Macedonian woman, albeit not from the upstart republic itself. The same blood, though, threaded throughout this land. His nieces and nephews were of the ancestry, too. In truth, there was little difference between the two cultures, apart from the names by which they called themselves.

Was it worth it? Lives squandered arguing over which set of ancestors back in the mists of time had created certain forms of pottery, had settled certain islands, had brought forth Alexander the Great. In today's world, growing smaller through commerce and the Internet, was it right to cling to those ancient claims to glory?

Yes. For without history, a nation had no basis for insisting on taking its place in the world community. Ancient blood ran in his veins, coursed through every inch of his body. Greece had earned its place in the world, and he would do his part to make sure it remained untarnished. And despite his revulsion at Arkady's conduct as an officer, Zentos knew that Arkady understood that as well. They agreed on the end—just not on the means.

"History is upon us," Arkady said out loud, breaking the silence in his office. "This question has been left unresolved for too many centuries." He stood and began pacing. "Not one more year. Not one more month or week. I will settle this matter once and for all." The general's voice grew louder as he recited the ancient list of wrongs between Greeks and Macedonians. "They are Greek, can't they see that? And they will be Greek, will admit it to the world. I will see them dead before they disgrace our blood. Every last one of them." The general appeared to have forgotten that his chief of staff was still in the room.

His words sent chills down Zentos's back. Had it come to this? Brother murdering brother, and in the interest of what? Old stories of glory and ancient birthright?

For the first time in his thirty-five years of military service, after campaigns ranging from fighting the British to the Italian incursions, the chief of staff began to wonder whether he had made the right choice in joining the Army.

"You will fly the mission, Colonel." Arkady turned to glare at him, his eyes refocusing and seeming to stare straight through the colonel. "Find the helicopter, the people onboard. And bring them to me."

As he left, Zentos felt a profound satisfaction that he'd volunteered. It was foolish, dangerous beyond any threat that the air could offer, but it was the right thing to do. If the consequences for his men were to include execution for an unsuccessful mission, then he could not order them into the air unless he was willing to face Arkady's justice himself.

If it must happen, let me die in the air. He went to check the flight schedule for the next scheduled mission.

Tomcat 304
Enroute USS Jefferson, *Aegean Sea*
1040 local (GMT −2)

Tombstone could see the aircraft carrier now, a barely discernible pip on the horizon. Not that visual mattered right now, though. It wouldn't until he was on final approach. *Jefferson*'s TACAN sang out sweet and clear on

his receiver, and he was on an inbound radial under the
control of an enlisted operations specialist in the carrier's
Combat Direction Center, or CDC.

The sound of a healthy Tomcat filled the cockpit, re-
verberating in his bones until he could feel the sound
merge with his own heartbeat. Twin turbofans, each capable of generating 20,900 pounds of thrust. Over the
years that he'd been flying, the Tomcat had seen contin-
uous upgrades. This bird, the F-14D, was one of the most
advanced fighters ever built. Even the older airframes had
gotten the upgrade, including a change-out of the engines
and avionics. Almost like new—except that eventually
metallic stress would win. You could only expect so much
from aging metal.

Still, this old gal had a few years left in her. He patted
the canopy affectionately, as though she were his favorite
dog. How lucky he'd been after Flight Basic to get Tomcats! It was a choice he'd never regretted.

"Three zero four, I hold you at forty miles, bearing one
niner two," a voice said in his ear. "Admiral, you will be
vectored in for immediate landing, sir. We have a green
deck at this time."

"Roger." Tombstone sighed. They had to do it that way,
of course. An admiral inbound on the carrier took priority
over all the other lowly aviators. He could see the faint
glint of sunshine on wings off to the right of the ship, the
starboard marshal pattern. Planes in air would be stacked
up there, waiting for their shot at the deck. They'd been
out flying missions, maybe even on a double cycle, and
were probably ready to get back on deck. His arrival
would throw the whole sequence out of whack, maybe
even forcing some of them to peel out and refuel if the
wait got too long. And it wasn't like someone could save
your place in line for you. You'd start over at the top of
the stack and have to work your way back down.

"I wouldn't mind spending some time in a starboard marshal," Tombstone said out loud, careful not to toggle the transmit switch. "Not one little bit."

His backseater, Commander Gator Cummings, heard him even over the cockpit noise. He clicked his ICS twice in acknowldgment. "Missing the stick time, sir?"

"You bet, Gator."

It had been a struggle to get his uncle to carve out a week's worth of time in Norfolk to allow him to requalify on Tomcats. It had been an abbreviated syllabus, one designed to bring a senior aviator who had been out of the cockpit back up to speed quickly. He knew the RAG personnel hadn't been happy, would've liked to have him for another few weeks, but there simply wasn't time. In the end, he'd managed to convince them that he was safe to fly after a couple of carrier qualification landings, and insisted that they sign off on his flight quals.

Now, feeling the warm reassuring thrum of the Tomcat around him, he knew it had been the right decision. The aircraft was a part of him, an extension of his own body. The avionics that fed into his and Gator's displays were extensions of his mind. The movements to control the aircraft were by now so automatic that he barely had to think of them. Instead, he could simply enjoy the flight.

"Tomcat 304, maintain 10,000 feet and continue inbound, sir," his operations specialist said. Tombstone clicked his mike twice in acknowledgment. He took the Tomcat down in a slow, controlled descent, gradually bleeding off his altitude while increasing his speed slightly.

"Roger, sir, hold you on course, on speed. Continued inbound on this radial. Say state and souls, sir."

Tombstone glanced down at the fuel indicator. "Six thousand pounds, two souls on board."

"Roger, sir, copy six thousand pounds and two souls.

Commander Cummings, is that correct, sir?"

"That's correct." For a moment, Tombstone wondered how Gator had managed to wheedle his way into a free trip to Sigonella to meet him, but decided not to ask.

Gator and Bird Dog had flown in together, and the pilot had been left to find his way back to the ship on a COD. Tombstone tried to feel sorry for the young pilot, but couldn't. Bird Dog had had his fair share of good deals, including having been paired so often with Gator. By now the two were a well-oiled team, with Gator supplying the raw brain power and Bird Dog the natural reflexes that made them a superb fighting team. Still, it had been Gator who had more than once pulled Bird Dog's butt out of the fire.

"Tomcat 203, turn right to course 010." The operation specialist continued on to rattle off the standard speed and descent requirements for an approach on the carrier, concluding with, "Tomcat 203, call the ball."

It was a request that Tombstone notified the landing signals officer, or LSO, located on ship's stern when he caught sight of the ball for the first time.

The ball, the common name for the Fresnel lens, was the mainstay of carrier aviation landings. It was a visual indication of the aircraft's relationship to the proper and safe glide path when approaching the carrier. Too low or too high, and a pilot saw a series of red lights. Right on course, the ball looked green. The LSO would keep an eye on the Tomcat's approach, checking for proper speed, orientation and attitude, and providing a visual confirmation that the aircraft landing gear was down.

The carrier was growing larger now, a solid, massive postage stamp in ocean ahead. Always, at these times, the deck looked impossibly small. Even after almost thirty years of landing on carriers, Tombstone still found it a miraculous way of landing.

He could see it now, the glint of green and red on the port side of the carrier. He made the call. "Tomcat 203, ball."

The LSO answered immediately. "Roger, 203. Ball. Looking good, sir. A little high—203, say needles."

Tombstone glanced down at the needles, crosshairs which indicated his relationship to the glide path. "Needles high and to the right," he said.

"Roger, sir, fly the needles," the LSO answered, indicating that Tombstone's cockpit indicators gibed with his own assessment of the Tomcat's approach.

Tombstone eased back off the throttle, decreasing his airspeed slightly, letting the Tomcat sink down through the air as gravity overcame his forward speed and lift. It always seemed so slow at this point, a gentle descent down to the deck. At least so far.

Then he hit the bubble, the wake of roiled air immediately astern of the carrier, created by the passage of the massive ship through the atmosphere. The Tomcat bounced around, and he made minor corrections to hold the aircraft on glide path.

"A little high, sir, that's right. Nose up a little bit more, looking good, looking good, attitude sir, attitude sir, power now, power now, looking good," the LSO sang as he coached him in through the final stages of the approach.

The deck loomed up at him, massive and spacious this close to it. The stern flashed by under him, and Tombstone slammed the throttles forward to full military power in case he missed the four wires spanning the deck below him. The Tomcat was barely airborne right now, sinking fast and approaching stall speed of 100 knots. Without full military power, he wouldn't have enough speed to take off the end of the deck if he boltered.

The wheels slammed down hard on the deck, the hydraulic shock absorbers taking most of the force. A controlled crash, that's what it always felt like. The impact slammed Tombstone forward against his ejection harness straps. The noise inside the cockpit crescendoed as the powerful engines sucked down air, mixed it with fuel, ignited it, and blasted out power.

"Three wire, sir," the LSO said. "Good trap." That meant Tombstone's tail hook mounted on the undercarriage of the Tomcat had caught the third wire from the stern of the ship. The three wire was considered the goal on every landing.

Tombstone kept one hand on the throttles, pouring the power on. Wires had been known to break, and only a fool took power off before he was directed to do so.

A yellow shirt walked out in front him, and made hand signals for decreasing power. Only that moment, when a member of the flight deck crew felt confident enough that the Tomcat was stopped that he was willing to step in front of the powerful aircraft himself, did a pilot risk his own life by easing off on the power.

The yellow shirt moved one extended arm in an arc underneath an outstretched arm, indicating that Tombstone should retract his tail hook. Tombstone did, and felt the Tomcat roll forward slightly, now free of the restraining wire. He taxied past the first yellow shirt, who handed him off to a second one. Tombstone was directed to his spot on the deck, and slid the Tomcat smoothly into his assigned slot. The second yellow shirt was still standing in front, making the signals now for engine shutdown. Tombstone complied, running through the shutdown checklist as he did so.

"Good trap, Admiral," Gator said. He was already powering down his own equipment and unsnapping his ejection harness after safing the ejection seat itself. "It's something you never lose, is it?"

Captain Coyote Grant, now commanding officer of

USS *Jefferson*, was standing at the bottom of the boarding ladder, waiting to greet him. Coyote was one of Tombstone's earliest friends in the F-14 community, just a few years his junior.

Coyote had followed Tombstone and Batman up the ranks, and had taken command of *Jefferson* just a few months earlier. It had been an easy relief process, since Coyote's previous assignment had been as Batman's chief of staff for Carrier Battle Group 14.

"Welcome aboard, Admiral," Coyote said. "Admiral Wayne's a bit tied up—he asked me to meet you and invite you down at your earliest convenience."

Tombstone held out his hand. "Nice to be back, Coyote." Salutes were never rendered on the flight deck, since headgear other than flight deck cranials was prohibited during flight operations. "We'll head down to flag spaces now." As they headed for the hatch that led into the island, Tombstone asked, "So how's it going?"

Coyote laughed. "Guess you'd be the one to tell me that, sir."

Inside the skin of the ship, they descended two ladders and ended up on the 0–3 level, the passageway which housed the flight spaces. Tombstone followed Coyote into the admiral's cabin.

"About time," Admiral Wayne grumbled. "Figured you'd show up sooner or later, Stony."

"Never pass up the chance at some stick time," Tombstone answered. Batman grunted an acknowledgment.

"So what's all this about, Tombstone?" Coyote asked, discarding the formalities now that they were in private. "All I know is I get a message telling me you're flying out en route an assignment in Greece. Might you tell me what's up?"

This was an old friend, one Tombstone trusted, so he gave him the full story. Everything—the details about his trip to Vietnam and Russia, the subsequent displeasure of naval leadership with his activities. He concluded by saying, "So be careful where you drop bombs, Coyote. I almost got taken out by my own former squadron."

"It's that serious, then?" Batman asked, leaning back in his chair. "I've seen the messages, of course. And there are always contingency plans. But now you're talking about bombing runs . . . where? And how soon? I need to get my people started on this."

"I don't know yet," Tombstone said. "But it looks like the UN is coming down solidly on Greece's side. At least if you read between the lines. They're going to try for peaceful settlement, of course." He spread his hands, indicating the futility of that. "You know how likely that is to work."

Coyote nodded. "Indeed, I do. So what can you tell us?"

Tombstone shifted slightly in his seat, uncomfortable with having so few answers. "For now, it's a question of what *you* can tell *me*. How is *Jefferson*? How ready are you? And if you're not one hundred percent, what do you need to get there?"

Coyote frowned, apparently slightly offended. "We're always ready, Admiral. Just like we were when you were in command here."

"Don't give me that crap, Coyote." Tombstone made an impatient gesture. "Okay, okay, your position is that the *Jefferson* is one hundred percent combat ready. Now that we've made that a matter of record, tell me the truth. What do you need?"

"A couple of spare parts, Admiral. That's really about it. They're already on high-priority replacement, so I'm not sure what else we can do to get them here. The main thing I need is for everyone and his brother to stop tapping me for liaison officers. I got enough people to man my squadrons, to fly and fix my aircraft, but I can't be sending my best people off the ship to join staffs."

Tombstone laughed, recognizing the eternal dilemma of a battle group. "That includes mine, I take it?"

Coyote grinned. "I would never say that, Admiral."

"You don't have to."

There was a moment of silence, then Tombstone said, "Formal briefing tomorrow morning?"

Batman nodded. "Are you out of here tomorrow afternoon?"

"Yep, unless I can figure out a way to get some more stick time," Tombstone said. To his surprise, Batman said, "We could make that happen, Admiral. I can move the briefing up to this evening and Coyote can get you in on the first cycles tomorrow. If you take a pilot with you, CAG will even loan you an aircraft so you can fly yourself to your final destination. In fact, Bird Dog should be back on board in a few hours. I'll toss him in your backseat, let him bring the bird back. How about that?"

Tombstone stood, now feeling the effects of transiting too many time zones in too few hours. "Sounds great. After the evening meal, then?"

"You got it, sir. And where exactly are you headed for?" Coyote asked.

"A little place up in northern Greece, right near the coast. A place called Tavista Air Base."

Tomcat Ready Room
Tavista Air Base
1400 local (GMT −2)

The Greek squadron duty officer averted his face from the woman standing in front of his desk. The small room was starting to fill up with pilots and NFOs wandering back after lengthy lunches, quick naps, and clandestine meetings with lovers—nooners, in military parlance—and he was hoping desperately that someone senior would walk in during the next several moments. Anyone, pilot or not, just someone who could answer the very difficult questions the woman was asking. Over the last five minutes, she'd becoming increasingly loud, and now her high-pitched voice was approaching a screech.

"You know where he is. Tell me *now*!" The woman darted around the edge of the desk and glowered down at him. "Is it another woman? You men—you hide each other, lie for each other—tell me the truth *now*!"

"I have not seen your husband for three days," the duty officer said, trying for some semblance of official dignity. "He is not on the flight schedule."

The woman snorted. "Excuses, excuses." She turned as a particularly boisterous set of officers came into the room. The aviators recognized her immediately and fell as silent as the rest of the group. "You," she said imperiously, pointing at one of them. "I know you. You fly with my Antipodes, yes?"

The RIO she'd pointed at turned pale. Dark circles around his eyes accented the haggard lines in his face. "No . . . no, I don't know him." He looked beseechingly at the rest of the officers. "I don't know him."

For just a moment, the woman looked uncertain. Then her expression hardened into determination. She abandoned the cowed duty officer and darted across the room and grabbed the RIO by his lapel. She shook him, then slapped him across his face. "You lie! You know where he is!"

The RIO seemed powerless to move, incapable of loosening the grip this madwoman had on his flight suit. The other aviators backed away from him.

"I . . . I . . ." the RIO stuttered, not knowing what he intended to say if he could ever regain control of his mouth. Then he had an inspiration. "Special duty—your husband is on special duty for General Arkady."

"Ha!" she spat, but she turned loose of him. "And you said you did not know him." She turned to fix a piercing glare on the rest of the men. "Cowards, every one of you. I shall go to General Arkady myself and demand an explanation." She shouted a curse at the duty officer, then let herself out of the ready room, slamming the door behind her.

The assembled men let out a collective sigh. The deep gloom in the room deepened. Finally, the duty officer picked up the telephone. "I shall call Colonel Zentos," he said to the room at large. "If he can reach her . . ." He let his voice trail off as he dialed the chief of staff's telephone number. The rest of his sentence went unspoken, but every man knew what he'd intended to say.

If I can reach Colonel Zentos before the general hears her, she may live another day.

FIVE

Saturday, 6 May

This time of year, the evenings in Greece were long and glorious. Sunshine hung in the air for an impossibly long time, keeping tourists out on a narrow cobblestone road. Traffic was light, since most people preferred to walk in this ancient city carved out of the hills. Roads ran at seemingly random angles up and down the hills, but all eventually returned to the main marketplace. The air was still warm, redolent with the sharp spice of cooking, the pungent smell of a city that spent its days drenched in sunshine. Whitewashed walls contrasted with the perfusion of flowers and foliage. Many of the walls had stood for centuries, refurbished on the outside with fresh coats of paint, but essentially structurally stable over the years.

For Brad and Clara Summit, it was the honeymoon of a lifetime. It was what they'd planned on, saved their pennies and scrimped for during the eighteen months they'd been engaged in order to afford their dream beginning to their life together. Married only three days earlier in Minneapolis, Minnesota, they had flown straight into Athens, rented a car, and driven north to Tavista.

"It's all too perfect," Clara exclaimed. She paused next to a streetside vendor, inhaling deeply and letting the spices suffuse her senses. "Everything I dreamed of—and you." She turned to face her new husband, love gleaming in her eyes. "It could not be more perfect, Brad. And neither could you."

Brad reached out and pulled her close, still marveling that this wonderful woman had agreed to spend her life with him. At thirty-three, he'd given up hope of ever finding the perfect mate. But then Clara had appeared in his life, a graduate student auditing his course in ancient English literature. He'd always insisted that it was her mind that attracted him first, but in his heart of hearts, he knew better. It had been her eyes, deep azure, a match for the unbelievable water they'd flown over in the descent to Greece. He'd never seen that particular color before, and spent hours musing over the fact that the very edge of her pupil was shot through with golden streaks. A lifetime would be too short to delve into all the mysteries those eyes held.

"Me, too," he said, then silently berated himself for not coming up with more perfect words. Shouldn't an English professor be able to do better than that? Maybe quote a sonnet, at least be able to put into words how very much he loved her. But he settled for saying it again. "Me, too."

They lingered for a moment, standing close on the sidewalk with their arms wrapped around each other. Pedestrians simply veered around them, some pausing to chuckle or smile wistfully at the sight of a couple so much in love. Finally, Clara pulled back slightly. "I'm famished. How about some lunch, then we go back to our hotel room?"

Brad chuckled. "Then what?"

Suddenly, he could hardly wait. He pointed at a café just off the main road. "How about there?"

Clara didn't even look at it. "Perfect. Come on, then." Brad led the way to the café, hoping the food would be good. It had been at most of the local spots that they'd eaten in, and he was thankful that neither of them were prone to Montezuma's Revenge.

They seated themselves, their eyes grateful for a break from the sunshine. Once their orders were placed, they went back to staring into each other's eyes.

Without warning, a violent explosion rocked the café. Clara, who had had her back to the door, was thrown over the table and landed on top of him. The table followed, slamming into the back of her head and driving her face into his neck. He could feel her teeth graze his skin, the hard weight of her body on his underneath the old wooden table. For a moment, his world consisted of nothing more than Clara's weight and a violent wash of sound.

There was a moment of silence. Then the screaming started, panicky wailing, as the patrons tried to make some sense of the world. Brad heard himself cry out, his voice harsh and anguished. He reached around Clara, and tried to shove the table off of her body. It resisted, then slipped partway off so the weight was resting on one edge to the side. He bucked, forcing it up for a second. As it moved, he slid to the side, dragging Clara with him. Cut glass slashed into his hand. He cried out again, for a split second oblivious to anything except the pain.

The noise, there was so much noise. It was overwhelming, a chorus of voices screaming out in pain and anguish.

Then it hit him. The only one not screaming was Clara. He bent over, his own pain forgotten, and cradled her face in his hands. "Clara? Oh my God, Clara!"

Her eyes were half shut, the perfect orbs that haunted his dreams rolled back under her eyelids. Her mouth was slack.

He bent over, moaning, trying frantically to escape the moment that he knew was careening toward him. It wouldn't be long from now, not long at all. It bore down on him with an awful inevitability that frightened him beyond all reason.

Clara's face was unmarked, the smooth clear skin still flushed by the blood that had moments before pounded in her veins. There was not a mark on the front of her, and he felt cold dread growing at what he must do.

Gently, no longer calling out her name, he rolled her slightly onto her side. Warm wetness flooded through his fingers. He moved his hand up her body to the base of her neck, then down her back. Mangled tissue slipped under his fingers, evidence of the deadly impact she had taken from behind. The noise in the room receded as his future crashed in on him.

Tavista Air Base
1820 local (GMT −2)

General Arkady heard the news first from Colonel Zentos. His command post monitored the police frequencies, and although the early reports were confused and incomplete, Arkady knew immediately what he was facing.

"How many casualties?" He asked, his voice cold and hard.

"At least twenty, sir. There are no exact figures yet, but it looks like the front half of the café was obliterated by the bomb."

"Is anyone claiming responsibility?"

The chief of staff shook his head. "Not yet. But it's early still."

General Arkady stood. "A cease-fire—surely they must now see the futility of it." He pounded one hand on his desk, and shouted, "It is one thing to kill another soldier. But to attack innocent civilians, to bring this war to the very streets of our city—no, I will not allow it. I will not."

"Was it the Macedonians?" Zentos asked.

Arkady turned to glare at him. "Who else would do this? Greeks killing Greeks—who else would possibly commit such an atrocity?"

Zentos thought he knew the answer to that particular question. Wisely, he kept his thoughts to himself. "Until someone claims responsibility, General, I think that—"

Arkady placed both hands on his desk and leaned across to glare at the colonel. "I do not need your thoughts at this time. What I need is for your actions to mirror your supposed commitment to me. The rebels have struck at the very heart of our city, and you talk to me about proof?"

The colonel kept silent, aware of the danger. Still, Arkady's reaction puzzled him. It wasn't the general's way to be worried about casualties, particularly not civilian ones.

"I want those reporters," Arkady raged. "Let them see the brutality of Macedonia, let them understand how they fight their war. And the UN would have us work out a settlement with these terrorists? Never. Not as long as I'm in command." He paused for a moment, and continued in a different tone of voice, "Your SAR mission—when is it scheduled?"

Zentos was slightly taken aback by the change of subject, but said, "Tomorrow afternoon, General."

The general nodded. "Bring me results, Colonel. Or suffer the consequences."

USS Jefferson
Admiral's Conference Room
1500 local (GMT −2)

Tombstone studied the chart outlining the disposition of the UN forces inside Greece. The troops were concentrated along the border, with most of them assigned to Tavista Air Base. "Lot of firepower for one air base," he noted. "How are they handling the logistics?"

"Pretty well, so far," Batman answered. "They've assured us that their maintenance facilities are more than capable of handling our Tomcats. We'll have to take some extra fly-away boxes in for the Hornets, but most of the consumables are interchangeable with the Tomcats. O-rings, cotter pins, that sort of thing."

"They've got a major rework facility co-located there," Coyote supplied. "The Tomcats should be fine for anything up to and including an engine change out."

"Let's hope it doesn't come to that," Tombstone answered. "In fact, let's hope all we end up doing is flying nice, quiet surveillance missions."

Both Batman and Coyote looked doubtful. "I don't think so," Batman said. He shuffled through the message traffic in front of him, selected one, and passed it to Tombstone. "You heard about that American couple that was killed in the bombing?"

Tombstone nodded. "They weren't the only ones. Lot of local folks were injured, too."

"Yeah, but they're the ones getting the big publicity push," Batman said. "And the Greeks are making the most of it. They know exactly which buttons to push with us."

"How so?"

Batman gestured to Lab Rat. "Fill the admiral in."

Lab Rat stood and pointed a clicker at the computer in the back of the room. A full face photo of a Greek general officer flashed onto the screen. "This is General Dimitri Arkady, chief of staff of the Greek Army and current commander of the UN forces. UNFORGREECE, it's called. He's a hardliner and he's been looking for an excuse to push this entire conflict to a military resolution. The terrorist bombing was just what he needed. He's calling for preemptive retaliatory strikes against known and suspected Macedonian forces."

"Hell of a peacekeeping mission," Coyote said, his face twisted with distaste. "Peace through superior firepower."

"It's gone further than we originally thought," Lab Rat said. "Intelligence reports indicate he's already got the first two strikes planned and weaponeered. And he's making a big push in the international media about how it's a duty he owes to his great friends the Americans."

"How's that playing out?" Tombstone asked. Pamela Drake's face flashed through his mind, and he felt a wave of grief surge through him. Whatever differences of opinion they'd had, and no matter that he was completely content married to Tomboy, Pamela had been more than just an acquaintance. A fiancée for several years, dangerously close to being a wife.

Pamela would have been able to cut through Arkady's bullshit. He could see her now as clearly as though she were in the room, hammering the general with tough questions, spiking follow-up questions into the broadcast. *How would she have slanted this story?* he wondered.

"Most of the media is going along with it," Lab Rat said. "They know how to hook their American audiences." He shook his head. "We think we can go anywhere in the world and be safe. Hell, we can't even go downtown after dark in some American cities."

"But it's going to be hard to back him into a corner over this one," Tombstone observed. "We've used American civilian casualties overseas too many times ourselves as a justification for military action."

Lab Rat nodded. "Exactly our assessment. When he's taking the same position we've held in public so many times, it's going to be difficult to counsel moderation in the UN."

Tombstone stood and stretched. "So you're telling me I'm stepping into a hornet's nest, right?"

Batman nodded. "That's about it. From what Lab Rat says, the Greeks are locked and loaded, and they're going to use the UN strike assets to conduct the attacks." His face grew somber. "Be careful, Tombstone. Arkady's a slippery critter, and the world's getting to be an ugly place again."

Tombstone looked at him levelly. "I'm just an advisor. But, yeah, I'll be careful."

SIX

Sunday, 7 May

Tomcat 200
0800 local (GMT −2)

Tombstone sat on the catapult, waiting for the launch. These were the moments he felt most fully alive, with everything on the line and waiting for that final salute from the catapult officer. Below him, the shuttle was already fastened to his aircraft, thousands of pounds of steam pressure behind it, waiting for release.

At the signal, he shoved the throttles forward to full military power. The jet blast deflectors, or JBDs, behind him shielded the rest of the flight deck and its people and aircraft from the hurricane blasting out of his engines.

It came then, that final salute from the catapult officer, who then dropped to the deck and touched his hand to the nonskid. There was a moment of hesitation, a slight thump as the shuttle took up the slack in the coupling. Then the pressure, hard and demanding, drove him back into his ejection seat. The world was noise and fury now, the Tomcat howling to be released from the unnatural confines of the deck to return to the sky.

Everything was happening too fast and too slow at the same time. The forward edge of the flight deck rushed toward him, the expanse of deck between his aircraft and the water shrinking to a thin sliver of baked black nonskid. Steam streamed out behind the aircraft as the shuttle vented, laying down skid marks of steam in the air.

And yet there was time still, time to think about the moment approaching when he'd be flung off the pointy end into the sky, time to wonder whether someone somewhere had made a mistake, forgotten to calculate the steam pressure setting on the shuttle correctly, missed a malfunction on one of his control surfaces, left the safety pins in the ejection seat points—too much could go wrong too fast, and yet there was time to think about it.

The last bit of deck slipped out from underneath him and he felt the Tomcat jolt down. A moment of panic, normal panic, as the aircraft fought off gravity, poised on the thin line between flying and falling out of the sky. He'd watched this too many times from the tower and knew what they were seeing: his Tomcat below the level of the flight deck, barely airborne, clawing for airspeed and altitude, the Air Boss holding his breath for the few seconds it took for the Tomcat to decide to fly.

He felt it then, as he always had, that odd shift in the feeling of the airframe around him that told him that he'd made it. No soft cat on this one, a launch too slow that would dribble him off the bow of the carrier like rainwater. No control surfaces sticking, no engines faltering— no, this Tomcat wanted the sky.

He kept her level for a few seconds, building up airspeed until he was confident that he was well beyond stall speed, judging the moment more by the feel in the seat of his pants than the heads-up display or the instruments arrayed before him. Then he pulled her nose up, banked hard to the right, and departed the immediate airspace of the carrier.

"Good launch," Bird Dog said finally from the backseat. His voice was high and tight, and Tombstone had to repress the urge to rag on him. Pilots were notoriously bad passengers, particularly when they were

stashed in the wrong seat—the backseat—of a Tomcat.
At least Bird Dog had kept his mouth shut during the
cat shot. Rank and formalities were stripped away in
those moments that both men's lives depended on the
pilot keeping his head, seeing trouble before it developed, and doing exactly the right thing at the right time
to keep them out of the ocean.

"Any sight of our escorts?" Tombstone asked. The
Greek government had insisted on allowing their aircraft
to serve as a formal honor guard for the admiral en route
Tavista Air Base. The carrier had been none too thrilled
at the prospect of allowing even allied fighters that close
to the carrier. A compromise had been reached—the *Jefferson* would move fifty miles offshore, ostensibly to
"pump and dump," to dump garbage and pump sewage.
American fighters would escort Tombstone to within
twelve miles of the coast and the Greek fighters would
take over from there. It was a workable solution, one that
saved face and avoided complicated coordination for both
sides.

"Yes, sir," came Bird Dog's voice from the backseat.
Slower than a real RIO would have been, but still sounding confident. "They're just feet wet, vectoring in our direction."

"Good. I'm switching to button three for coordination
purposes," Tombstone answered. A few moments later,
he heard a voice speaking slightly accented English come
over the channel.

"Tomcat 00 this is Greek one, on station to join you
for escort."

Probably trained in the United States at some point,
Tombstone reflected. Most Tomcat fighters did. Or, if not,
their training facilities were built and operated by American corporations that employed former fighter pilots. It

was no surprise that English was the *lingua franca* for free world fighters.

"Roger, Greek one. Copy you loud and clear. Request you take station on either side of me at standard distances." Tombstone clicked off the mike and said, "I presume they know what that means?"

"Probably so, sir," Bird Dog said, slipping back into a slightly more formal tone now that the catapult shot was over. "And if they don't, that tells us as much as if they did."

Tombstone nodded, pleased by the younger officer's insight. Sometimes it was just as important to know what an allied didn't know as what he did.

"Tomcat 00, this is Viper lead," a definitively American voice came over button three. "Sir, we have a visual on your escorts. Recommend we move off and let them vector in without interference."

"Go ahead, just like we briefed." The announcement had been made to remind all parties that there was a plan—and that they were expected to follow it.

Tombstone could pick out the Greek fighters now, duplicates of the Tomcats in CVBG14's own air wing. His own aircraft rocked slightly as his two escorts peeled off, heading for altitude to oversee the entire evolution.

The Greek fighters came in low, giving him a moment of disorientation as they disappeared from view. He could hear Bird Dog shifting in his seat, straining his neck and trying to stare down at them. They reappeared a few seconds later, on either side of him, slowly climbing and falling in the correct formation.

"Tomcat 00, Greek one on station and at your disposal, sir."

Solid airmanship, Tombstone thought. Nothing flashy,

nothing sloppy. Just good, solid, by-the-book airmanship.

Tombstone made a few small course corrections, checking the Greeks' proficiency in staying on station. They were welded to either side of him, indicating that they were paying attention.

Two miles off the coast of Greece, Tombstone had a clear view of the land. Blue spread out below him, brilliant green land against the stark blue of the Mediterranean. At this altitude, the marks humanity had made on the land even after centuries of occupation were still insignificant against the grandeur of the earth itself.

Suddenly, a flurry of Greek questions and answers crowded the circuit. Although he didn't understand a word of Greek, Tombstone knew what a worried pilot sounded like. He waited for a pause in the transmission, then asked, "Someone want to fill me in?" There was a moment of silence, then a new voice said, "Tomcat 00 this is ground control. Admiral, now that you're safely over our land, I will be detaching your escorts slightly early. Please continue on this course and speed pending further approach instructions." The voice broke back into a string of incomprehensible Greek.

First the Tomcat to his left, and then the one to his right peeled away, shucking altitude as they did. Tombstone made a minor course change to correct for the effect of their jet washes.

"Well, look at that," Bird Dog said. "Man, these people take their escort duties seriously."

Tombstone glanced over at the Tomcat now streaking off to the north. "Lots of escorts carry weapons, Bird Dog. It's just symbolic—probably training loads."

"Maybe so, sir," Bird Dog said, but Tombstone could hear the frown in his voice. "Only thing is, I wouldn't pick iron bombs as the ordnance to slap on a wing just to impress us. Clumsy mothers to fly with. A couple of Sidewinders would have been better, wouldn't they?"

Iron bombs. Tombstone had seen them, of course, wondered the same thing himself at the time, but hadn't said anything. Now, with his escort detached unexpectedly, that old feeling started to gnaw at him, that sixth sense that had saved his ass so many times before.

"It *is* odd, Bird Dog," he said slowly. "And I don't think I like it at all. Anything else in the area?"

"Nothing out of the ordinary," Bird Dog answered. Tomcat 00 was still in the LINK, receiving the combined picture from all the ship's radars as well is its own sensors.

"I wonder where the hell they were going?" Tombstone asked. *And, more importantly, why bombs?*

Greek Tomcat 01
Just south of the Macedonian border
1025 local (GMT −2)

The Greek pilot maintained altitude until he was well clear of the American dignitaries he'd been escorting. This mission had been briefed and rebriefed as a contingency so many times over the last several months that he thought he could fly it in his sleep. There had been a final update before they departed on this escort mission. It could happen at any time, all of them knew it.

Why me? he wondered, as he glanced over at his wing man. Why not another pilot with another section of Tomcats? After all, any one of them could have flown this mission. To break him off escort duty—even though he welcomed the interruption—to undertake this mission hadn't been the only option. When the Americans heard of the bombing run, of course they would make the connection. How could they not?

But perhaps that was exactly what General Arkady intended. To send a message to the Americans by using the escort forces to conduct this mission.

"Two minutes," his backseater said. "On course, on time."

He grunted an acknowledgment. He could see the first landmark now, the small village just south of the border. There, that water tank. Just as briefed, just as he'd flown before. He descended to one thousand feet, turned east and commenced his final approach. His wingman settled in behind him. At two miles out, he descended another five hundred feet. Then he bore in, mentally checking off the landmarks as his backseater called them off.

"Five seconds," his backseater said. He continued to count off the seconds. At precisely the right moment, the pilot toggled off the bombs. His Tomcat jolted upward, suddenly relieved of the two thousand pounds of drag.

He rolled his Tomcat out hard to the right immediately, at right angles to his earlier course. He jammed the throttles forward and went into afterburner. The Tomcat climbed quickly, putting distance between his aircraft and the target. It was only a matter of seconds now.

He ascended to five thousand then continued his turn to the right, giving him a view of the impact point. The land was still and quiet, and for one cold moment he thought they'd missed the target. Then he spotted the iron bomb, curving down in a graceful arc toward its target. He experienced a mild surge of excitement.

The white building in the middle of the clearing exploded. He had one brief second to see the structure start to crumble, then the entire area was consumed in a boiling mass of flames and smoke. It billowed up, mushrooming in clear air and rapidly expanding. A second explosion then, followed by a third and a fourth. The entire area was now a flaming mass of destruction, details invisible inside the conflagration. Then the mushrooming cloud seemed to double its rate of growth—his wingman's weapon had found its target as well. The tactical circuit filled with cries of congratulation and victory.

There was much to be proud of, that was true. According to the intelligence reports, they had just destroyed a major covert headquarters facility operated by the rebel Macedonians. The hurried briefing from the ground controller was that the mission had been authorized as retaliation for a terrorist bombing just hours earlier in Tavista.

Destroying the HQ now would save countless Greek lives down the line, both Greek and Macedonian. After all, the Macedonians were Greek as well, weren't they? A small segment of them were rabid nationalists, misleading the rest of the populous with their inflammatory accusations of racial cleansing. But Greece—his Greece—would never engage in such conduct. No, it was the Macedonians that killed women and children, that brought their terrorist devices into peaceful towns and cities. And while he hoped and prayed that no civilians were killed in the bombing, as would any good Christian, the fact remained that they had brought it on themselves.

"Better than baby-sitting the Americans, is it not?" his wingman cried out. "It was beautiful—did you see it?" And he rattled on with another description emphasizing the size and quality of the blast.

The pilot nodded, made the right sounds at the right moments. But something else had replaced the joyous victory he felt initially. A premonition, perhaps, of what was to come. It seemed that the future held nothing but death, dying, and more bombing runs.

The prospect of that didn't bother him nearly as much as the fact that he enjoyed it.

SEVEN

Sunday, 7 May

United Nations
1130 local (GMT +5)

"The resolution condemning terrorist activities by Macedonian forces inside Greece and authorizing UNFOR-GREECE strikes in retaliation is hereby approved." The secretary general's voice made it clear that he was just reporting the results of the vote. His own arguments against military action were already on the record. "The ambassador from China has moved that all military forces be placed under direct UNFORGREECE command. The United States opposes the motion. China has the floor."

Ambassador Sarah Wexler gazed out across the assembled delegates to the United Nations. The mood running through the room was ugly, a mixture of strident righteousness and false bravado that so often characterized the proceedings at their worst.

There was such potential for good in this organization, she thought, studying the faces of the delegates. At least half of the men and women in this room were possessed of an innate goodness that she cherished. The other half were solidly entrenched nationalists incapable of seeing any viewpoint other than that supported by their own narrow concerns. In a way, the latter were easier to work with. She could draw on the resources of the United States, promise them improved foreign aid or economic advantages, and generally get them to do the right thing . . . if not necessarily for the right reasons. The deals were made behind closed doors, out of the sight of the rest of the world. She regretted many of them, while simultaneously appreciating that the end result was for good.

The ambassador from China fell into the latter category. At least for now. As a growing powerhouse, China would soon be in a position to spurn those benefits that friendship with the United States offered. With nearly two billion people residing inside her boundaries, she possessed a military and economic power untapped at present time but intimidating in its potential. China was just beginning to wake, and she feared if the dragon ever fully uncoiled, the world would feel the consequences.

"I am surprised, Madame Ambassador," the ambassador from China said, "that you oppose this motion." He paused for an appreciative murmur to sweep across the room. "Surely the United States is concerned about the massacre of so many civilians, women and children among them?"

"Of course we're concerned," she said immediately, silently damning him for even daring to play that card. As if China had any right to protest the massacre of countless civilians, given their own record on human rights. "Our forces are now standing by to augment and support the UN peacekeeping efforts in the area."

The ambassador laughed softly. "Peacekeeping. An aircraft carrier loaded with missiles, bombs and fighter aircraft is an excellent weapon—I mean to say, tool—for peacekeeping, yes?"

"Many nations have thought so," she shot back. "Including your own, I believe."

"The United States confuses peace with imposing its own wishes on a region." T'ing nodded at the shouts of agreement now, primarily from China's client states. The young Asian Tigers, she thought bitterly, sweeping her gaze over them and counting their numbers. The world applauded their economic aggressiveness, sought to emulate them in ways that would never ever work in the American culture. But let China follow the path she feared it was taking, and they would be the first to cry for United States intervention. If China ever moved to dominate the region, there would be no stopping her. At least not without another world war. Couldn't they see that? That someday in the not too distant future they would need the aid of the other country they now tried to humiliate in this very forum?

"The USS *Jefferson* is at the United Nation's disposal," she said.

"A careful choice of words," the ambassador replied. "But of course, it is not under the direct command of our UN task force commander, is it? No, it sits there willing to provide resources to support this noble effort only at those times that the United States deems it appropriate. In reality, it is no more than a pawn in these games we play."

Aha, got him! "It is hardly a game, Ambassador. Not when so many lives are at stake."

"Is the United States serious about peace in Macedonia?" he asked. "Prove to me that she is serious. Prove it to the world."

Do not ask the question. Alarms were going off in her mind as she saw what he intended to do. *Do not ask it, oh no, do not ask it. Not because you do not know the answer—but because you do. And what he's about to propose is completely unacceptable. Completely.*

"We're following the well-established and eminently sensible practice that characterizes UN actions today. Our forces are available. As are the forces of other nations that have agreed to participate."

The ambassador nodded sagely. "Oh, yes. As in the previous UN peacekeeping forces that were actually a front for American aggression. As in the Persian Gulf. As in Hong Kong. Infringing on the rights of other nations under the pretext of international relations."

Is that what this is about? Hong Kong? Probably . . . and I'm afraid I don't like what it is going to cost us this time.

She thought of Hong Kong as she had known it over the decades, an amazing, teaming center of financial activity and commerce in the midst of isolation and ethnic suspicion. It had survived because it must. That part of the world needed a Hong Kong in order to trade, as a buffer zone between their own isolationist cultures and the rest of the world. But since the Chinese takeover of administration of the area, the Chinese government had come to a startling realization: given enough money, enough power, and sufficient reason for action, the Chinese political ideology was as vulnerable to corruption as any of the Western governments. With the economic well-being of so many tied to the political maneuverings, it was no wonder that China was still smarting over the last U.S. intervention in the area.

"The only way, I believe, that the United States can demonstrate her complete commitment to this force is to place operational command of USS *Jefferson* in the hands of the UN commander. That, and that alone will prove her sincerity." He said the words carefully, throwing down the challenge in dulcet tones.

I had not expected you to be so blunt. What do you know that I do not, what makes you so sure of yourself that you'd make this move in public? There's something we're missing—something that will get too many of our men and women killed if I don't find out what it is.

Now speaking out loud, she said, "Of course, this is outside my range of expertise." No one missed the sardonic expression on the Chinese ambassador's face. "But

I can consult with the president and determine his wishes. It is unlikely that we would be willing to do that unless every other nation committed to this effort did so as well."

"Then I suggest an immediate poll of the other ambassadors," he said. "Perhaps hearing how the rest of this world views the notion might have some impact on your president."

Is that what it is? You already have your supporters lined up?

"It is certainly something to be discussed," she said calmly. She turned to the current secretary general, the ambassador from Iceland. "In fact, it is so important a question that I suggest a special subcommittee be appointed to investigate."

The secretary general, who'd been watching the entire play-by-play with no expression on his broad impassive face, said immediately, "Of course. An excellent idea. If the following members will agree to serve, they may consider the matter and advise us of their recommendations. Britain, Yemen, Ethiopia, and Singapore. Do the members consent?"

And what drives you? You're usually on our side for one reason or another. I see the point to Britain and Yemen and Ethiopia as well—they're all probably on our side. But Singapore? What is it that you know about them that I do not? Is that what the Chinese ambassador is worried about, something to do with Singapore? She glanced over at T'ing. His face was a carefully orchestrated mask of outrage. But the secretary general's order required no vote from the membership.

"Do the members agree to serve?" the secretary general asked.

The British Ambassador rose. "Of course. We are honored to be a part of such an undertaking with such possible broad implications for both this august body and others in the world. This question of sovereignty, of co-operation between peoples to achieve world peace—it is a difficult matter. And this one central question often arises."

And what did he mean by that, other bodies such as this? She stared at the British Ambassador for a moment, hoping to pick up some clue from his expression. He turned in her direction, offered a bland smile that revealed nothing, then turned back to his notes. Yemen and Ethiopia accepted in short order, as did Singapore, although apparently with some hesitation and confusion on the part of its ambassador.

"Well, then." The secretary general had the expression of a man who should be rubbing his hands together vigorously, please with a difficult task well done. "Shall we table this matter until our subcommittee reports in?"

And there's no telling how long that could take. Is that what he's doing, simply kicking it over to the subcommittee to buy me some time? But then Singapore . . . what is it about Singapore?

No matter. This would bear investigating later, but for now she had achieved what she'd hoped for. Murmuring her thanks, she returned to her seat. At least for the moment, this particular crisis had been averted.

Tavista Air Base
Joint Forces maintenance facility
1200 local (GMT −3)

"What's this?" Airman Smith asked. He stared at the shoulder patch and the oddly faded blue beret the chief had just handed him. "I brought my own gear. What color is this, anyway?"

The chief sighed. "Just take them, Smith. Sew the patch on your right shoulder, about where your crow would go if you put it on that side." He stabbed a finger at a spot on Smith's shoulder and dug into the muscle still sore from carrying tie down chains.

"I'm not wearing any stupid beret," Trudeau announced.

"You guys would bitch if we assigned you to duty in a whorehouse," the chief snapped. "You're on a UN peacekeeping force, so you wear what they wear. Got it?" He turned away from them to the line of sailors queued up to receive their UN-issued gear.

Smith and Trudeau walked off slowly. Smith stared down at the blue felt beret in his hand. It wasn't a color for a sailor accustomed to dreary khakis and whites, too bright for a real military uniform. He tried to imagine himself wearing it, glanced around at the rest of his troops to see what they looked like in it, and decided he didn't like what he saw. No, he didn't like it all—not one little bit.

"How are we supposed to sew these things on, anyway?" Trudeau grumbled. "Like I brought a sewing kit with me?"

"We go find the parariggers," Smith said. "Just like always." The division in charge of maintaining all the flight gear, including parachutes and ejection harnesses and cranials, was particularly adept at getting things sewed on. More than one junior sailor too broke to afford the prices the cleaners charged relied on their expertise.

"Okay, but where does the patch go?" Trudeau persisted. "Dungarees? Coveralls? Man, I hope it's not the dress uniform. This will screw up the sleeve. I'll have to buy a new set after we leave."

Smith spotted a bunch of people walking by sporting the blue beret. A babble of foreign languages reached his ears, some vaguely familiar from high school classes and others completely beyond his understanding. Russian, maybe? That sounded like Chinese or something?

"So we wear the same uniform as the rest of those guys?" Smith said slowly. He shook his head, bothered in a way that he could not completely define. "I don't know, Steve . . . doesn't make a whole lot of sense to me. We're here to take care of our birds, fly some missions. But we're supposed to be on one unit?"

Trudeau shrugged. "I guess so."

"I don't know," Smith repeated. He shoved the beret and patch into a pocket in his coveralls. "I don't have time to do it now anyway. It'll have to wait."

Four hours before, the chief had come to them while they were hiding in the chain locker and told them they were on the team going ashore. "And it's not like we have much time," he had snapped. "So get your asses in gear and get turning. The COD leaves in two hours."

"What do we take, chief?" Smith asked.

"Hell if I know," the chief muttered, more to himself than in answer to the question. "You start sending birds ashore, and who the hell knows where we'll wind up? Spare parts, lubricants, hydraulic fluid—and the one thing we're going to need the most is whatever we forget to take." He glanced over the two young airmen. "You don't have to worry about that—the lieutenant says they got a spare parts depot ashore for their own Tomcats. Supposed to be interchangeable with everything on our birds."

Smith and Trudeau exchanged a telling glance. They had heard that particular line before from the more senior sailors in the squadron, and knew that it never worked out the way it was supposed to. Now, staring at the throng of foreign military men, he was even less convinced that his bird would get the proper care while ashore.

"So what do you think all this is about?" Trudeau asked.

"I mean, it's great be off the ship for a while, not to mention the liberty. But sort of weird to be flying here, you know?"

Smith nodded. "I don't know. I haven't heard anything about the missions. Not specifically."

Trudeau shrugged. "Yeah, well, our job is to keep the birds flying, isn't it?" As Smith walked back to the flight line, one question kept bothering him. Was that all his job was? To keep the birds flying? That was why he was in a uniform?

"I joined the Navy, dammit," he said, as they started across the tarmac to locate their birds. "The Navy, and not the United Nations."

"Life in a blue suit, shipmate," Trudeau answered.

"Is it?" Smith asked.

For once, Trudeau had no ready answer. And neither did Smith.

"These damned things don't fit," Trudeau complained as he stuffed the O-rings into a pocket of his coveralls. "Interchangeable, they said. Right." For all the good the consumables were doing, he might as well have tossed them on the ground, but no good airmen ever intentionally fouled his own deck.

"None of this is any good," Smith said. "And I'm going to do something about it." The indignation over the blue patch on his shoulder had been building throughout the day, and now, faced with another unworkable aspect of this peacekeeping mission, it was too much. He stormed into the line shack and pulled his beret out of his coverall pocket. "Not going to wear it, Chief," he said. "I'm not in the United Nations. I'm in the United States Navy. I'm just an airman, but I know that much."

Much to his surprise, the chief had no immediate reaction. Smith had been prepared for an ass chewing, coupled with some new profanities Chief had not yet used on them. But this silence, that was something new.

"Sit down, Smith," the chief said finally. He pointed to the battered wooden chair in front of his desk. "You and I need to talk."

Smith sat, feeling definitely uncomfortable. This wasn't what it was supposed to be like it all. Nothing took the impetus out of righteous indignation like reason.

Outside he could hear the noise of four different types of aircraft engines turning. The flight schedule this afternoon was an unholy mess, and the tower crew had finally settled for simply spacing fighters and attack aircraft at thirty-second intervals within a twenty-minute window allotted to each aircraft type. The end result was that no one knew exactly who was airborne and who wasn't until the entire twenty-minute window had expired.

The problem was further complicated by the fact that many of the flight line workers didn't speak much English. So far, they'd been able to resort to the universal hand signals all international airports used. But that didn't do much for getting the right O-rings for a bird. Not with half the wrenches measured in centimeters and the other half in inches. "The sleeve patch, is that it?" the chief asked. There was something oddly reserved in his voice that worried Smith.

He shook his head. "It's not the uniform, Chief. I guess I sound out of line, but it's the whole idea. I mean what we're doing here. This isn't our fight."

"Don't you think a lot of people all up the chain of command, including the president, have thought about that?" the chief shot back.

Smith nodded. "Yes, Chief, I do. But I think they came up with the wrong answer."

"You do?"

"Yes, Chief."

The chief studied him in silence for a few moments, then let out a heavy sigh. "You follow orders, son. That's all there is to it. This isn't your call."

"I think it is." Smith's earlier uneasiness was fading.

The chief exploded then. "You have no idea what you're fucking with, Smith. These Greeks, they're in command around here. You think everything works out here like it does back home? Do you realize what could happen to you in a foreign country?" He leaned closer, and Smith could smell the stale rankness of beer on his breath. "These people don't kid around about orders, son. Not for their own people, and not for airmen under their command. People disappear when they disobey orders around here, you got that?" The chief stopped suddenly, as though he'd said too much.

"I'm not your son," Smith said. *Gramps would never talk to me this way. Dad wouldn't either, if he'd lived. They wouldn't be shitfaced in the middle of the day, either.*

"No, you're not. You're a stupid kid who doesn't have a clue. Let me tell you what happens to people who screw up out here." The chief was shouting and the stink of the alcohol was overpowering. "I went to the little welcome aboard lunch they had for us over at the Chief's Club. I *heard* what happens here. One of their pilots, he screwed up a mission last week? Shot down that helo, they said. Well, as soon as he came back to the flight line, the general had him in his office. He hasn't been seen since. His wife, neither. And you want to piss them off over a crappy hat and patch? You willing to bet your life on them being understanding?"

Dad, Gramps . . . what would they do? By rote, Smith felt the outlines of his Gramps's last letter in his pocket. Comfort and conviction radiated out from it, suffusing his whole body.

"There's right and there's wrong, Chief. And this is just plain wrong." Smith stood and walked out of the line shack, leaving the chief shouting after him.

United Nations
1600 local (GMT +5)

Jack Tarkington had been Sarah Wexler's aide for the last ten years. In that time, he'd come to know her moods so well that the rest of her United Nations staff accused him of reading her mind. So when he heard her footsteps padding over the heavily carpeted passageway outside the reception area, he knew that something was wrong. Based on her telephone calls over the last two days, along with the Chinese ambassador's angry appearance in her office just yesterday, it was probably Greece.

Greece. As if there were any easy answer to that one. Not that there ever was with any form of ethnic warfare. During their days in the state department, he'd seen the futility of that.

The junior rank-and-file at the State Department was filled with young, idealistic political science majors bent on changing the world through deep and culturally appropriate understanding. Then there were several layers of increasingly cynical career State Department personnel, who differed only in their degree of disillusionment. At the very top, the ambassadors. Political appointees, the power to represent a mighty nation in international relations conferred upon them based on campaign contributions.

As a rule, the State Department tried to do a good job— and failed miserably. So often at odds with the military over how and when to use force to resolve a situation, the

State Department started howling for troops the moment it appeared that opposing parties simply would not, beyond all reason or rational understanding, listen to United States orders on how to conduct their affairs. They took themselves and her families to remote locations, were surrounded by cultures they might understand intellectually but could never be a part of emotionally, and were surprised when some local hothead took a pot shot them. Let one of them die, and every last one of them turned into a hawk.

Almost every last one, he amended. There was the standard fare of the State Department—and then there was Sarah Wexler. The current administration had appointed her to the position of Ambassador to the United Nations from the State Department based on the strength of tough career decisions and her personal relationship with the president. It was a decision neither party had had reason to regret. Ambassador Wexler often took heat off the present president, and her own forceful and well thought-out positions were often floated as possibilities to assess public and international reaction before the president took a stand. So far, the relationship had worked for both of them.

Ambassador Wexler strode into the room, the picture of complete confidence and dignity. Two assistants trailed behind her, carrying boxes of documents as well as her own prepared speech.

"Tea?" Jack asked.

She looked at him, and he saw the true story in her eyes, but her words were calm and professional. "How thoughtful. Yes, tea would be quite nice. Thank you."

And that, he thought, summed up Sarah Wexler. Grace under pressure, and instinct for human kindness coupled with an understanding of the necessity for force when needed.

After so many years working by her side, he knew exactly how she liked her tea. He left his desk and went to the small kitchenette area, and busied himself for a few minutes bringing the water to the correct temperature before carefully pouring it over the tea leaves. He heard movement behind him, and was not surprised when he turned and saw her there.

He handed her a cup, knowing that he should have steeped the leaves a little longer but guessing that the restorative effect was more important than gourmet considerations. "Bad?"

She nodded. Here, away from the rest of her staff, she let her true emotions show on her face. Hopelessness, and anguish that he saw all too often these days. "They won't listen to reason."

"Do they ever?"

Instead of answering, she slumped down into one of the plastic chairs pushed around the edge of the room. "Not often enough. I've tried everything I can think of, called in every favor. But I think they're going to win the cote on the strikes."

He poured her a refill of the tea, now at the correct strength. "You expected that, didn't you?"

"It doesn't make it easier." She drained the rest of the second cup, although he knew it was too hot to drink that quickly. "There's one last thing I can try, I suppose," she said, almost herself. "It won't work, but at least I'll know I've tried."

"What?" Jack asked, a cold shiver running down his spine. Not since the Spratley Islands conflict had he seen that look on her face: deep regret coupled with iron determination.

"I'll have to talk it over with the president first," she said. "It's risky, but it might work."

Jack felt a deep sense of foreboding. "What might work?"

"China," she said softly. "T'ing holds the keys to this, and I don't know what locks they fit."

The White House
1800 local (GMT +5)

The president listened carefully as Ambassador Wexler briefed him on the previous day's maneuverings. He nodded appreciatively at her description of the secretary general's action. "Good teamwork. You bought me some time, anyway."

"There's too much that troubles me about this entire situation," Wexler said after a moment. "The problem is, they are raising some good points. If the United Nations is truly supposed to be a force for peace in the world, then it makes sense to have all forces under one command. As it stands now, you can withdraw from participation at any time."

The president nodded. "And that's exactly the way I want it. Sure, I could give operational command of our forces to a UN commander. And most of the time, it would be no problem. If things started going wrong, I would simply revoke that chain of command. The other side of it is that I've got good men and women on the front lines out there. I suspect that if the NATO commander gave an order that was truly inconsistent with our national security policy, they'd find a way to stall until I had a chance to act. At least that's the theory. But out there on the edge of a conflict, there's never enough time. I won't put them in the damning situation of having to evade a lawful order that's damning to our national interests. That has to remain my decision. I can't have them making national policy by proxy."

"So it would really be just a sham," Wexler said. "If we agreed, that is. I suppose it's naïve to believe that the UN could be what it's supposed to be." She felt a sense of disappointment. They had talked so often about the potential for good in the United Nations, but sometimes she'd wondered just how much of it the president believed.

He shook his head. "Not at all. The UN is a powerful force. If every member nation were as concerned about world peace as we are, then you can bet that I'd probably support allied command of U.S. forces . . . in some situations. But they're not. Each one has his own rice bowl and their interests don't always coincide with ours."

"The other thing is this entire Macedonia/Greece issue. I'm fairly certain that the UN counsel will authorize military sanctions against Macedonia. But the truth is that Macedonia has some very real, valid complaints about Greece's conduct. The whole idea of self-determination for nations is a central part of our national philosophy. But is that just for us and not for other nations around the world?" she asked.

"I haven't really decided what role I want the U.S. to take in any action against Macedonia," he said finally. "For the same reasons I've just mentioned. There are no easy answers, and I don't want us to be part of a bad one."

"So what do we need to accomplish in the UN?" she asked. "It's coming to a head soon."

The president stood, indicating the discussion was concluded. "If I knew, I would tell you. I'm intrigued by China's connection with Singapore as it relates to Greece. I trust your instincts on this—it's important, or the secretary general and Ambassador T'ing wouldn't see it as an issue. See if you can find out what that's about."

She stood as well. "I'll try, Mr. President. I'll try."

She left his office with no real answers, but in some way unaccountably cheered that the president was grappling with the same issues that bothered her. She would try to untangle the threads of self-interest that ran through her brethren and sistern in the United Nations and get the answers they both needed.

He's a good man. He'll do the right thing if he can. But until we know more about what's happening, none of us know what the right thing is. The only thing I know for certain is that it normally doesn't involve bombing civilians.

Tavista Air Base
2100 local (GMT +5)

Colonel Zentos twisted uneasily in the left seat of the helicopter. It had been years since he'd spent much time airborne, and he found he disliked it now just as much as he had before. The terrain looked alien, unfriendly, particularly now with daylight finally fading.

They'd almost finished combing their assigned search area. So far there had been no trace of the downed helo, but there were still over one hundred and fifty square miles of ground to cover. From this altitude, it should have been easy to spot a twisted mass of metal wreckage on the ground.

Then why haven't we found it? Why haven't the previous patrols found it? Colonel Zentos kept circling around the question, worrying at it from different angles, gnawing at it while another part of his mind automatically translated what he was seeing from the air into what he'd be facing if he were on the ground. It was an old habit, one he'd developed as a major when he'd realized that airborne spotters and ground pounders like himself spoke entirely different languages. He'd forced himself to volunteer for spotter missions, concentrated on learning to extrapolate what his troops would see from what he saw from the air until he felt certain that he'd be able to direct air assets on target every time, no matter where he was.

The shuddering noise inside the helo changed pitch slightly, ratcheting higher. A few extra knots of speed, eked out from the fuel reserves, so that they could cover the entire area before darkness fell.

It hit him all at once as their speed over ground increased noticeably. Their minds were attuned to the wrong mental picture—the helo wasn't in sight, it *couldn't* be. The earlier patrols, no matter how screwed up the pilots were, would not have missed the wreckage.

Therefore, the wreckage wasn't in sight. So what they should be looking for was signs of where a helo *had been*—and no longer was. An entirely different frame of mind altogether.

Seven minutes later, scanning the landscape with his new perspective, he saw it. At the edge of a field, a dark swath of raw land amid the green. Not a farming track, not a cattle path. No.

"There," he shouted, waving the pilot over toward the edge of the field. "Near the trees."

The pilot shot him a puzzled look, but cut sharply away from his course toward the spot.

Hovering over it, Zentos felt relief surge through his body. "Can you set it down?"

The pilot nodded. He eased back on the power and drifted down. As soon as they touched the ground, Zentos popped his hatch open, ducked under the rotor blades, and jogged to the edge of the field. The first stars were visible overhead.

As soon as he reached the area, he knew he was right. The helicopter's downdraft had kept the smell from reaching him at first. Aviation fuel—burnt aviation fuel. And the ground, not gashed—burned.

Then where was the helo? He walked around the perimeter of the burned spot, looking for signs that the helo had been moved. At the edge closest to the woods, the sod had been hastily replaced over part of the burned area. Beyond that, under the canopy of trees, he saw moonlight glinting off metal. He walked over to it and checked quickly to see if there were any bodies. None, but parts of it were so twisted by both the fire and the impact that he couldn't be certain.

No matter. At that moment, he was simply relieved to have found it at all.

Zentos trotted back to the helo. "Call the Command Center. Get a full team out here." He waited to make sure the pilot was complying then walked slowly back to the wreckage.

EIGHT

Sunday, 7 May

Tavista Air Base
Tavista, Greece
1000 local (GMT −2)

Although he couldn't pinpoint why, Tombstone's first impression of General Arkady was not favorable. There was no reason in the man's physical appearance for the trace of revulsion Tombstone felt upon meeting him. Arkady fit the stereotype of a classically handsome Greek: black curly hair, olive skin, the elegant angles and planes of his facial bones had been memorialized for centuries in classical sculpture. Arkady was a bit taller than most of the Greek men Tombstone had met so far, but still a few inches short of Tombstone's own height.

Nor was there anything in Arkady's manners that Tombstone could fault. His welcoming speech sounded genuine, if slightly rehearsed. He spoke of the historic friendship between Greece and the United States, of their long history together. He touched briefly on Tombstone's prior experiences and noted that he was honored to be advised by such a man of experience.

Advised. Perhaps that was the word that rankled slightly with him, Tombstone thought. Advice was something you could take or leave, sort of like Tomboy's opinions on what tie ought to go with which suit in his civilian dress.

Is it my own resentment at being sent here as an advisor rather than being in command myself? Tombstone considered the matter for a moment, then decided it was not. Sure, it stung his ego a bit, but he was a big boy. He could live with it.

Then what is it? Try as he might, he couldn't put his finger on it. Something about Arkady's bearing, the way his men looked at him, the way Arkady's chief of staff stood slightly away from his commander. That wasn't like most chiefs of staff that Tombstone had worked with. Your chief of staff was like a second skin, an extension of your own body, closer to you than damned near anyone, a fucking mind reader—or you got a new one.

"We should have some final word on the helicopter crew and passengers later today," Arkady was saying as Tombstone's attention returned to the conversation. "Frankly, I don't hold out much hope for them. The fire destroyed most of the helicopter, and the remains are being sorted out as we speak. It may take weeks for the DNA analysis to prove who died in this tragedy."

"Is there any possibility that anyone survived?" Tombstone asked. The possibility that Pamela was irrevocably gone seemed inconceivable.

"I don't see how. The fire . . ."

"What if it didn't catch fire immediately?"

Arkady was silent for a moment, then turned to his chief of staff. "Is it possible?"

To Tombstone's surprise, the man seemed to go pale. "I don't think so," he said finally, but his voice lacked conviction.

Arkady let his gaze linger on the chief of staff for a few moments, then returned his attention to Tombstone. "If there were survivors, we would have heard from them by now."

"How near is the crash site to the Macedonian forces?" Tombstone glanced at the chief of staff as he asked the question and was surprised to see that he was even paler than before.

"Ten kilometers, a little more," Arkady answered. "Determining exactly where their forces are at any one time is one of the diff—"

"So it's at least possible that there were survivors who could have been captured by the Macedonians?" Tombstone interrupted.

Silence, chillier than before. "I suppose so. But we would have heard something by now. A demand for ransom, perhaps some propaganda about the cause of the accident. These people think nothing of using tragedy for their own purposes."

"There won't be a ransom demand," Tombstone said, suddenly certain that he knew exactly what was happening. "No, that won't be the first thing we see from them at all."

"The first thing? Admiral, I realized that you are intended to be my advisor, but you do not know these people. I do. What else could there possibly be?"

Tombstone smiled. "A story."

Line Shack
Tavista Air Base
1020 local (GMT −2)

The commanding officer of VF-95 was perturbed. More than that—clearly pissed off. She glared at Airman Smith, bringing the full force of nineteen years in the Navy and three full stripes on her sleeve to bear against Smith's eighteen months in the Navy and three small slanted stripes.

"You put it on. No more of this bullshit, Smith. Get

that damned patch on your uniform by tonight and you'll get off with some extra duty. You understand that?"

"Yes, ma'am," Smith said.

The captain appeared relieved. "Good. Then this matter is settled." Commander Joyce "Tomboy" Flynn-Magruder snapped the manila folder shut.

"Not exactly, ma'am," the maintenance chief said. "We ran across this little problem earlier. I said the same thing to him."

"What do you mean, not exactly?" Tomboy said, menace plain in her voice.

"Skipper, you asked him if he understood. You didn't ask him if he'd do it."

Tomboy swore silently. The chief was right. She turned to look at Smith. "Well?"

Smith was shaking his head before he even started to answer. "I can't do it, Skipper. It's just wrong to put someone else in charge of American forces. I can't."

"Won't, you mean," she said.

"Can't. The oath said I'd protect and defend the United States. I put this on, I'm going back on my word."

Tomboy sat back down at her desk. "What if I told you that in my opinion, this is entirely legal?"

"No disrespect intended, ma'am. But I'd have to disagree."

Tomboy looked at the circle of men and women formed up behind Smith. His LPO, Chief, Division Officer, Department Head, and the XO looked back. In each face, she saw the emotions that were churning her own guts up.

The easy way out would simply be to ship him back to the boat. Get him out of the way, wait for this all to blow over.

Yesterday that would have worked. But today . . . Tomboy sighed and reluctantly opened the folder again. "You realize what's going to happen, then?"

"I get court-martialed, I guess."

Tomboy checked off one box on the disposition section of the report chit. "Right." She closed the folder and handed it to her XO. "Make sure he gets to see a lawyer immediately."

"Yes, ma'am."

"And XO?"

"Ma'am?"

"Make sure they give him the best one they've got. He's going to need it. We might all need it."

NINE

Sunday, 7 May

ACN crash site
Ten kilometers south of the
Macedonian border
0600 local (GMT −2)

General Arkady stood just outside the line of trees as the mishap investigation team combed through the wreckage. A support team was erecting a command tent and running field cabling for the generator. Darkness had cut short the inquiry the night before, but wouldn't slow them down now. By that afternoon, giant floodlights would bathe the area in high wattage night.

"We need proof," Arkady said as he watched the team clad in white jumpers approach the twisted masses of metal. "You and I, we know who is responsible. But proving it to the world is a different matter altogether."

"No one has any doubts," Colonel Zentos observed.

"From a lack of doubts to military action is a large leap," Arkady said. "Wouldn't you agree?"

And when has he ever asked my opinion in that way? Zentos had spent all night setting up the investigation at Arkady's orders, and the general's oddly congenial and mild mood was somehow all the more ominous. He would never understand this man, never, and the assignment which had seemed so much of an honor was becoming an increasingly difficult minefield to traverse.

"We will find it, if it is there," Zentos said finally.

"Of course it's there," Arkady snapped, his mood changing abruptly. "Why wouldn't it be?"

"It is hard to tell with aircraft mishaps, General," Zentos said carefully.

Just then one of the technicians broke away from the crash site and trotted back to them. He sketched off a hasty salute and said, "I think we've found some of the equipment, General. Would you care to inspect it?"

"What is it?" Arkady asked.

"We can't tell yet. It's buried under some debris. But it appears to be an overnight bag of some sort, perhaps belonging to one of the reporters. They're going to try to move—"

The area under the trees exploded in the light and noise. The shock wave from the explosion hit them like a cannon, knocking Arkady and Zentos onto the technicians. Zentos shouted, and rolled over to cover Arkady with his own body. Debris rained down on them, one hard shard of metal piercing the colonel's left shoulder, lancing through soft tissue and muscle like a bullet.

Zentos felt Arkady trembling underneath him and felt a moment of disgust. In danger, one acted. There was time to be afraid afterward.

"Get off me," Arkady snarled. Zentos waited a few seconds longer to make sure there were no secondaries, then rolled off of his commander. "You presumptuous ass," Arkady continued, then stopped when he saw the blood coursing down Zentos's shoulder. Arkady stared for a moment, then turned away indifferently. "What happened?"

The technician was just pulling himself to his feet, his face drained of all color. "An explosion," he said stupidly. "It exploded."

"It was a trap," Arkady said. He turned hard, cold eyes back to Zentos. "Did you not warn them that it might be booby-trapped?"

"General, I . . . no, sir. I did not specifically warn them of that possibility." Zentos noted that Arkady's hands were trembling.

"You are a fool." Arkady walked over to the tree line, picking his way through smoldering debris. The technician shook off his shock and trotted after him, shouting for the medic to come with him.

I didn't warn them because they know to check. They are . . . were . . . the experts. Zentos stared after Arkady for a moment, watching him move among the wounded, closer to the downed helo than he'd been all morning.

"Sir?" a voice asked behind him. "Sir, shall we radio back to the command center for additional teams? A medical helo at least, sir. Colonel?"

Things look different from the ground and from the air. From inside and outside. I wonder . . .

"Yes, immediately," Zentos said, consciously steering his mind away from that train of thought. "And alert the base hospital to stand by to receive casualties."

As the rest of the men began the careful process of extracting the survivors and the casualties, Zentos tried very hard to ignore the suspicions crowding his mind. Everything had gone wrong, so wrong. There was only one consolation. Zentos might be a fool, as Arkady claimed—but Arkady was a coward. If not worse.

Tavista Air Base
Command Center
0800 local (GMT −2)

Tombstone stood to one side as the command elements of the investigation filtered back into the center. Most of the men were still in shock, but a somber, angry undertone was starting to surface in the snippets of conversation he understood. You didn't have to understand Greek to know that every one of them took it personally, just like any military officer would. Somehow falling victim to sabotage made the deaths seem pointless, devoid of the honor of dying in combat.

But this was the way of modern combat, with attacks on civilians and guerilla tactics substituting for conventional warfare. You didn't have to approve of it to realize that it was the wave of the future.

He felt a vague sense of guilt as well, and saw the accusation in the survivors' faces. It was an American helicopter that had killed them. Civilian, perhaps, but American nonetheless. Coming on top of American objections to the UN command of their forces, the tragedy of the ACN helicopter simply added fuel to the argument that the United States was not really a part of any peacekeeping force that didn't serve their own agenda. He supposed it was reasonable from a Greek point of view, if one ignored the countless contributions Americans had made in other parts of the world, most particularly in virtually single-handedly shouldering the burden of keeping the explosive Middle East under control.

He waited until General Arkady retreated to his inner office, then quietly approached and rapped on the door. "Come in," a voice said in English. Tombstone paused, trying to fit the fact that they were expecting him into his intelligence picture. He shoved the door open.

"My deepest condolences, General," Tombstone said. "Is there any way in which I can be of assistance?"

Seated behind his desk, General Arkady simply stared at him. Finally, he shook his head. "No. America has done so much for us already."

Tombstone started to answer, then stopped himself. The aircraft involved might have been civilian, operating with its credentials approved by General Arkady himself, but now was not the time to point that out. Not when Ai ·dy had just lost ten men at last count. There might be time later to discuss it, but for now Tombstone let it be.

"I'll leave you, then," Tombstone said.

"Wait." Arkady held up one hand. "There is something that you might be able to resolve for me. Until the transfer of command power to my task force"—*the UN task force, but I'll let that pass*, Tombstone thought—"I am in a difficult position in a particular matter. Since it involves a U.S. serviceman, I would like to appoint you as investigating officer."

"Investigating officer? For a court-martial or a JAG investigation?"

"Perhaps either one," Arkady said. He picked up a file folder from his desk and held it out. "Review the facts. Interview the witnesses and the man in question. I shall require your assessment of the situation."

"I'm not certain—"

"Read the file. Keep in mind that regardless of the status of your military forces, you are still assigned to me as an advisor. So do that. Advise."

"Of course." Tombstone took the folder and eased out of the office, aware that he'd been summarily dismissed. Once out in the corridor, he started leafing through the sheaf of papers, skimming the acts. He let out a low groan when he saw the squadron—VF-95.

He knows—he's got to know—that I'm married to the skipper. That it's my old squadron. Conflict of interest written all over it. Tombstone started to head back to Arkady and explain why it was simply unworkable.

He stopped two paces from the door. Conflict of interest was an American concept—would it apply to the Greek way of looking at things? And would Arkady care one way or the other?

You're not thinking about this the right way. Of course he knows about the conflict of interest—he has to. He's making a point, assigning me to investigate this case. Making the point that America's got too many conflicts of interests to remain a distinct and separate force.

Well, he'd do the investigation. Find out what was behind it all, see if he could nip it in the bud. He skipped back to the first page and read the sailor's name again, fixing it in his mind.

Tomorrow, Airman Greg Smith, I'm going to find out exactly what was on your mind when you started this. You're a pawn in this power struggle, and you've just given Arkady another piece to play on the board.

TEN

Monday, 8 May

Tombstone stared at the young sailor popped tall in front of his desk. The youngster's uniform was immaculate, freshly pressed and starched. The rank insignia and rating were meticulously positioned, the Dixie cup hat placed squarely on his head, and the haircut high and tight. Airman Smith stared at a point somewhere over Tombstone's head, unblinking and seemingly frozen at attention.

"At ease," Tombstone ordered. Smith snapped immediately into the correct position, no more relaxed that he had been at attention.

"You're aware of why I asked to see you," Tombstone said.

"Sir, yes, sir. The admiral is assigned as the investigating officer in this case and will make a recommendation to the convening authority as to whether court-martial charges should be preferred against me." The voice shook slightly but was clear and level.

"That's correct. They've explained your rights to you?" Tombstone asked, glancing through the file to make sure that the correct form, signed and dated by Smith, was in it.

"Sir, yes, sir."

"And you know you don't have to talk to me unless you want to?"

"Sir, yes—"

"One sir per sentence will do, Airman Smith."

"Sir—yes. I understand my rights."

"And having those right in mind, do you wish to speak to me now?"

At this, Airman Smith seemed to relax infinitesimally. "Yes, sir, I do."

Tombstone leaned back in his chair. From what he could tell, the case was relatively open and shut. Airman Smith had been given a direct order to wit: wear the UN beret and sew the patch on his uniform. Said Airman Smith had refused to do so, violating Article 92 of the Uniform Code of Military Justice, or UCMJ. There was a lot more verbiage accompanying the charges, phrases having to do with the lawfulness of the order, the fact that a commissioned officer was involved—all sorts of legalese.

Disobeying direct orders was an offense that didn't allow much leeway. Unless Smith could prove that the order was unlawful, that he didn't understand it, or that he had no way to obey it, it looked like he was screwed.

And over what? A hat and a piece of cloth. There was no doubt that Smith understood the order and he was physically capable of placing it on his head. Maybe an argument about how you get a patch sewed on when you're ashore in a detachment, but Tombstone suspected Smith could have worked that out, too.

That left only the legality of the order in question, and Tombstone didn't have much doubt about that issue either. If the order to participate in a UN peacekeeping force was illegal or unlawful, then a hell of a lot more people than Smith were in deep shit.

"So explain this to me, son. Tell me why you won't wear the beret."

Smith took a deep breath. "Sir, my lawyer told me not to talk to you, but I figured if anyone would understand it would be you. I know who you are, Admiral, and what you've done. Everybody does." Smith laughed nervously, his words tumbling over each other. "I'd probably ask you for an autograph if it weren't for . . . for all this."

"Go on," Tombstone said.

Smith began outlining his initial excitement about being part of the team, then the reality of working side by side with the other nations on the flight line. Some of his complaints were simply the disgruntled opinions of a very junior sailor who didn't have the big picture. But when he got to the details of maintenance on his Tomcat, Tombstone paid close attention.

"It wasn't safe, sir. Not what they wanted me to do. Chief, he would never have let me do it that way."

"And you told the chief?"

Smith nodded. "But the Greek lieutenant said we had to do it anyway. That's when I knew it wasn't right, what they wanted us to do. Being under his command. Because what he wanted us to do could have gotten a couple of guys killed in my bird, and that's not going to happen."

"Maybe he knew something you didn't know about it," Tombstone suggested.

Smith shook his head, now more animated than he'd been since he first entered the room. "No disrespect, sir, but no. You wrap the cotter pin like that and don't safety wire it, it's too dangerous. What if it comes loose in flight?"

"What if this lieutenant had been an American officer?" Tombstone asked. "Don't tell me that you've never had one of our officers tell you to do something that was stupid?"

"Sure, that happens," Smith said. "But then you've got a chain of command. I tell the chief, we go to the division officer, the maintenance officer, all the way up if we have to."

"And what if your skipper still told you to do it?"

Smith was silent for a moment. "It would depend, sir. I'd probably do it because the skipper knows more about the Tomcat than I do. So does the maintenance officer. But this guy, he didn't. And there was no one else to ask." He dropped his gaze from the distant spot on the wall he'd been staring at. "We shouldn't be trusting them with safety of flight, sir. Not unless the guy making the decisions knows what he's talking about. And they don't."

"Why do you say that?" Tombstone asked. From what he'd seen of the Greek forces, they operated pretty much like the American ones did, albeit with a few cultural differences.

Silence again, then Smith said, "They shot one of their pilots when he screwed—excuse me, Admiral—when he messed something up. We don't do things like that. So what would they do to me if something happened to my bird?"

"They shot a pilot?"

Smith nodded. "Everybody knows about it."

Everyone but the person who ought to. Tombstone took a deep breath, trying to calm down before he blew up. "Tell me what you know about this pilot getting shot. Tell me everything."

"He flew a mission a few days ago, the same day that helo went down. When he got back, he had to go see the general. Nobody's seen him since then. His wife, they said, she showed up at the squadron looking for him, all crying and everything. They took her to see the general too. She hasn't been back."

"And you think they shot him . . . and maybe his wife as well?"

Smith nodded. "The Greek guys that speak English, they say it's not the first time, either."

After Tombstone had heard Smith's entire collection of rumors, he called the Judge Advocate General officer in and sent Smith out to the reception area. Tombstone briefed the lawyer, asking him to take a complete statement from Smith. "And do it yourself," Tombstone said. "I want this close held until I can find out what's going on. Don't grill the kid, just ask him enough questions to keep him talking and to get it all. Then come see me." He dismissed the lawyer and picked up the telephone. After accessing a satellite telephone line, he punched in the telephone number for *Jefferson*'s flag spaces.

Batman's chief of staff answered the phone, then put Tombstone on hold for a few minutes while he tracked down his boss. Finally, Batman picked up the line. Tombstone said, "How far along are you on the turnover of our squadron to the UN command? Officially, I mean."

"It's going well," Batman said, although his tone of voice indicated that he was far from pleased with it. "We've got a ton of inventory lists to work through, but we're getting there. I expect to be done late tomorrow."

"Find a way to stall. We need to drag this whole thing out for a few days—weeks, if we can."

"Why? What's up?"

Tombstone glanced at the telephone to make sure that the crypto light was on, indicating that the circuit was encrypted. "You're not going to believe this. Hell, I'm not even sure that I do. But until we get to the bottom of it, don't submit the final documents, okay?" Tombstone filled him in on Smith's story, concluding with, "And not a word to anyone. Red circuits only, no message traffic on it. Got it?"

"I got it. Let me know when you have something solid and I'll take care of things on this end."

Tombstone hung up the telephone, satisfied that he'd done what he could to buy the United States some time.

Four buildings away, General Arkady hung up his telephone as well, scowling.

The United Nations
1130 local (GMT +5)

Ambassador T'ing regarded Wexler gravely. "You ask too much."

Wexler glared back at him. "I don't think so. A simple explanation isn't all that egregious a request, is it?"

"China simply acts on behalf of the struggling people of Macedonia. Their cause is just, and China has a long history of supporting those who fight for the right to determine their own futures."

"Ah. Like Vietnam? Like Taiwan? Or like Tienaman Square?"

T'ing drew himself up to his full height. "There are many parts of the world that the United States has never really understood. For all your talk about democracy and Wilsonian ethics, you've never understood the question of nationalities. In fact, you make it a national ethic to ignore the very question with this melting pot myth of yours. Ha. You end up with a nation of mongrels."

Wexler sighed, suddenly sick of the all too predictable path the argument was taking. It had been a long day—hell, it had been a long week—and it showed no signs of being over any time soon. "Give it a rest, why don't you? All I'm really interested in is Greece and Macedonia and this blasted insistence of yours that we turn over command of an aircraft carrier to the UN commander. Just once—just this once—would it be too much to ask for a straight answer?"

"I am answering you," T'ing said stiffly.

"No, you're not. Not really. What's really behind this? Teaching the U.S. a lesson after Hong Kong and the Spratleys? That's it, isn't it? Or do you have some sort of trade concession you'll wring out of me eventually when I simply have to know what's going on?"

T'ing fell silent for a moment, clearly put off by her approach. She understood why—this was not the way diplomacy worked. Her conversations with the Chinese ambassador should be mere formalities to cement agreements worked out by their underlings who could speak frankly without making national policy or committing her to anything definite. By the time it reached their level, all the shouting should be over, reduced to sterile phrases on international accords.

She knew this—knew it too well not to know how uncomfortable she was making T'ing.

Knew it, and was tired of it. Frank talk, like the kind that she'd grown up with in the Midwest, where people worked out their differences out in the open. She understood that that approach was antithetical for the Asian nations, but why did it always have to be the United States that had to try to understand other cultures? How about a little understanding from the other side as well?

"So what is it?" she said, feeling a sense of release of the strictures she'd practiced and perfected over the years. "Talk to me."

T'ing drew back, a look of deep offense in his eyes. She took a step forward, physically backing him into a corner. "Come on, just this once. I won't tell anyone that you broke the code. Play ball with me and let's see if we can come to an understanding instead of dicking around with words for a few years. You want fighter aircraft? The Spratleys? I'm not saying yes to either of those, but I'm willing to discuss it."

"We do not need your aircraft," T'ing replied. "And as for the Spratleys, they are not yours to give or to take away."

Wexler sighed. She'd had a moment of hope, of crazy enthusiasm, that this blunt approach might work. She should have known better. In all the time she'd known T'ing, since their paths crossed during their younger years, she'd never seen a crack in his inscrutable reserve. "Let our staffs talk, then. I had just hoped . . ." She let her voice trail off, knowing that T'ing would get the point even as he refused to concede an inch.

Then inspiration hit. Right idea, wrong approach. She was asking T'ing to go first.

"You know, the U.S. really doesn't have that much interest in what happens in Greece," she said, and watched a shadow of shock race across T'ing's face. "Not like the Middle East. What we really hope is that there'll be some way to make Europe solve her own problems for a change."

"Then why the task force and your public support?" T'ing said.

She shrugged. "What else could we do? The only point is to make sure our historic allies understand that we'll be there if there's ever another Hitler on the march. Somehow, that whole idea's gotten out of hand, made us the nine one one force of the world. You have to know that we're not happy about that."

"I see." She watched T'ing's face, seeing the subtle changes in his expression that told her he was thinking furiously. "If I might make a suggestion, then," he said. He stopped and waited.

"It would be welcome," she said, and for once she

meant it. "China's been at this business of government quite a lot longer than we have. You've got a civilization that stretches back centuries. Maybe your solutions aren't ours, but they're worth listening to."

T'ing glanced around to see whether anyone else was watching them. They were, of course, but they were standing back at a polite distance. Both coteries of aides were holding back the rest.

"I think," he began slowly, "that none of us wish to be the world's nine one one force. China has had her own problems with the rest of the world in recent times."

Wexler nodded. Recent times—to T'ing, that would cover the last several centuries, she knew.

"What we wish most is to be left alone," he said. "It is hard for the rest of the world to understand that, but it is precisely what we desire, what we work for. Yet as the world shrinks, it becomes increasingly difficult to achieve that. Energy demands . . . the point of the Spratley Islands was not only that we do believe that we have a valid claim to them, but that China has energy requirements growing at a tremendous pace. We've seen how your country has been crippled by your reliance on the Middle East—ensuring that you maintain that flow of petroleum from foreign sources has cost you billions in military spending, and yet you are still not assured of access to oil. China does not wish to go down that path. We prefer for all our needs to be satisfied internally. We have learned from the American experience."

"And this has implications for the Macedonian problem?" she asked, wondering if she'd gone too far. For T'ing, his remarks had been astoundingly frank.

"You might consider that possibility," he said. "Just as a starting point for discussion."

Discussion—might that actually be possible? She felt a

thrill at the very prospect, not at the advantage that it would give her in her own career, but in the possibility that the U.S. and China might actually be able to reduce the level of aggression and hatred in the world.

"I shall," she said, and meant it. Then another thought occurred to her. "Would you by any chance be free for dinner this evening? I'm without commitments myself for a change, and was considering dining alone. I'd welcome the company and perhaps a chance to hear your opinions on a number of issues. As a representative of a more experienced country, of course."

For the first time since she'd known him, T'ing actually looked flustered. "I had not . . . my plans are . . ."

"Forgive me," she said instantly. "I'm afraid I—"

"No, not at all, it is just that—"

"I insist we—"

"If you would—"

They both fell silent. Finally, T'ing inclined his head slightly. "I shall be dining in the Executive Hall this evening. At perhaps nine P.M."

"Perhaps I shall be as well," she said tentatively.

"Perhaps," he answered, his voice giving her no clues.

Suddenly Wexler broke out laughing. "I do not yet understand you, T'ing, not even after all these years. But I do understand the UN. Whatever you've got in mind, you're likely to prefer to have a bit of uncertainty stirred into the pot. And don't you think that if the two of us are seen dining together that that will set some people talking?"

T'ing almost smiled. "The fact that tigers are dangerous does not alter the fact that there are tigers in the world. At nine, then. Perhaps." He bowed, gestured to his entourage, and departed.

Wexler stared after him with a bemused expression on

her face. Jack edged up to her and asked quietly, "What the heck was that all about?"

Wexler stared at T'ing's departing back and smiled. "I honestly don't know. But it felt like progress."

ELEVEN
Tuesday, 9 May

Tavista Air Base
Tavista, Greece
1900 local (GMT −2)

Tombstone stared down at the paper map laid out in front of the assembled staff of American, Greek and other nation's pilots comprising the UN task force. The plan seemed simple enough, with the ingress and egress routes characterized by easily recognizable landmarks. The weaponeering on the entire mission seemed to be sound, and there had obviously been some thought given to allowing each nation to participate to the best of its capabilities.

Why, then, were alarm bells going off in his head?

He tapped one site marked in red. "This radar installation—how did you determine it was inoperable?" It was critical to using limited resources effectively to know whether a target had been suppressed, neutralized, or destroyed so that weapons could be allocated where needed.

"It is already destroyed, Admiral," Arkady replied without looking up. "Our intelligence sources are quite capable."

"How was it destroyed? And how exactly did you make that determination?" Tombstone persisted. "Satellite? Recon? Or reports from civilians on the ground?"

"I'm afraid that information is sensitive," Arkady said, finally looking up from the map. "There are certain sources that we choose not to disclose at this time. Naturally, I have reviewed the assessments personally, and I'm quite satisfied that the installation is inoperable."

"Inoperable—or destroyed?" In Tombstone's mind, the words were hardly synonymous. The need for precision in describing BDA was one of the first lessons the U.S. Marines had taught him. A suppressed target was simply incapable of intervening in the conflict. A neutralized target was damaged—a tank, for instance, that was knocked off its treads was neutralized because it was no longer mobile. It was not, however, destroyed. That term was reserved to describe smoking holes in the ground formerly occupied by a target. One didn't ask the Marines to destroy something unless smoking holes were what you wanted.

"It will not be a factor," Arkady said. "The matter is closed."

Dead silence in the room at that. Tombstone tried to control his temper and think of a way to make his point. It was obvious to him that the BDA from the previous day's strikes was sorely inadequate, particularly since restrikes were not planned on some of the more critical installations. Like this radar site, which prior to the first strike had provided an excellent picture of the area surrounding the location of the suspected rebel headquarters. If they managed to repair and rearm it before the next day's mission took off, the cost in lives and equipment could be devastating.

"I think the admiral has a point," one of the Israeli pilots said.

I can count on them. They know what combat is about.

"I don't," Arkady said, compounding his earlier discourtesy. The American pilots in the room bristled. Every last one of them knew Tombstone; had either served with him in combat or knew his reputation as a top fighter pilot. They trusted his judgment a good deal more than that of the UN commander.

"I'd like to know more about the BDA as well," Tomboy Magruder said. "Before we put our people in harms way, we need to know what risks they're taking."

Arkady drew himself up to his full height and glared at the assembled officers. "Timid pilots don't win battles. If you have doubts about your ability to cope, then you may request to be removed from tomorrow's schedule. If necessary, my pilots alone will fly the mission. I'm confident enough of this information to risk their lives. That should be all the confirmation you need."

Right. And then you'll explain to the rest of the world that the Americans were chicken. Besides, I'm not so sure that risking your own pilots' lives says all that much— not if you're willing to shoot them if they screw up.

If that was in fact what had happened. Tombstone experienced a moment of doubt as the eyes of the rest of the pilots were fixed on him. How reliable was Smith's report? Was it anything more than mere disgruntled gossip from the troops? If only he had a name, a few details other than the date of the alleged incident, he might have felt more confident in interrogating Arkady about his commitment to his own pilots' safety.

But with nothing but Smith's word to go on, it wasn't enough. Too few details . . . and then there was Smith himself, facing court-martial charges for disobeying orders. A reliable witness? Tombstone suspected he was, but there was no way he'd be able to convince a Board of Inquiry that he was right.

Not that that would stop him if he could convince himself. So far, all he had were grave doubts.

Arkady snatched the flight plan from the table and threw it to the ground. "My men will go first." He gazed at the rest of them, disgust in his eyes. "We will prove to you that the site has been destroyed. And any others that you are feeling less than confident about. I would not want you to take unnecessary risks, of course."

"That won't be necessary," the skipper of VF-95 spoke up immediately, her eyes hard and angry. Tombstone felt a surge of pride coupled with his concern. Nobody accused an American of cowardice and got away with it—nobody.

"No, I insist," Arkady said. His voice left no doubt of his opinion of the rest of the UN forces. "You will fly in a supporting role." He turned and walked from the room, tossing the flight schedule at his chief of staff as he left. "Arrange it."

Tomboy walked over to Tombstone and said quietly, "You know I didn't have a choice. Not after that."

Tombstone nodded. "I believe you didn't *think* you had a choice." He left it at that.

United Nations
1900 local (GMT +5)

Over dinner, T'ing proved to be a surprisingly congenial companion. While he could hardly be called charming, Wexler discovered that he had a dry sense of humor coupled with keen observations on the various personal quirks of the other ambassadors. He also seemed to take a quiet pleasure in the consternation their dinner caused the other diners. By the next morning, Wexler was certain that rumors would have circulated through the building.

Only once did they touch on the question of Macedonia. When she made an innocent remark about Greek food, T'ing apparently took it as a request for information. He stared down at the vegetarian meal on his plate—another surprise, that was—and said, "The enemy of my enemy is my friend. It is something you should keep in mind." All attempts to get him to elaborate failed.

As her driver took her home later that evening, she kept trying to tease meaning out of the statement. She had a feeling that T'ing was trying to warn her, was actually making a good faith effort to reciprocate her earlier candor. But coming right out and saying something was too foreign to his culture and to the way of doing business in the UN that had enabled him to survive for so long. It might not be much, but she suspected that it was the best he could do.

The enemy of my enemy—well, who would the enemy be? Macedonia? China? Probably the former, she decided, since she could see no immediate reason for China to be an open enemy at this time. Or maybe he was explaining China's position? Then who was China's enemy? Greece? But why?

The first strike was due to launch in two hours or so, given the time difference between Greece and D.C. Maybe she should let JCS know, tell them to . . . to what? To be careful? To expect treachery? They would be taking all necessary precautions anyway, and she had nothing definite to be factored in to their decision-making process. The cryptic words of a man who'd stood too often on the opposite side—what would they make of that?

Yet there was a kernel of meaning in T'ing's words, she was certain. The only question now was whether she was smart enough to figure it out. And if he'd had the guts to give her a warning of some sort, then she would have to find a way to decipher it.

Macedonian Camp
1800 local (GMT −2)

Pamela Drake put her hands on her hips and glared at
Colonel Xerxes. "I'm not going anywhere," she announced. She pointed at the all-terrain vehicle waiting for
her. "You can forget it."

"You don't understand the danger," he began.

Her temper erupted. "I've been in more wars in the last
two years than you've seen in your entire lifetime," she
snapped. "I didn't run when the Cubans took me hostage,
and I'm not running now."

"If you were a hostage, then by definition you couldn't
run," he pointed out. "This is a different situation entirely."

"Not as far as I'm concerned." She took a step closer
and laid one hand on his biceps. "This is what I do for a
living. Don't you understand that?"

"Crash in helicopters?"

"When required. Listen, if I'm not here, someone else
is going to get the story. Someone who may not be as
open-minded as I am. You need me here if your side of
this thing is going to get a fair airing in the international
news."

Xerxes was silent for a moment, seemingly fascinated
by a small patch of dirt next to his shoe. Finally he looked
up, and she was shocked by the anger she saw in his eyes.
"Do you think that this is what this is about? Sides, stories, photo opportunities? Have you learned nothing about
war in this oh-so-glorious career of yours?"

"I've learned plenty about it."

"But not the most important thing." He pulled away
from her and headed for the vehicle. "And until you do,
you're a danger to me and my men."

"What are you talking about? I've seen dead bodies

before, if that's what you're worried about."

He turned to face her, sadness crowding out the anger. "I'm sure you have. But the one thing you haven't seen yet is dead friends. And until you understand that, until you're capable of leaving your precious objectivity aside long enough to understand the human cost of this, you don't understand anything other than the facts."

"I have to be objective. That's what makes it reporting."

He shook his head, and turned away again. "That's what makes it sad. You know, you've never even asked me what happened to the bodies of the other people on the helicopter."

Pamela watched him go, confusion raging in her mind. How dare he—did he have any idea who he was talking to?

Of course he did. He knew from the moment she was brought to his camp who she was. Other than not being permitted to leave—not that she'd have gone if offered the opportunity—she'd been treated well, in accordance with her standing in the international community. So he understood who she was, what she did. Why then these comments about dead friends, about the other people on the helicopter? They all knew the risks when they'd gotten on board.

What was his name? The cameraman. Something inside her cringed a bit at that, and not for the first time. Hadn't it been one of the first things she'd thought of when she'd regained consciousness? What would it be like, to die in a foreign land where no one knew your name?

He probably had a family somewhere, maybe a wife and kids. Did they know what had happened to him? The news had reported the helicopter as lost, but there'd been no discussion on the disposition of the bodies. Surely his family had been notified privately and they knew the awful truth—that he wasn't coming back in one piece.

Tombstone. His face flashed into her mind as she thought about the cameraman's family. She knew what Tombstone had suffered over the years, not knowing the fate of his own father, and that had lasted for decades. It had finally driven him into Vietnam and Russia in search of answers.

Would it bring the cameraman's family to Macedonia? And if they came, would she see them? How would she answer their questions about his final moments?

I can't tell them I didn't even know his name. Even for her, that act would be too cruel.

Xerxes vaulted into the vehicle and tapped the driver on the shoulder. He pulled away, did a U-turn, and headed back toward the camp.

She watched him go, a tall, passionate man, one who asked questions that disturbed her certain world immeasurably. Another chilling question crossed her mind, one that bothered her more than she would have liked.

What if he's next?

TWELVE

Wednesday, 10 May

Tavista Air Base
Flight line
0900 local (GMT −2)

Bird Dog ran through the prelaunch checklist, calling out
the steps as he went. From the backseat, Gator double-
checked him at every step. It seemed to Bird Dog that his
RIO was moving slower that usual. Was Gator pissed at
him? He ran back through the last few days, trying to see
if there was a reason for it.

Nothing as far as he could remember, and neither of
them had had enough time off to get drunk enough to
forget something truly significant.

"Hey, what's up with you?" Bird Dog asked. "You on
the rag or something?"

Gator snorted. "Right. And I suppose you've been doing your usual sterling job of paying attention at briefings?" He read off the next step in the checklist and
waited for Bird Dog's response.

"I was there. And I took notes, too."

"And?"

"And what?"

"And you're entirely satisfied with the mission planning?"

Bird Dog could tell from Gator's tone of voice that
there was a right answer to the question, and it wasn't
"yes." "Maybe," he said. "I might have done it a little

differently, but I'm not on staff anymore. I've got an ingress route and a place to drop ordnance—what's not to like?"

"And what did you think about Tombstone's concern over those SAM sites?" Gator pressed. "Bothered you a little?"

Of course not. Just one of the hazards of naval air, shipmate. "Sure it did. But Arkady seems pretty certain he's gotten it taken care of. Hell, his boys are going in first. You think he'd do that if there was a reason to worry?"

"Ah. I see. You're willing to risk your ass—and mine as well, I might point out—based on the word of a Greek general that you've never worked with before. Even over Admiral Magruder's objections."

"Tombstone didn't put a kibosh on the mission," Bird Dog said, now feeling a bit defensive. What the hell was the big deal about one SAM site more or less? They'd been up against them before and gotten out all right.

"I know he didn't. But he's not in command right now. Let me put it this way. Based on what you observed at the briefing, do you think Tombstone would have tanked this mission if he'd been running the show?"

"You're so smart, you tell me."

"He would have," Gator answered, no doubt in his voice.

"And so what? You saying we should have sniveled out of this one just because of a SAM site when our own skipper says its good to go?"

Gator fell silent for a moment, sighed, then said, "No, of course not. You just be careful, that's all I'm asking. Pay attention to your RIO from time to time."

Bird Dog read out the next couple of steps on the checklist, verifying that his altimeter setting was correct and his backup hydraulics were working. In the back, he heard Gator bringing his gear on line in standby mode. "You think those SAM sites are still there, don't you?"

"Yes. Don't you?"

"Probably." The plane captain in front of them was giving Bird Dog the start-engines signal and the conversation terminated as the low, throaty grumble of the engines starting up drowned them out. The plane captain ran them up to full power, then signaled for a final check of control surfaces. Bird Dog obliged and was finally turned loose to taxi and take his place in the waiting line of aircraft. He turned slightly out of the straight line approach to avoid the jet wash from another American Tomcat.

"You listen up if I start yelling, you hear?" Gator said over the ICS. "No hotdogging."

"I hear." Bird Dog taxied forward, pivoted to his left and saw the broad expanse of runway stretched out before him. A few moments later, the tower cleared him for take-off. He slid the throttles forward smartly and let the Tomcat accelerate smoothly through one hundred and forty knots. Finally, as he could feel her straining for the sky, the sensation of the wheels light underneath him, he pulled back and eased her into the sky. As soon as he was clear, he retracted the landing gear, slammed the throttles forward and headed for the open sky.

Hill 802
Just west of the Macedonian camp
0910 local (GMT −2)

"They're coming, Pamela." Xerxes touched her gently on the arm. "We need to take cover."

She pulled away from him. "We're far enough away from headquarters for it not to matter." She glanced around the lush hills. "Besides, there's nothing around here that would keep a five hundred-pound bomb from killing us. Let's keep going."

She'd spent the last hour trekking back toward the camp, still furious at Xerxes for dragging her out in the boonies. Getting the little woman to safety—god, would this crap ever end? What, he didn't think she'd be able to get away from him, figure out where she was and get back some way? Short of hog-tying her, there was no way that they could stop her. After a few vehement protests, including a pointed reminder that he'd evacuated his own staff, Xerxes had finally given up. He'd tossed her in an all-terrain vehicle, hopped in the driver's seat, and simply taken off. As soon as he'd stopped, she'd jumped out of the truck and started hiking back toward the camp. Xerxes followed, alternately pleading and threatening.

There was a grumble off in the distance, like thunder over the horizon. Pamela paused, straining to hear. As it grew louder and more distinct, she nodded authoritatively. "Tomcats. Couple of sections at least."

"You're right. Please, Pamela . . . at least until the attack is over, let's stop."

"Are you kidding? This is the perfect time. Come on, that hill over there. We'll get some altitude, maybe see them make their run." She set off at a brisk trot, her Nikon banging against her leg. Maybe she couldn't shoot rolling footage, but a couple still shots right at the exact moment would have to do.

Xerxes kept pace with her easily, leading her to reassess her earlier guess of his age. They trotted up the gentle lower slope of the hill in tandem, slowing only at the steeper craggy slope near the top. Finally she had a good view of the surrounding countryside. She turned to glare at the Macedonian commander. "You could have told me we weren't that far away."

He shrugged. "You know how long the ride was out here. Can I help it if you didn't notice we went in circles?"

She swore silently, acutely aware that she'd been distracted. Xerxes, the ass. Why had she let him get her talking, started sharing some of his own stories about Greece with her? It'd been a ploy, all of it. If she'd been paying attention, she wouldn't have spent the first two hours lost, would have known how to get back to the camp.

The Tomcats were visible on the horizon now. They were coming in low, nap of the earth stuff, flying that Tombstone had always said was the best thing since Disney World. Automatic terrain navigation capabilities enabled the Tomcat to stay a set distance from the ground, relying on its auxiliary radar to hold the aircraft in position. She watched them porpoise in over the low hills, eerily following the exact contours of the terrain.

The camp—yes, that was the target. Good intelligence—they knew exactly where they were headed. Tomcats first, four of them. Thirty seconds behind, the smaller form of the Hornets boring in. Then more Tomcats. Then . . .

She held her camera up and focused in on the campsite area spread out below her. It was well camouflaged, with netting and brush spread over every part that could conceivably be seen from above.

All to no avail. The aircraft clearly knew exactly where they were going. Unhesitatingly, they inchopped the valley between two hills and seemed to pass over her so close that she could make out the pilots' faces.

The first two went by, their thunder washing over her like a storm. She looked up to gauge their speed and when they'd be over target, and noticed the tail markings—the Greeks first, it seemed. Well, that made sense. It was their fight, after all.

When it started, the spitting hum of antiair rounds were almost swallowed up by the sheer fury of the Tomcat engines. At first she thought it was an insect, then turned to see the tracers spiking up from the trees on the opposite hill.

The lead Tomcats were well out of range, but not so the Hornets immediately in the Tomcats' wake. The first Hornet cartwheeled in the sky, tumbling forward along its former course completely out of control. She saw the canopy fly off in a different direction, then the chute emerge. So close to the ground—could it possibly open? It did, billowing out against the blue sky, lines invisible from this distance but not the green figure suspended below the chute as though by magic. For just a moment, she thought they might make it.

Then the chute completed the arc it had been making, swinging its cargo up and over it. The pilot hung overhead for a moment, suspended above his parachute. Then he descended on the opposite side, pulling the parachute over with him and spilling the air out of its folds.

She cried out a warning, knowing already that it was too late. The pilot was still alive, waiting, knowing that any second he would start that last fatal uncontrolled descent to the ground. At least a thousand feet up—was there any chance he could survive it?

Suddenly the distance between the pilot and the chute increased dramatically. He'd cut the useless chute off and was deploying his backup. But was there time for it to deploy, to fill with air and brake his descent? She watched as the chute streamed down through the remaining eight hundred feet, never completely billowing out.

Maybe it had been enough. It had to have been.

The second Hornet was jinking around the sky, weaving and bobbing as it tried to evade the antiair fire while still remaining on course and on time for its mission. She watched it maneuver, wondering whether the pilot would make it.

Devil Dog 220
0915 local (GMT −2)

Thor swore automatically while he mentally worked out the trajectory of the antiair fire. That hill over there—he double-checked his memory and kept swearing. It was the same one that Tombstone had questioned Arkady about.

So much for the effect of letting the Greeks go first. Whether they'd needed time to acquire the targets, had had a start-up fault or what, the antiair site had let the first two aircraft pass without attacking, lulling the Americans that followed into a false sense of security. His wingman, Marine Captain Buddy Murphy, had just paid the price for that false sense of security.

The Hornet was a light aircraft, much nimbler than the Tomcat. It was also a single-seater, and the primary reason that Thor had chosen to go Marine rather than Navy out of the Academy. There was something primal about fighting the battle alone, even surrounded as he was with a host of sophisticated electronics, the LINK picture, and all the decision and targeting aids embedded in the complex black boxes that lined the interior of the fuselage.

He pulled the Hornet into a hard turn, held it for two seconds, then cut back in the opposite direction and slammed the afterburners in. The Hornet cut hard arcs in the sky, dancing through the SAM site airspace like a running back. A low hill off to his left—he remembered it from the briefing. A quick visual told him what he needed to know, that it was probably large enough to shield him from the site if he could get behind it.

But where was the IP? Could he maneuver that far off the ingress route and still get ordnance on target?

Like he had any choice. If he didn't find some cover from the SAM site, his ordnance would still be on his wings when he hit the ground nose first.

He porpoised up two hundred feet, then back down, cutting back and forth as he changed altitudes, careful not to fall into a rhythm with it. Two more seconds—if he could just get a few more knots of speed, he might just . . .

The ESM warning system screamed that he was out of time. Missile launch . . . and Thor was the closest target.

Thor dove for the deck, pulling up just fifty feet above the ground. He'd traded his altitude for speed and distance, but the ground now posed almost as much of a threat as the missile. He kept his eyes glued to the earth racing by below him. At least this far out from civilization there weren't any telephone wires or gondola cables to run into.

Wait for it, wait for it—now! Thor toggled off two chaff canisters and three flares, hoping to sucker the missile in. If it were IR or dumb homing radar, it might go for it.

Another second. He pulled up, trying to avoid the missile's path but desperate for some altitude. He needed another fifty feet to clear the hill unless he wanted to go around, and he didn't think he had time for the scenic route. Whoever was at the controls at the SAM site already had one Hornet to his credit—Thor wasn't going to let him make it two. Besides, there was a little matter of payback for Murphy.

The missile symbol was sprinting across his heads-up display, homing in on the hard metallic target that his aircraft represented to most targeting systems. Just as it reached the point at which he'd ejected the chaff and flares, Thor cut hard to the right, rolling the Hornet into right angles with the ground. He circled back around now heading one hundred and eighty degrees off his previous course.

He could see it now, the real missile instead of just the radar paint on his HUD. It was coming for him at an impossible speed, too fast and too hard to evade. There was no time, no more at all. He jerked the Hornet up and away from the chaff and flares and waited.

A hard buffet rocked the Hornet as the missile took the decoys, the noise drowned out by the scream of his engines.

Bingo. Fire and black smoke scarred the sky, and a few small pieces of flaming chaff shot out from the main fireball. Thor turned hard back to his base course heading to avoid FODing his engine and headed for the hill.

Two seconds later, he topped the summit of the low, rounded him and dove down. The ESM warning cut out as the earth shielded him from the radar waves saturating the air.

How far off course and time was he? He made a hasty mental calculation, popping up briefly from behind the hill to take a visual on the rest of the strike. Forewarned by the destruction of Buddy's Hornet, a Prowler had toggled off a HARM missile at the radar. The HARM sucked down radar waves, following them back to their sources before detonating, and was the weapon of choice against a radar or SAM site.

The rest of the strike was scattered along the ingress route, still maintaining their precision spacing but dispersed along the straight-line course they'd planned on. They were regrouping quickly, though. Part of every standard navy preflight briefing was to expect the unexpected.

The hill that housed the disguised SAM site exploded into an inferno of smoke, flames and shattered foliage.

The fire spread down from the crest, pumping heavy black smoke into the air and degrading visibility.

"Strike leader, Devil Dog 220," Thor said over the common circuit. In a few words, he outlined his position. "I saw a chute, repeat, had visual on a chute. Request permission to rejoin in tail position on third wave."

"Negative, Devil Dog 220," the accented voice of the Greek Tomcat strike leader came back. "RTB at this time."

RTB? Now why the hell should I turn tail and return to base when I've still got weapons on the wings? If anything, he ought to order me to orbit overhead Buddy until SAR gets in. But I'm not hearing anything on his PRC and I saw the chute streaming. This is fucked, totally fucked.

"Strike leader, nothing heard. Out." Thor clicked the mike off, hoping that the American leading the third wave had heard him and got the message. He wasn't landing wings heavy, no way. And if the Greeks didn't like it, they could kiss his scarlet and gold ass.

Thor pulled out from behind the hill and vectored in on the last incoming wave. He maintained separation, but caught a wave of welcome from the third wave leader. He gained altitude to maintain separate then turned back in behind the last Tomcat, easing into station as though it were part of the briefed strike plan.

The ground thundered past below, mostly clumps of trees and fields. There was no sign of human structures past a few shacks clearly intended for occasional use. He debated turning back on the radio, but decided that he might as well continue to experience "radio difficulties" until after he'd made a few Macedonians rue the day they'd ever even thought about such things as SAM sites. For Buddy—this one was going in hot and sweet for his wingman. And if he couldn't hear anyone ordering him back to base, well, then how could he be accused of disobeying an order? It was always better to ask forgiveness rather than permission.

Hill 802
0920 local (GMT −2)

Pamela watched the second Hornet spoof the missile shot then dart behind a hill. There was no sign that he was bugging out—another wave, then, and maybe—yes, there it was. The missile shot hard and true through the air and found its target. Seconds later, another strike wave loomed on the horizon.

The pilot, the one that had ejected. Where the hell's the SAR? They never fly a mission without it. Someone will be coming.

But when?

She started scrambling down the slope, ignoring the inbound strike aircraft and Xerxes's protests. Maybe if she got to him in time . . . he could bleed out before a rescue helo could get to him, even with the SAM site destroyed. It might make a difference—maybe just enough of a difference for the man to survive.

Or the woman. The Marines were now letting women fly close air support in their Hornets.

Where had she seen him? Over to the left a little, right near that taller clump of trees. She remembered seeing a shack—goatherder or something—nearby. She got her bearings, changed course slightly and headed into the hills.

Xerxes caught up with her easily and snagged her by the elbow. She tried to jerk away, but it was as though he were planted in the ground on which he stood. "You're not going there," he said, stating it as a fact. "It is too dangerous."

"There's a man hurt over there. Maybe dead."

He pulled her back toward their earlier location. "Perhaps. We'll find him eventually."

"Listen, you can't do this. What if we can do something to save him? We've got to try—we can't just leave him there." She was panting now, twisting and pulling and trying to break the iron grip on her elbow. *"Let me go, dammit."*

"This isn't your fight."

"He's an *American*, you ass. If he were one of yours, would you leave him there? And if you would, what makes you any better than the Greeks?"

He didn't loosen his grip on her elbow, but he did stop pulling her away. "Do you know these men?"

"Yes," she said. *Probably. I've been on Jefferson enough times that I ought to. And if I don't know this particular guy, then I know someone just like him.* "It's personal to me. It's a friend."

He rubbed his chin with his free hand for a moment, clearly troubled. Whether it was from the possibility that she actually did know the pilot or thoughts of how she might eventually report this entire incident, she couldn't tell. And didn't care. As long as she could get away, maybe try to make a difference.

The cameraman . . . I didn't even ask his name.

"You follow me," he said finally. "My way, you understand."

She nodded. It was better that way. He knew the terrain, probably could pinpoint exactly where the man went in. They'd save time, precious time. "Hurry." She followed him at a trot, rummaging through her backpack as she did, hunting for the first aid kit. It was small, mostly intended for traveler's stomach and minor injuries, but she remembered stuffing a couple of bottles of painkillers in there as well. That, and some bandages if he needed a tourniquet or something of that nature. With a sinking feeling, she realized she hadn't actually checked on the condition of the material inside the kit since Xerxes had returned it to her. That it had survived the crash and she actually had it seemed miraculous.

A miracle. Just one, please, God. Whoever you are, wherever you are, let me get to this pilot in time. Maybe it will make up for . . .

Her thoughts veered away from thinking about the whole question of her objectivity. Later, when there was time. Maybe.

She patted her camera. Either way, it would be a hell of a story.

Devil Dog 220
0930 local (GMT −2)

Out in front of him maybe two miles, Thor saw two people running across the long field laid out along their ingress path. A man and a woman, judging by the way the smaller one was running. Their presence registered long enough for him to notice that the woman was rummaging in a pack of some sort as she ran.

Stingers. The ubiquitous antiaircraft missiles were the weapon of choice for terrorists like the Macedonians. They were easily obtainable on the international arms market and were effective for close in air defense.

Maybe they weren't part of the resistance force. After all, it was pretty normal to see people running away from the projected location of an air strike. Nothing wrong with that.

Except they were running the wrong way. People ran *away* from aircraft, not directly across the ingress path. And the pack—

He swerved slightly off course, just enough to bring them into line with his gun.

Hill 802
0932 local (GMT −2)

"Run!" Xerxes shoved her from behind then locked one arm under hers and dragged her along with him. She lost her balance but couldn't fall, not with his arm locked under hers. He was carrying her, practically dislocating her shoulder in the process.

"They're ours," she screamed back as she moved her feet, trying to keep some of her weight off her shoulder. It was like a controlled fall. "They're American."

"They don't know who you are," he said, moving faster than she thought possible. "Those rocks—hurry, it's our only chance."

She saw them now, a dingy set of gray boulders cropping up along one edge of the field. She glanced up, saw the Hornet was now nose on to them. Xerxes was right— the Hornet had seen them and was not too pleased about it.

I'm only trying to help. Shit, the one time I try to do the right thing . . .

"Get down!" Xerxes tossed her over the boulder head first then followed her himself. He landed on top of her. She heard an odd, sickening snap and pain radiated through her rib cage.

Xerxes was still on top of her, holding her facedown in the small field of rocks and debris surrounding the boulders. He crossed his arms over the top of his head and tucked his chin in, digging it into her back.

There was a sound like a buzz saw, a moment's pause, then another spate of sound. Rock chips flew up over them, arcing off from the side of the rock facing the aircraft. Pamela screamed, the noise muffled by the dirt being ground into her mouth.

Then the aircraft was almost directly overhead, the hard beat of its jets drowning out everything else in the world. The ground underneath her shook as it beat against her body, penetrating skin and muscle to resonate in her very bones. Xerxes's weight, the pain in her side, all of it was insignificant compared to the overwhelming blast of sound energy. It went on for seconds, minutes, hours it seemed.

Then the sound down dopplered and dropped in volume. It was now mere noise, not the world-ending fury she'd felt before. She tried to move, but the Macedonian commander held her down. The pain returned, harder and more demanding now.

Finally, she felt him roll off of her. He laid on his back for a moment, breathing heavily, Then he levered himself up to his feet, dusted off the front of his uniform and said, "We have to go. He'll be back, and then he's going to have time to take another run on us. This time, we were lucky."

Pamela started to stand, then let out a yell as the pain lanced through her. A hot knife, gleaming dull red, was turning in her chest. She tried to speak, then felt the world go dim gray around her.

"You cannot do this," Xerxes said. He knelt down beside her and with no regard for any sort of personal privacy, ran his hands exploringly over her body, searching for the injury. He paused as his fingers skated over her ribs. Pamela let out a moan. He prodded her rib cage, sending new flashes of agony arcing up her spine. She tried to roll away, make him stop the torture, but his free hand held her firmly clamped in position.

"Cracked ribs," he announced. "You'll feel better once you stand up." He grabbed her under the armpits and hauled her into a standing position. "Come on."

Pamela put one hand on the boulder for support, now certain that she was near passing out. "I can't walk."

"Sure you can. I've had plenty of cracked ribs. As long as you're not having trouble breathing, you're okay for now. And you're breathing just fine. So come on."

"I can't."

He continued walking without turning around. "You said this was important. Or is that only when it's convenient?"

Pamela bit back a harsh reply. If he could do it, then she could. "It's important. Hold on, I'm coming."

Devil Dog 220
0935 local (GMT −2)

Thor swore as he saw the bullets digging a deadly furrow in the rich earth. The rounds tracked into the rock, blasting off the front face of it. Maybe some of the shrapnel got them, but he didn't think so. They'd found just the right angle behind it to shield themselves from the gunfire.

Maybe he could go around, circle back behind them and keep hammering at them until he either got them or blew their rock to gravel. He considered that option for only a few moments before rejecting it. He might pull some crap with the Greeks over this RTB bullshit, but that Tomcat driver would never buy it.

He veered back into the formation, bringing up the rear.

There was a chance they hadn't even noticed his strafing run, although the plane captains certainly would when he brought the Hornet back in with rounds expended. Not that that mattered—his plane captains were Marines, and they'd understand.

On the way back there might be time. That is, if they were stupid or wounded. At least he hadn't had to dodge a Stinger, if that's what she'd been pulling out of that pack.

Now that he thought about it, the pack wasn't really long enough to accommodate the bulk of a Stinger missile tube. But if that's not what it had been, then why had they been running into the path of the oncoming strike.

Buddy. The thought rang icy cold in his mind.

They were after his wingman.

He started to turn back, but the strike wave was already descending for their final run in on the target. He divided his attention between the IP ahead and trying to crane his head around to see if he could still see them, then realized that was a hell of a good way to get killed. Who knew what else was around the IP? And not paying attention at this altitude was sheer insanity.

Like a good Marine, he made his choice. Dump ordnance, then break off and orbit over Buddy's location. Ninety seconds from now he'd be headed back in, and to hell with any Tomcats who tried to force him to RTB. No way he was going anywhere, not until he saw a SAR helo taking off from an LZ with Buddy in it. One way or another.

Hard choices, harder answers. But with the decision made, he locked the question of his wingman out of his mind and concentrated on flying the aircraft.

Ninety seconds. Then he'd settle that score.

Hill 802
0936 local (GMT −2)

Pamela ran with her hands wrapped around her, trying to hold the shattered rib in place. Each breath was agony, piercing and hot. She bit the inside of her lip, determined not to make a sound. Now that the first shock of being injured was over, she was learning how quickly one could learn to live with pain.

"This way." The Macedonian shoved aside some bushes, took a quick look, then put out one arm to hold her back. "No. They are always armed. If he doesn't know who you are, he will shoot before you can explain." He pulled her behind a tree. "Tell him now."

She took a deep breath automatically in preparation for shouting at him, then let out a low moan as the pain intensified. She stifled it just as it started, shutting her eyes for a moment to paste her iron control back in place. When she opened her eyes, she saw a grudging respect in the Macedonian's eyes.

"Hornet pilot, my name is Pamela Drake. The reporter on ACN. Can you hear me?" She waiting, holding her breath. There was no answer.

"He's unconscious," she said.

"Or pretending to be. I would. Wait until you come to check, then take a better shot."

"Could you tell which way he was facing?" she asked.

He shook his head. "His feet were toward me. I could not tell if he was conscious or if his eyes were open."

"Well, then, I'll just have to find out." She raised her voice and said, "You'll recognize me as soon as you see me. I'm not armed. I'm going to step out so that you can see me, okay?"

There was no answer. She started to move away from

the bulk of the tree, but Xerxes stopped her. "You know that he was going to bomb my people. If he's alive, he's a prisoner of war."

She nodded, oddly uneasy at having the point made clear to her. If she convinced the pilot to give up his sidearm, Xerxes would take him prisoner. So was she committing treason by not telling him that the Macedonian was hiding here behind the tree? The words from an old training film she'd watched one night while onboard *Jefferson* came back to her. Aid and comfort to the enemy, something like that?

But at least he'd be alive. They'd treated her injuries, hadn't they? They'd probably treat him all right, maybe set up a prisoner exchange. It wasn't like he'd be a POW in Vietnam. As soon as this all blew over—unless they needed to make a point to the United States. Then what better example than an American pilot held prisoner?

They'd be misjudging the American psyche if they thought that. The reaction to Americans shot down during Desert Storm had been overwhelmingly supportive of the military.

"I'm coming out now. You'll see me if you look over your feet, I think. Just take a look . . . you'll know who I am." She started out again, and this time Xerxes let her go.

Devil Dog 220
0938 local (GMT −2)

Thor could feel the briefed path stretching out before him like a yellow brick road leading him straight down to Oz. So far, there was no sign of antiair activity, not even of a Stinger squad, much less anything more sophisticated.

That worried him, but not too much. Maybe they'd only had the one truck-mounted site left and Arkady's men had destroyed the rest.

But Stingers? Everyone had Stingers. Even the most impoverished rebel forces could find some larger power somewhere that would be glad to supply them in exchange for the opportunities created by internal turmoil in a country. Russia, China, even Italy—plenty of ways to get them if you wanted them.

The seconds were slipping by quickly now, along with the ground under him. The lead Tomcat was almost in position . . . there. The first aircraft in this wave jolted up as the bombs left his wings, then banked hard away from the IP. They continued on in, each one lofting the bombs in on target from slightly further away to avoid being blinded by the debris thrown up by the earlier aircraft.

It was his turn now. His internal clock was counting down the seconds. Maybe twenty seconds since he'd left the two stretched out on the ground behind the rock. He hadn't seen them move—maybe he'd gotten lucky and nailed them, but he didn't think so. Still, it was always better to be lucky than good.

Three, two, *now*. He pickled off the bombs and broke hard to the right as he accelerated away from the danger. The Hornet carried fewer bombs than each Tomcat did, but he'd made certain that his counted.

He reached out for the radio switch, then hesitated. No—not now. He'd see if he could locate Buddy and the two terrorists after him first. He wasn't sure he could. The trees looked pretty thick back there, and Buddy could be hidden under any one of them. Hell, if he'd survived the ejection, he was probably in deep cover by now, waiting for the SAR helo.

But there was no chatter on the Military Air Distress, or MAD, frequency. No single tone locator beacon or mayday call from Buddy. The radio could have been broken in the ejection, or he could be unconscious. There was no way to tell from here.

He vectored back in over the rock he'd shot up and started expanding search pattern over the area.

Hill 802
0940 local (GMT −2)

Pamela stepped out into the open, holding her hands over her head. "Can you see me?" She waited for an answer, but there was none. She took a step closer to the body stretched out on the ground. "Look, you can see me now. I'm not going to hurt you."

There was an odd stillness to the figure, and it took her a moment to quantify what she was seeing. When it finally hit her, she darted forward, ignoring her own pain, and knelt down next to the pilot. He wasn't breathing.

Oh, god, how long has it been? Four minutes before there's brain damage—maybe he was breathing when he hit and I can do CPR. Where the hell is the damned SAR extraction helo?

Xerxes was on the ground next to her now. He'd moved silently, simply appearing there.

Pamela ripped down the zipper on the front of the man's flight suit, then bent over to press her head to his chest while her fingers sought out the pulse point in his neck. She thought she felt the vein flutter under her fingers. He still wasn't breathing, though.

She tilted his head back, holding her ear close to his mouth. Still no breath sounds, but if his heart were still beating, he had a chance. A big if . . . she was finding it hard to distinguish between the shaking of her own hands and his pulse.

Shock. It's starting to set in now from the ribs. I can't afford it—this can't happen now.

Xerxes was watching her, his face impassive. She glared at him. "Do something."

He shook his head. "It won't matter." He pointed at the blood coming out of the pilot's ears. "Even if he starts breathing, he's too badly hurt. He'll never survive."

She swiped at the blood. "It's just a slash on his ear. There's still a chance." She administered the first deep life-giving breath of artificial respiration, then another, inflating his lungs and saturating them with oxygen. She stopped, waiting to see if his own breathing reflex returned.

Suddenly, the aviator gasped. He sucked down a deep lungful of air, then started coughing. Pamela hovered over him, praying that he'd keep breathing.

Spluttering and hacking, he did. The breaths were irregular for a few moments, then finally settled down into a steady rhythm. After another minute, he opened his eyes and stared up squinting and trying to focus on her face.

"What happened?" His voice was a harsh croak.

"You punched out," she said. "Your parachute got fouled and you came down hard."

"Where am I? Where's the bird?" Murphy, or so the name patch on his uniform said, was regaining situational awareness at an astounding rate.

"The helo is on its way," Pamela said reassuringly, not knowing whether it was true or not. Even if it had been nearly on top of them, she wouldn't have heard it. Not too far away, the strike was pummeling the ground with hard iron bombs. The noise this distance from the strike still made it hard to even be heard.

That seemed to satisfy him. His eyes fluttered, then started to close.

"Keep him awake," Xerxes said. "If he has a concussion, he must not sleep."

She touched the pilot gently, not wanting to risk injuring him further. "Murphy—Murphy, wake up. You've got to stay awake."

His eyes opened but his gaze was unfocused. "I'm so tired."

"I know, but you can't go to sleep. Not now." Pamela looked over at the Macedonian. "We can't move him."

"We have no choice."

"I do. Have a choice, I mean."

"No. You don't. You're going back to the alternate camp. Whether or not you wish to bring this man with you is irrelevant. You knew the price from the beginning. Now he must be moved."

"We went through all that to get here and now you're going to risk killing him?" she asked incredulously.

"If the helo shows up, they will try to kill me. It is a simple choice." He leaned over and slapped the pilot hard. "Stay awake. You must stand up now."

The pilot moaned, then tried to move. His arms and legs seemed uncoordinated at first, but he quickly gained control of his limbs. A few moments later, with Pamela's help, he was on his feet.

"Come, now—quickly." Xerxes prodded her from behind and pointed to the north. "I've got responsibilities to attend to. There's another detachment there, and I do not see any flames. We will go there."

Pamela draped Murphy's arm over her shoulders and let him lean his weight on her. "Can you walk?" she asked, already aware of a deepening pain in her own body. "It's not too far."

Murphy nodded. He moved mechanically. He'd evidently recognized her and decided to rely on her. She felt another twinge of conscience as she realized that.

They skirted the edge of the cleared field, edging through the trees and occasional rocks to try to keep to a northerly course. But the field ran northeast, and it became clear to her that they'd have to cross in the open soon.

The noise from the air strike was louder now, especially the sound of the aircrafts' engines. They were returning, she realized, and felt a frisson of fear. That Hornet pilot—he'd be looking for his wingman. It didn't matter who it actually was, she knew with a deep certainty that he'd be back.

"We wait," Xerxes said, and drew them further into the cover. "They will be gone shortly, then we will assess the damage."

At that, Murphy stiffened. Pamela had the distinct impression that he was far less disoriented and groggy than he'd let on. She started to speak, to reassure him once again, but realized that anything she said now would just make her own situation worse.   •

The sound like thunder grew stronger now, the distinctive howl of the Tomcats mixed with the slightly lighter whine of the Hornets. Murphy was fully alert now, though masking it for the benefit of the Macedonian. She felt him tense up, his muscles shaking under the effort. Then without warning, he broke free from her supporting grasp and started staggering toward the open field, arms waving and shouting as he stared up at the aircraft.

Pamela caught up with him twenty yards later. By that time he'd expended his reserve of energy and was moving slowly, still headed directly into the path of the oncoming aircraft. She joined him in waving her arms, signaling to the other pilots. The sole Hornet in the group peeled off and headed directly for them.

Devil Dog 202
0942 local (GMT −2)

"Murphy," Thor shouted. He flipped back on the radio and said over the common circuit, "It's a friendly. That's my wingman."

"Roger, Devil Dog," the American Tomcat pilot said. "SAR is inbound at this time. Remain in orbit over him pending pickup."

"Roger, copy all. Interrogative ETA of the SAR bird?" Thor asked.

"So you have repaired your radio?" another voice broke in. Thor recognized the voice of the Greek strike leader. "Then join on my wing. We will make sure that you are within visual communications range until we land."

There was a short pause, then the American Tomcat pilot said, "Negative, strike leader. Devil Dog 202 must remain on station to protect the landing zone."

"Any threat to the landing zone has already been neutralized," the Greek shot back. "Obey my orders immediately."

Thor didn't even bother answering. There was no way he was going to leave his wingman, no way. He shouldn't have left him the first time, but the seconds and the miles had flashed by and he'd been over the IP. He felt a wave of regret and shame. If he'd orbited over Murphy's position, he might have been able to keep them off of him.

And just who the hell were they, anyway? One of them was a soldier by the looks of him, outfitted in green camouflage uniforms. The other, he wasn't so sure. In a fight like this, just being a woman didn't earn her any points. They were just as dangerous as the men.

And where was the guy, anyway? The woman was standing in the field with Murphy, waving like a mad dog. But the guy—was he off in the brush to the side, sighting down on Thor with a Stinger even at this moment?

Probably so. Thor took on some altitude, not enough to put him out of range but enough to give him some maneuvering room. Or at least the illusion of it. His odds of getting away form a Stinger at this range were nil

"Devil Dog, helo inbound in three mikes. How copy?"

"Copy three mikes. Advise the helo that the LZ may be hot."

"That woman with him?"

"There was a man with her earlier, military."

Silence then, and Thor knew what the Tomcat lead was thinking. The woman, out making happy faces and enticing the aircraft in with the downed pilot. The man, ready in the bushes as soon as a target came within range. It was a trap, pure and simple. And without forces on the ground, there was no way to extract Murphy, not without risking the SAR helo.

"I can hose down the area to either side," Thor said finally. "Lay down some suppressing fire."

"Roger, I'll advise the helo. Do you have communications with Murphy?" Tomcat lead asked.

"Negative. That's him, though."

Another long silence. Without communications, there was no way to direct the pilot to a safer pickup area. They were playing a come as you are game, and in a dangerous situation.

"Roger, Devil Dog. Be advised that SAR helo is standing off one mike out waiting for clearance to the LZ. You take the left side—I'll take the right. If anything's standing after we've expended our rounds, you owe me a drink."

"Roger, copy all. Murphy will know what's up and he'll stay put." Thor had been orbiting overhead, and now he descended again, pushing the Hornet into a maximum rate of descent. He pulled up hard, cut back on the power, and walked a stream of rounds down one side of the LZ while the Tomcat took the opposite side. Just as they reached the midpoint, a figure broke out of the cover and headed for the center of the field—and for Murphy.

"Get him," Thor shouted. "Now, lead!"

The ground around the running man exploded as the bullets rained down on it from the Tomcat. Thor tried to maneuver around to get a shot at him himself, but he couldn't do so without fouling the Tomcat's field of fire. He took another pass down his side of the field, hoping to scare out another tango.

Hill 802
0943 local (GMT −2)

"That's Thor," Murphy shouted as the Hornet passed down the side of the field. "The helo is here—look." He pointed off in the distance at a helicopter well out of range. "We're getting out of here."

"Stop them," Pamela screamed. "You've got a radio, don't you? You've got to stop them."

"Why the hell should I?" he snapped, the earlier confusion and apparent weakness now completely gone. "They don't clear the LZ, we don't get out of here."

"You're leaving. I'm not."

"What?"

"I'm not," she repeated. "I'm not military . . . I'm a civilian."

Suddenly a figure broke of the tree line and started running toward them. He danced across the open field, zigging and zagging in an attempt to foil the targeting of the Tomcat. The rounds stopped falling as he came closer to them, and when he stopped he grabbed them by their arms and held one on either side of him.

Murphy was reaching into a pocket on his flight suit, and Pamela could see the outline of a handgun pressed up against the fire-retardant cloth. He fumbled as he pulled it out, and Xerxes's hand closed around his wrist. He shook Murphy's wrist once, then twisted his arm up behind him. "No guns. It's her fault I'm even here, and I'm not getting shot for my troubles."

Murphy yelped, then dropped the gun as Xerxes's fingers dug deep into the bone. The Macedonian scooped it up and deposited it in his own pocket.

"They won't come in if you're here," Pamela said, her words slightly slurred. It was getting harder and harder to stay focused—the shock creeping up on her, she supposed.

"That's the idea." The Macedonian pulled her hard up against him. "They're not coming in."

"We can leave," she said. "We go back into the trees, let the helo come in and pick him up. They won't shoot at me."

"You've got the wrong idea again about who will shoot at who and why. Right now, he's our only protection," Xerxes said, shaking the pilot lightly. "We let him go and they'll kill us both. You see what they did to the land on either side of us?"

"Murphy would tell them who I am," she insisted. "They won't take the chance of hitting me."

"I think you're missing the whole point of this. They're *supposed* to be shooting at me—and I'm supposed to be keeping them from doing that. Now let's get moving."

Devil Dog 202
0944 local (GMT −2)

"Weapons tight, weapons tight! We've got friendlies in the area." Thor was shouting now, venting his frustration over the circuit. "Dammit, they've got Murphy. I saw them go into the trees."

Silence greeted his demand. They all knew the score.

"Break off, Devil Dog. We can't take the chance," the Tomcat lead said finally. "RTB."

Every Marine is a ground soldier first, and Thor was no exception. His hands ached for a rifle, a sniper scope, anything that would be useful in picking off the two terrorists that had custody of his wingman. The Hornet was a powerful weapon, but it was a blunt one. This situation called for precision fire, something he couldn't produce no matter how much he wanted to. To watch his wingman being led away, moving slowly and awkwardly in the custody of the two Macedonians was almost more than he could bear. Sheer impotent rage swept through him and he howled his frustration and anger in the cockpit, the scream echoing off the canopy around him.

But the Marine Corps habit of obedience under the most dangerous of circumstances was already reasserting itself, taking over. He was gaining altitude, falling back into position on lead, maintaining a rock steady formation flight position even as every atom of his being ached to stay overhead, waiting, hoping for some chance to kill the two captors.

Tavista Air Base
Tavista, Greece
1010 local (GMT −2)

"If your pilots had followed the flight plan, there would have been no danger." General Arkady's voice was implacable. "Yet they chose to deviate from it. They put themselves at risk."

Tombstone watched him impassively, hiding the wild rage storming through him. "No mission goes exactly as planned," he said. "That's why we brief contingencies. So pilots will know how to compensate for the unexpected."

Arkady shrugged. "In combat, one must learn to expect losses. Do you know how many men I have lost in the last six months before the United States so generously decided to come to our assistance?"

"You could have told me about the SAM site," Tombstone said. His voice was harder and colder than it had been a moment before.

"I thought it had been destroyed. We only learned otherwise this morning. If we had deviated from the briefed plan, we would have put sensitive intelligence assets at risk. Once they are burned, they are no longer of any use, are they?" Arkady asked, as though his reasoning were eminently clear with it to anyone with the slightest common sense.

Shock and horror settled over the room, among both Greek, American and other foreign aviators alike. Tombstone glanced around room and saw that only Arkady's general staff failed to react. One man had the good grace to look ashamed.

What's his name? Colonel Zentos. I've seen that look on men's faces before.

"The point of intelligence is to save lives of pilots," Tombstone said. "At least in my service." General Arkady met his harsh glare without the slightest trace of regret on his face.

"Many men have died, Admiral. Many more will before this is over. And not just men—women, children, the very old. How easy it is for us so far away to panic over the first loss of life." He gestured to encompass the entire room. "Ask my men how many we've lost? Then tell me that I should risk my sensitive intelligence assets that are now making a difference.

"And may I point out, I sent my own men in first. Had your pilots stayed with the plan, followed their strike leader, they would have been home even now." General Arkady settled back into his chair and made a dismissive gesture. "Now, for tomorrow's strike, we will—"

"You will disclose every bit of intelligence you have." Tombstone leaned forward and placed his hands flat on the table, splaying his fingers and nailing down the edge of the paper Arkady was reading. "Do I make myself clear? Every bit of it, General. Or my forces don't fly."

Arkady looked up, quiet amusement on his face. "You forget yourself, Admiral. They're no longer your forces. They're under my direct operational control. You're here as a matter of courtesy—*my* courtesy in allowing an advisor from America to participate in command decisions. Perhaps that is the mistake." He leaned back in his chair and clasped his hands behind his head. "Perhaps I should have you removed."

"If I go, so do my people."

"Are you so sure?" Arkady asked. "I think before you make such rash statements, you should consult your authorities at home. They may have other ideas."

"Come on," Tombstone said, gesturing to the assembled Americans. "I want talk to you—alone."

Arkady waved them away. "You have my permission to consult with my forces, Admiral. But don't forget who owns the firepower around here. They're *my* men and women—not *yours*."

The Americans, without exception, followed Admiral Magruder of the conference room and down the hall to an unused ready room that had been assigned to them for temporary usage. Away from the other nationalities, the stolid veneer they had all applied to their faces cracked and shattered. The skipper of the VF-95 slumped down in the front chair and buried her face in her hands. Tombstone sat down next to her, resisting the urge to place an arm around her shoulders. "I know how you feel," he said softly. "Don't worry, we'll get them back."

Tomboy looked up, anguish on her face. "Admiral—Tombstone—what he said is true. I chopped to his command and control yesterday—didn't Batman let you know? Except for administrative matters. If he tells me to fly mission, I have to or face the consequences. How am I supposed to explain court-martialing Smith if I pick and choose what orders I'm going to obey?"

Tombstone nodded. "I know. But no one back home had this in mind when they did that. It was political maneuvering of the worst possible sort, an attempt to curry world favor by placing forces the Greeks can't begin to imagine at their disposal. If they had had any idea that Arkady would be wasting lives like this, it never would have happened."

"Are you so sure?" Tomboy shot back. "Hell, I don't know what to believe right now. Maybe that's all we are anymore—cannon fodder."

Tombstone stood now, and addressed the assembled man and women. "Any of the rest of you feel like that?" he asked. A few guilty nods, eyes averted, answered him. He felt something crumple and die inside his chest. "If that's the way you feel, that's all you'll ever be. But you've got it wrong, every last one of you." He strode to the podium in front of the room and turned to address them. "What you are is the world's most elite fighting unit. Sure, the Greeks have Tomcats. You've seen how they maintain them—and how they fly them. Is there a single pilot among you who doesn't know deep down in his heart that he's better than anyone they can field?"

The expressions were brighter now, the aviators leaning forward on the edges of their seat. Tombstone continued, "I won't lie to you and tell you that I like the situation we're in here. But it's not the first time, and it won't be the last time. We've all been in tough situations before. But what American pilots do, they do better than anyone else in the world. I don't like the command structure we're in here. Nor will I tolerate any of you disobeying General Arkady's orders. It's my job to get this mess straightened out, and I promise you, I will. Until then, I need you to hold together. Just for a day, maybe two. Once JCS and the president hear about this little incident, there's going to be hell to pay."

And there would be hell to pay, but not exactly in the manner that Tombstone had envisioned. Nor were the results to be anything he could've anticipated.

THIRTEEN
Wednesday, 10 May

"Damn them to hell," Wexler swore, throwing the message board down on the floor. "T'ing—he knows something about this. He knew and didn't tell me—not in so many words, nothing I could use."

Jack picked the clipboard up and studied the top sheet. He'd already heard the general story on CNN, but the details were even more chilling.

The commander of the UN Forces, General Dimitri Arkady, was demanding that the United States withdraw its special advisor, Admiral Tombstone Magruder. The body of the message was filled the vitriol and hate, posing as a complaint about Tombstone's performance while embarking on a ranting diatribe against America's foreign policy and political systems. It ended with an appeal to all member nations—and with dismay, Wexler noted that every nation was an info addee to the message—band together to force the Americans to stop using the UN as their own private rubber stamp for the American agenda overseas. It concluded with thanks to the General Assembly for taking the opportunity to achieve a lasting peace in the area, and expressed every confidence that the rest of the nations would understand the deep, grave, and sincerely held objections that Arkady had to Tombstone's continuing presence in the region.

"What are you going to do?" Jack asked after he'd read the message twice, more to be polite and give Sarah Wexler the illusion that he didn't already know what she'd say.

She sighed. "I'm going to see the president. I argued against this whole idea when he proposed it, but he wasn't listening. Maybe now he'll understand why foreign command of American troops is a pipe dream." She stabbed on finger at the offending message. "This is just one of the things that can go wrong."

Tombstone Magruder. Jack had met him several times, traveling in the surprisingly small circle of people whose opinions mattered, who actually had some well-thought-out views on international affairs. Smart man, for a naval officer. He didn't pretend to have all the answers, nor did he try to fake understanding the details of how the UN and its member nations worked. That took years, and Jack was just starting to get proficient at the standard fare of back-door deals and negotiated compromises that were the UN's stock in trade.

Even apart from his relative naivete, though, Tombstone had managed to impress both Jack and his boss with his understanding of how they worked, even if the actual details eluded him. That Tombstone had understood immediately made Jack consider the possibility that perhaps the Navy had more going on inside its senior ranks than Jack had thought before. He'd always had the impression that all senior military men and women were idealistic and ethical, a perception that had not changed since the days that his own father was a senior enlisted man in the Army. Power plays, rice bowls, personal power—he'd thought them all a little too good for the sort of down and nasty horse-trading that international politics required. You did the dirty with the other nations and called in the forces when everything else failed.

But with Tombstone, it had been different. Even back in the Spratley's conflict, when Tombstone had forged together an alliance of unlikely allies to defeat the Chinese surge into the oil-rich islands. In Cuba, when he'd faced down the island nation supplied with nuclear warheads from Libya.

It had been Hong Kong that had made the difference, Jack decided. In tacking down the source of advanced technology used against the American forces during a period of infighting in the Hong Kong administration, Tombstone had been exposed to international intrigue on a level that few active duty military officers experienced. Coming on the heels of the admiral's search for his father in Vietnam and Russia, it had obviously seasoned him from a superb war fighter to a potent force with a frightening insight into the realities of everyday international politics.

"What do you think the president will do?" Jack asked, aware that he'd been silent for some time as he sorted out the pieces to this particular puzzle himself.

"I'm hoping he refuses," Wexler said. "I'm not certain he will, though."

"You actually think he'd recall Admiral Magruder?"

She nodded. "There are too many secrets being kept around here, Jack. T'ing knows something and the president knows something that they're not telling me. I'm not sure how the president thinks I can do my job without knowing, but he does. We've got to find out what's going on. And do it on our own . . . at least until they decide to be on the up and up with us. I'm counting on you to pull this one off."

Jack thought about it for a moment, about the explosive combination of Tombstone Magruder and General Arkady, the equally uneasy relationship between T'ing and Sarah Wexler. The dinner Jack wrote off with a cynical check mark. T'ing was after something big, and if he thought a few dinners might make Wexler more receptive, then Jack was certain that T'ing would be the most entertaining dinner partner around. No matter how Sarah perceived the overtures, Jack would never believe them. The Chinese had allies, not friends.

"I'll see what I can find out," he said slowly, wondering as he did whether his mouth was writing a check that his butt couldn't cash. "Might be nothing," he added, trying to prepare her for that possibility.

"No." There was not a trace of doubt in Sarah Wexler's voice. "T'ing's up to something. The president doesn't know exactly what it is, or he would have told me. Not that he tells me everything"—an understatement, Jack thought—"but he would about this."

Maybe, Jack thought. *And maybe not. He's got his own problems these days.*

"Besides," Wexler continued, "If it's important enough to T'ing to try to make friends with me with all these nice little dinners, then it's important enough for us to go digging for." Jack was gratified to see a hard smile creep across her face. "My new best friend, the one with so much advice for our country. Just giving us the benefit of his centuries of experience, you understand."

So she's not fooled. Jack experienced a mild rush of relief then looked at his boss with new respect in his eyes. "But that was your line, the one about a more experienced culture."

Wexler's smile broadened. "Yeah. And he bought it hook, line and sinker."

Jack stared at her for a moment in amazement, and then started laughing. If T'ing thought he was winning this war, he was in for a rude awakening.

A rude awakening. Now what does that . . . oh. Yes, that would do. Jack felt a slow smile spread across his face.

Wexler noticed it immediately. She leaned forward. "Tell me."

"It's not much," Jack said slowly, "but it might be enough to tip the balance with T'ing. And it's a long shot. But here's how it'd work." He outlined the idea, filling in the details as he went. After the first few moments, Wexler started nodding. It would have been unkind, Jack thought, to call her smile slightly evil.

"Oh, yes," she said finally. "Yes, that would do quite nicely. I'll set it up later today."

For a moment, Jack almost pitied the ambassador from China. He had no idea what he'd started.

Northeastern Greece
1800 local (GMT −2)

The Macedonian commander decreed that it was too dangerous to return to base. Oddly enough, he commented sardonically, they'd managed to prepare for that contingency. "We're a small force," he said. "We can't afford to risk them all in one location."

The secondary camp was proving to be farther away than Xerxes had let on. They'd tramped through open hills and forest for most of the day, stopping only for two skimpy meals.

Pamela led the way, with Xerxes bringing up the rear as they headed back toward the camp. Murphy had started off berating her, accusing her of everything from treason to aggravated cruelty and had finally settled into a frigid silence broken only occasionally by quiet groans of pain. Though he curtly denied being injured in the ejection, it was clear from the way that he moved that that was at least partially untrue. He brusquely rejected her attempts to at least ascertain the extent of his injuries, and had settled into what Pamela privately characterized as traditional male bullheadedness.

So let him sulk. It's not like I could do anything about it. Xerxes wasn't going to let him go—he'd have shot him first. I'm a reporter, dammit, not a player in all this.

Or was she? Hadn't she intervened, pleading with Xerxes not to shoot down the American aircraft? For all the good it had done. And what had it gotten her?

Nothing. The only thing it had done was shatter her credibility with the Macedonians. So much for getting this particular story out.

She glanced back over her shoulder and saw two faces that mirrored each other. Cold, grim determination in the eyes belied the granite expressions carved into the two faces. One dark, Mediterranean, with the classic features and curly black hair of this region; the other corn-fed blond hair and blue eyes that would have looked more natural wearing the open, easy-going expression of a farm boy. But not now—boiling oil wouldn't have tortured out a single expression of emotion from either face.

"Turn left at the fork," Xerxes ordered.

She obliged, following the narrow trail that broke off the main path. After years of reporting on conflicts all over the world, she'd come to recognize the normal signs that one was at the outskirts of a military camp. Guards, maybe scouts, well-concealed yet inclined to shoot first and ask questions later. The smell of cooking, wood smoke or gasoline camp stove, the necessary sanitary arrangements, and the odor of men under pressure living in close quarters without regular baths. She glanced around the woods, pristine and quiet. If the base camp were located anywhere near here, they'd done an excellent job of disguising it.

"Are we almost there?" she asked, keeping her voice low.

Silence from behind her, then Xerxes said, "We're not there yet. We're stopping here for the night."

"Why?" A longer silence this time, as though he were debating exactly how much to tell her.

That tears it, then. Whatever little trust we had is gone. I should have known it would come to this—these people are all alike. They can't understand what it is to be impartial, to have a responsibility to the rest of the world. I'll be lucky if he doesn't tie me up for the night, much less tell me what's going on.

"It's too far to the camp tonight," Xerxes said finally. "We'll make it in the morning."

"If it's still there, you mean." Pamela shocked herself with the small note of vindictive glee in her voice.

"It's still there."

"How do you know? I mean, if it's not nearby, then you can't possibly know whether or not it survived the bombing runs, can you?" she asked, her voice louder now and strident. Behind her, she heard what she thought was a grunt of approval from Murphy.

"I saw where the aircraft went," Xerxes said.

"Where *this* strike went, you mean. How do you know there weren't others?" *This is insane. Stop taunting him, you idiot! What about the story?*

"I will know shortly," Xerxes said, a sad note of triumph in his voice. She heard a noise and turned in time to catch Murphy as he stumbled and fell forward against her, his hands still tied behind him. She caught him and controlled his descent to the ground. The Macedonian was holding his weapon by the barrel, pulling back from jabbing Murphy in the back with it. "Because he's going to tell me. One way or the other."

FOURTEEN

Wednesday, 10 May

The White House
1115 local (GMT +5)

Wexler had always thought that the Oval Office was not conducive to frank discussion. It had seen too many ceremonies and was drenched in the polite compromises signed with smiles on faces that represented final victories after dirty knife fights. Everyone had seen it too many times on television, it was too much a part of their national heritage for words such as she must speak to be palatable here.

Yet she must speak frankly, brutally even. The president had to understand that the consequences of his decision affected more than just the next election, more than his perception of the impression that they were creating with their allies. Lives were at stake here, not just in this conflict, but in the potential for bloodshed in every conflict yet to come. By ceding command of his troops—America's troops—to a foreign commander, he was setting a precedent that would echo down through history.

History—perhaps that was the way to approach him, for President Williams had a clear and overriding concern about carving out his own spot in it. If she could just put it in the right words, he'd know how very dangerous this game was.

"Thank you for seeing me on such short notice, Mr. President," she began quietly.

He chuckled and patted her hand. "There's a Girl Scout troop from Boise cooling their collective heels in the waiting room, Sarah, so don't flatter yourself that I've cleared my calendar."

"Maybe you should."

He paused, taken aback by the serious note in her voice, as she'd intended. Their relationship had been for so many years one of mutual respect and friendship that she wondered if they occasionally let it distract them from the very real trust imposed on them by the American people.

How easy it is to forget that, she mused, watching her friend and her president switch gears. *But if we ever truly forget it, then we're no better than the people we fought so hard to defeat.*

"Serious talk, I take it," he said finally just as the silence was becoming uncomfortable. "Okay, shoot."

"Mr. President, you're aware of the pilots that were shot down over Macedonia yesterday, I assume?" she began.

He nodded. "I've got other advisors besides you, Sarah," he said, gently but with sufficient force to make his point. Other advisors who would have other points of view on whatever she was proposing to discuss. Other advisors he'd consult, so she'd best not count on a quick and easy concession on anything.

Alright, if that's how we need to play it. And we do, I suppose. Because this isn't about either one of us personally—although I'm hoping to make it seem that way to you. It's about the country. And you're right to seek other opinions, my friend. Because I'm not the one who's going to be judging you—history will be.

"I'd like to give you the perspective on how this chain of command question is playing itself out on the international side of things," she said, making it clear that she understood the message he'd sent.

"That's your job. Go ahead."

She began with a discussion of T'ing, quickly sketched in the background, and then brought up T'ing's veiled warnings. "I'm not sure what it means, Mr. President. But it means something. I thought you might know."

Bingo. She saw a fleeting trace of guilty knowledge on his face, and was aware that she probably could not completely mask her own expression from him.

"Not that I'm asking what you might know," she clarified, careful to back away from a confrontation. "There are probably some considerations I'm not aware of."

And again. Whatever it was, she could see in his eyes that he'd debated telling her about it, maybe sought counsel from his other advisors, and decided against it. Now he was second-guessing himself, wondering if it had been a mistake.

It had been. Of that she was completely certain. And why would he not tell her? They had enough history together that there should be no question of her trustworthiness, of her loyalty to his administration.

Bad advice from somebody. But who? And why?

No matter. She wouldn't get any answers by pressing the point now, even though the urgency beat inside her like a drum. No, all she had to do right now was make the point, put the idea of history into motion in his head, and let time do its work.

If they had any time at all.

The president stood, indicating the meeting was over. He held out his hand and said, "Thank you for your advice. I'd like you to talk to Defense and make sure they know about the Chinese ambassador's warning . . . if that's what it was."

Her heart sank at that. She had never been more certain of anything than she was of this—T'ing *had* warned her. And that the president was not taking it seriously.

"Using aircraft alone was a mistake," he said finally, his face now completely controlled. "Next time, we go in the way we were trained to fight, with an all-platform attack. Ships, bombers, satellite intelligence, the whole nine yards." He gazed at her levelly. "The problem this time was that we weren't committed. To correct that, I'm placing additional resources at the UN force's disposal. They'll constitute the heart of UNFORGREECE."

"Under UN command," she said.

He nodded. "This is the way of the future, Sarah. And you and I are going to forge the way."

Or bury the dead. She gazed at him hopelessly.

FIFTEEN
Thursday, 11 May

Tavista Air Base
Tavista, Greece
0900 local (GMT −2)

Tombstone skimmed quickly through the preliminaries in the message, running his finger down the margin as he read the standard words of most OPORDS. Timing, targets . . . important, but not his major concern.

There it was. His finger paused over the offending paragraph. Command relationships—*damn*.

He looked up into Arkady's genial face and scowled. "Just what is this second strike supposed to accomplish?" he said quietly.

"What the first did not. To cut the throat of the Macedonian command and control forces. Had your pilots done as they were ordered, this second strike would not be necessary," Arkady said in the same tone of voice, his words intended for Tombstone alone.

Arkady turned away to face the rest of the assembled forces. In addition to the pilot commanders from previous briefings, the commanding officers and their weapons officers from the two cruisers were there. "My staff—the UNFORGREECE staff—will discuss with you the details of your particular roles in the next twenty-four hours. As you can see from your packages, this will be the single decisive blow against the rebel forces. I am pleased to welcome you to UNFORGREECE and look forward to working with you."

Arkady nodded in the direction of Admiral Magruder. Looking at him, Tombstone could never have guessed that just days earlier Arkady had been agitating to have Tombstone removed from the theater of operations.

Why did he change his mind? Tombstone thought that if he could find the answer to that one question, he'd know the answers to the rest of them.

Arkady was speaking now, his voice warm and congenial. "As you can see, we have a wealth of talent here to advise us on the best use of UN forces. However, I also direct your attention to paragraph four. All mission decision will be made by UNFORGREECE in order to deconflict disposition of forces. Any questions regarding that provision should be addressed to my staff immediately."

And not to Admiral Magruder. The unvoiced caveat was clear.

No one moved. All eyes were fixed on Tombstone. While the habit of obedience was deeply ingrained, so was the loyalty they felt to this one man, the one who'd brought them safely home from so many other battles.

Tombstone sat immobile and considered his options. The gauntlet had been thrown down. Right now, right here, Arkady was challenging him. And in front of his own people.

Yet not his people, not this time. He felt the cheap paper of the message slide between his fingers, negating anything he could possibly say about the procedures Arkady had outlined. As wrong as it felt, and terribly wrong—Arkady was right.

Tombstone gave a small nod, an almost imperceptible inclination of his head. He felt the tension in the room break as each officer realized that while they might some day be called to choose sides, to make hard decisions, it wouldn't be just now. That moment was postponed—not finally settled, but at least held in abeyance while they occupied themselves with matters that they knew better.

Arkady beamed in triumph. "Well, then." He turned to Colonel Zentos, who was standing off to one side. "My chief of staff will conduct the remainder of the briefing. I will see you in battle, my comrades." He turned and left the room, leaving a deeply worried Tombstone behind him.

Tavista Air Base
Flight Line
1010 local (GMT −2)

The noise of forty aircraft in various stages of startup flooded across the tarmac, warm and welcome to Thor's ears. There was nothing like it, not even on the flight deck of a carrier. This was a real strike.

"Sucks, doesn't it?" The Marine Corps lieutenant colonel assigned to the detachment was blunt. "They blow the SAR effort last mission and expect us to roger up on following them in again." He pulled his shoulders back and stuck his chest out. "At least there's some serious SAR planning this time. And better intelligence on the SAM sites."

"We asked for that last time," Thor said. Maybe the bird colonel could extract more information from Arkady's staff than Thor had been able to, but he doubted it. Their orders were clear—regardless of how they personally felt about the mission that had been laid out for them, the president had made his wishes clear.

Not that there was much to complain about in the mission planning. On the face of it, it seemed competently done. A wave of Tomahawk missiles to soften up the area, specially targeted to seek out suspected command and control points. Then electronics birds with HARM missiles leading the charge, taking out any remaining radar sites to avoid a repetition of the disaster of the first strike. Two waves of fighters again, the first composed of Greek aircraft, the second a mixed bag of U.S. and other forces. A final sweep through by a couple of Tomcats, one loaded with TARPS, the other with dumb bombs and orders to pick up any targets that the more structured waves had missed. A couple of drones for BDA, some of the high-tech ones that had been flooding the fleet since Hong Kong. He wondered a little at that, exposing that much advanced technology to possible compromise.

Five SAR helos, all with fighter protection. The Americans had drawn four of those assignments in addition to their attack tasking. Special forces on standby for any hostile extractions. Even the Marines hadn't been able to find much fault with that part of the plan.

The only real problem was the attack itself. The whole thing was starting to remind Thor entirely too much of Vietnam. Telling who was a civilian and who was a combatant was the first problem. The second was that rebel forces such as the Macedonians rarely operated out of fixed positions. Sure, there'd be some structures that could be identified as command centers. But if the Macedonians had any sense, their actual commanders would be somewhere else.

Thor started his walk-around of the aircraft, running through the checklist. Some people might skimp on the routine items, counting on the ground crew to catch any major problems, but not a Marine. And most particularly, not this Marine.

Finally, he was ready. He popped down the first rung

of the boarding ladder and started crawling up the side of the Hornet. Her skin felt smooth and thin under his fingers. He pulled himself up and over the edge of the cockpit, easing down into his seat. A plane captain followed him up and helped him buckle in. At the last moment, the young corporal pulled the safety pins from the ejection mechanism.

"Semper Fi, sir," he said.

"Semper Fi, Marine." Thor flipped open the pre-start checklist, worked his way through it, then followed the corporal's hand signal to start engines. When they were both, major and corporal, completely satisfied that the Hornet was good to go, the corporal snapped into a picture perfect salute. Thor returned it from the cockpit and released the brakes.

"This one's for you, Murph," he said aloud as he taxied toward the runway. "And for me."

USS John Paul Jones
1015 local (GMT −2)

The ship rocked slightly in the gentle current. She was making bare steerageway, just enough forward speed to enable her to retain rudder control in case she needed to maneuver. At two knots, she seemed to rest gently upon the surface of the ocean rather than steam through it.

"All stations report ready, Captain," the TAO said.

Captain Daniel Heather nodded. "Any last words from UNFOR?"

"No, sir." The TAO held up a sheet of paper. "The last message we got was that the strike was airborne and would remain in orbit over the airfield until we'd launched."

"Very well." Captain Heather glanced at the chronometer on the wall, then double-checked the time displayed on the edge of the computer screen. "Thirty seconds, I make it."

"Yes, sir."

He waited, watching the digital figures click over on the screen. A routine launch—if any weapon launched in anger could be called routine. But if anything, there was less tension in Combat than there'd been during their last exercise firing. Then the spacious compartment had been stuffed with civilians, contractors, and CRUDES staff all wanting to offer their opinions and assistance.

Assistance. More like a pain in the ass than anything. In Navy tradition, it was one of the three great lies in the world: "I'm from the staff, I'm here to help." What they were really there to do was grade the entire ship on how the evolution was conducted, looking at everything from how well the watchstanders in Combat did their jobs to whether the galley managed to get meals on the table on time.

Well, this time there was just one grading criteria. And that was how well *JPJ* put a huge, smoking hole in one particular spot in the ground.

In actual fact, the Tomahawks were relatively easy to fire. A separate weapons console housed the software, but the actual targeting package for the terrain-following missing was loaded into the missile from a CD. The shape of the terrain, the points it could check its flight path against, the speed of the missile, all were out of the control of the ship. As long as they were in the basket, in the piece of area designated as the launch area, and as long as they got the weapon off on time, everything should go just according to plan.

"Ten seconds," the TAO announced. "Weapons free. Tomahawk, you have permission to fire."

"Permission to fire, aye, sir." The petty officer first class perched on a stool in front of the Tomahawk Engagement Console, or TEC, had his finger poised over the keyboard. "Five seconds, sir."

The final moments clicked by without incident. A low shudder ran through the ship and a faint ringing as the launch warning buzzer on the forecastle sounded. It was almost anticlimactic when the petty officer announced, "Missile away, sir."

Almost immediately, the Tomahawk sprang into existence on the tactical console, a missile symbol with a long speed leader attached. It headed off at an angle from the ship for the first waypoint.

The waypoints were intermediate stations that the missile would pass through on its way to landfall. Constructing them was one of the few tasks a ship had, and the final waypoint and course change were designed to put the missile exactly over a point its electronic memory would recognize. From that point on, it would be guided solely by the terrain map, with an ever-decreasing tolerance for errors.

USS *Jouett*, a cruiser, would be launching her missiles as well in thirty seconds. Two missiles, each with its own target, and then the air bombardment. With any luck, there'd be nothing left of the rebel forces.

"Good work. Now comes the hard part," Captain Heather announced. He settled back into his chair to wait.

Tavista Air Base
1020 local (GMT −2)

"Devil Dog 202, you are cleared for takeoff." The tower's voice sounded almost bored.

"Roger, Devil Dog 202 cleared for takeoff," Thor acknowledged. He shoved the throttles forward, feeling the Hornet surge forward around him. God, but this was an aircraft that loved to fly!

He rolled out and rotated with plenty of runway left, old habits learned the hard way in carrier aviation dying hard. He was the third aircraft in the launch sequence, behind two Tomcats. Queued up on the runway behind him were an assortment of other fighter aircraft, some quite capable and some barely airworthy. It had been clear to him that the Americans had better make damned sure they hit their targets, because he wasn't sure how many of the others would be able to find their IP, much less their targets.

The Hornet burbled for a moment close to ground, then the full effect of the engines kicked in and she soared like a bird. Thor hauled back, climbing at a hard angle, wondering whether he'd catch any flak from the air traffic controller. From the two-dimensional radar now tracking him, it would appear that he was virtually standing still in the sky, showing a remarkably low speed over ground with all of his power poured into gaining altitude.

"Three, you got a problem?" the lead Tomcat asked. "Maybe with your horizon?"

"Negative, Lead, all green back here," Thor said. "Just heading for altitude."

"Right." Lead appeared to be about to let it pass without further comment, then said, "Tanker's not for another fifteen mikes, Three. You think you can wait that long?" A double click of the mike from Two substituted for a laugh.

"I'm fine, Lead. Thanks for asking." Thor cut back his rate of ascent to that of the more heavily laden Tomcats.

That was the one drawback to the Hornet—at least from the Tomcat's point of view. The lighter, more maneuverable Hornet could carry less weapon weight, and had correspondingly smaller fuel tanks. They needed a quick plug and suck at the tanker just about any time they could get it.

But there were advantages to being the smaller fighter, too. They could meet the MiG on a MiG's terms, not expending fuel in the vertical game a Tomcat had to play. And, even more importantly, the Hornet was the platform of choice for close air support, providing firepower to troops on the ground. For a mission like this, one that required precision bombing to hit small, easily concealed targets, the Hornet was the airframe of choice. Finally, the Hornet had one last feature that none of the Tomcats could claim—each airframe was younger and required far less maintenance hours per hour of flight than the massive, aging F-14s.

The first landmark slid by on Thor's right. He checked his chronometer—right on schedule. The Tomcats were formed up in a tight pair ahead of him, and Thor's own wingman was tucked in tight. He craned his neck around for a visual check and got a thumbs-up from the young captain in the cockpit.

Four more minutes. That was the one good thing about fighting a war in Europe—everything was closer together.

Command Center, Tavista Air Base
1021 local (GMT −2)

Arkady stared at the radar picture of the surrounding area, then transferred his gaze to the small-scale topographical map mounted on the forward wall. The suspected locations of the enemy camps were laid out in red, a square enclosing an X marking what his staff believed were the headquarters. More symbols denoted the light mechanized infantry, the two lone tanks that the Macedonians had acquired from defectors from the Greek forces, and the antiair sites now annihilated. The ingress and egress routes were laid out in white.

"Sir. The Tomahawks." His radar technician pointed at the screen. "Right on time, General." The missiles symbology coupled with the impressive speed leaders left no doubt as to the identity of the airborne contacts.

"No," Arkady said immediately. "Those can't be the Tomahawks. They're off course—they're antiair missiles."

"General, the speed doesn't fit," the technician said, a puzzled expression on his face. "Antiair missiles go much faster." He tapped the symbols on his screen. "These have to be the land attack missiles, sir."

"You're contradicting me?" Arkady snapped.

The technician turned pale. Every soldier in the camp knew what had happened to Spiros, and there was a silent pact among them all to never suffer the same fate. "General, my apologies. Clearly, I'm mistaken. Antiair rounds inbound on . . . uh . . ." The technician paused, at a loss.

"On the lead wave of the strike," Arkady supplied. "They know that the first wave is composed entirely of Greek aircraft. This is clearly an attack by the American forces on our units."

"On our aircraft," the technician said eagerly.

"Warn them," Arkady said. "In Greek, not English."

The technician picked up his microphone, his thoughts whirling, and tried to compose a standard phraseology warning to his forces, but he couldn't get his mind focused on the problem. Finally, he settled for, "Attention, all Greek aircraft. The Americans are firing antiair missiles at you from their ships. You are ordered to . . . General?" He looked up for guidance.

"Continue the mission as briefed, regroup at Point Delta, then destroy the American aircraft. They have committed a hostile act," Arkady said. He listened while the technician repeated his words verbatim, then turned to his chief of staff. "Have the guards take all American military personnel into custody. And bring Admiral Magruder to me here."

Macedonian Camp
1030 local (GMT −2)

Xerxes had roused them an hour before first light. Three hours later, they made it to the camp. Pamela was exhausted. She was used to roughing it while reporting from the field, but at least she usually had a decent sleeping bag, sometimes a tent. A cold night curled up against a rock with a thin blanket for protection from the wind had left her exhausted. What little sleep the cold hadn't stolen fell prey to her own speculations about whether or not the Macedonians intended to torture Murphy.

She'd tried talking about it with the Marine, but he'd refused to answer her questions. Whether it was exhaustion or his own dread of what the next day might bring, she couldn't tell. When she persisted, Xerxes threatened to gag her.

When they'd finally made it to the secondary camp, untouched by any bombing run, Xerxes had had them separated immediately. An old, taciturn sergeant had silently showed her to a tent and taken up a guard position outside the front flap. When she'd tried prying up a back corner, exploring the possibilities for regaining her freedom of movement, he'd been there waiting for her. Finally, she gave in to the exhaustion and collapsed on the cot. For the first time in thirty-six hours, she was warm.

The noise outside had awoken her two hours later. She groaned as she crawled out of the sleeping bag, every injury aching anew. She pushed aside the tent flap to discover her guard was gone.

In the small clearing in the center of the camp, Murphy lay sprawled on the ground. She darted out and knelt down next to him, staring in horror at his bloody face. When Xerxes had said that Murphy would talk, she hadn't wanted to acknowledge the menace underlying the words. Now, confronted by the bloody evidence of the Macedonian's handiwork, she could no longer avoid it.

She turned to face Xerxes. "Torture."

Xerxes shook his head. "He fell."

"Right."

He took two steps toward her and reached out one hand for her shoulder. She flinched back. An expression of disappointment and regret flashed across his face, to be immediately replaced by something colder. "I had thought more of you. Think this through. If we had truly resorted to torture, would I bring you here? Give you the opportunity to talk to him, to see what we'd done." He shook his head.

"I can talk to him?" she asked cautiously.

"Go ahead." Xerxes looked sullen now. "Ask him what happened."

She knelt down beside the battered figure stretched out on the cot and touched his shoulder gently. Murphy groaned, then his eyes opened, staring out in the distance unfocused.

"Murphy? Can you hear me?" she asked.

He groaned again then tried to speak.

"Water," Pamela snapped. Xerxes filled a plastic cup with water and handed it to her. She leaned over the cot and tried to prop him up while she held the cup to his mouth. He was just barely conscious enough to try to help her guide the cup. He sucked down two noisy gulps then paused to take a breath.

"More?" she asked. He nodded, his expression already clearly more focused. He levered himself up into a sitting position and took the cup with shaky hands. As he drank the second cup of water by himself, his eyes refocused and found Xerxes standing quietly in the corner. Murphy stared at her impassively as he slowly drained the cup.

"What happened to you?" Pamela asked after he declined more water.

"They caught me trying to depart their hospitality," he said, his face still expressionless. "A couple of guards were trying to drag me back to camp. I wasn't too wild about the idea."

"They beat you?" she said, still not looking at Xerxes.

He shook his head reluctantly. "No. I tripped. Once I was down, one got handcuffs on me. Then the rest of them showed up and hog-tied me for the trip back. I got in a couple of licks though—kicked one guy in the face pretty hard."

"And broke his jaw," Xerxes said, speaking for the first time.

"Too bad," Murphy said, no trace of remorse in his voice.

"And you," Xerxes continued, crossing the room to tower over the Marine pilot. "How are you feeling?"

"I'm just peachy, thanks."

"Good. Fit enough for a little hike?"

"Probably." Murphy's eyes were guarded now, as though he were trying to decide whether to admit it. "If the ribs hold up."

"What's wrong with your ribs?" Pamela asked. She reached out as though to examine him, and he flinched back.

"Cracked a couple in the ejection, maybe. Might be just a strain. It's no big deal," he said reluctantly. She got the impression that little would be more distasteful to him than admitting physical weakness.

"Good. You'll let me know if they get too uncomfortable, then," Xerxes said. "I'm sure we can arrange other transportation for you."

She stood, feeling the pain in her knees as she did so. "Where are we going?"

"Somewhere else. I thought you would have learned by now not to bother asking that sort of question."

"I always ask questions."

"I don't always answer them."

For a moment, it was as though they were the only two people in the room. Murphy was forgotten as their eyes locked and something more passed between them than just a simple question for information and a refusal to give it. Finally, Pamela looked away.

"There's likely to be another strike," Xerxes said finally. "We're moving camp."

"You've got pretty good intell," Murphy said. Xerxes didn't answer.

Moving camp. Pamela glanced at Murphy and knew immediately why he'd minimized his injuries. Movement meant a degree of disorder, and maybe another chance to escape. He'd take that opportunity any time it presented itself, no matter how small the odds for success, no matter how many beatings they administered.

Just like the Marines would be back to get him. That was one of the primary tenets of their brotherhood, that no Marine left another.

So Xerxes was right. They'd be back, both to finish what the earlier strike had started and to look for Murphy.

And to kill as many of the rebel Macedonians as they could in the process.

So where does that leave me? Rooting for Murphy or for the Macedonians? Every time she thought she finally had the answer, some new angle or perspective upset her carefully reasoned approach to the question. Now, staring at the two faces so much alike, both grim, haggard and determined, she knew what her only choice could be.

A sense of peace descended on her, coupled with not a little sadness. The comfort of righteousness, the strength one found fighting for a cause would forever be denied to her. She thought of Xerxes's charge that she would never know what it was to lose friends in battle because she chose no sides.

But he'd gotten it wrong. It wasn't that she had no side—it was that they were all hers. The Macedonians, the Greeks, the Americans . . . despite her nationality, each death was one that mattered to her as a person, as the story of how the war affected that individual. She was denied the luxury of seeing the other side as inhuman, faceless creatures. To her, and to the other men and women who brought the rest of the world to each conflict, each warring faction was composed of human beings. They mattered. They had to. Because only when she could show that side of war to the rest of the world would the civilized nations bring enough pressure to bear on the combatants to stop the bloodshed.

That was her role as a reporter. To bring the facts to the world, to force the international community to intervene. And if she had to have a side to claim as her own, then let it be that one—the side of peace.

Xerxes must have seen something odd in her expression. He stepped away from her to the door of the hut and barked out an order, his voice harsher than she'd heard before. Running footsteps answered him, then a sound like early summer thunder far away.

No. Not thunder. Fear surged through her, shattering

the peace that understanding had brought her.

Not thunder at all. Bombers.

Hornet 202
1035 local (GMT −2)

Thor dipped the nose of the Hornet down slightly for the barest moment, exposing more of the ground under him to view. Not that he really needed a visual, not following in the path of the Tomcats, not with his own HUD indicating he was on course, on time. And especially not with the streamer of smoke and fire billowing up to his left, evidence of the deadly accuracy of the Tomahawk attack on a fuel and weapons dump. No, visual contact with the ground was simply a final confirmation of what he already knew—that they were dead on in their ingress run.

"Five seconds," Tomcat Lead warned. "Hold your positions and don't screw up the egress. Break left if you get hit. SAR and Special Forces are only one mike out."

Thor waited for Two to acknowledge, then said, "Three." His wingman followed with, "Four."

"Alright. Let's give them hell." Tomcat Lead began his descent, falling away in a graceful arc, his wingman dropping in slightly to the left and behind him. Thor counted off three seconds, then followed them down.

Closer to the ground now, with trees rushing by underneath him he could truly feel the effect of the Hornet's speed. Individual trees whipped by, barely visible long enough for him to take note of them before they flashed out of view. Three small buildings spaced perhaps a mile apart, a herd of something—goats, perhaps?—between them. An older burnt-out house, all details he recognized from the satellite photos.

There, just ahead and to the left. An odd patch in the undergrowth, natural enough from a distance but with hard glinty highlights in it as they approached. Could have been quartz formations or rocks if they'd been in a different part of the world, but not here. He'd seen the blow-ups of the area, taken note of the carefully outlined trucks and encampments the photo intelligence technicians had picked out. It would have been clear enough even without the infrared shots that showed warm engines, campfires, and people moving about underneath what was trying to appear as a simple forest. Smoke from the Tomahawk attack was blowing across the area now, further obscuring the picture.

The camp. Human intelligence sources had confirmed with the locals what the intelligence specialists already knew. And what the people on the ground, in a few short seconds, would know beyond all hope of redemption.

Macedonian camp
1036 local (GMT −2)

Xerxes shoved Pamela to the ground then rolled her under the cot. "Take cover!" He followed her in under the scant shelter of the flimsy wooden frame. It bent then flexed upward. Although her vision was partly blocked by Xerxes body, she caught a glimpse of a darkly tanned foot flashing toward the door.

"No!" She tried to shove him out of the way so that she could escape the illusion of the safety of the cot. Better to take her chances in the open away from the structures.

Xerxes shoved her back against the wall of the hut as though determined to hold her in the death trap that she

knew this building surely was. She started to fight back
by reflex, her hands clawing at his face, then realized that
there was only one way out. Instead of reaching toward
him, she flattened her hands and jammed them straight
up.

The cot bucked up. It started to settle back down on
them, one aluminum leg headed straight for her face, but
she got her feet up and kicked. It rose again, rolling now,
and clattered over on its side. The noise was lost in the
all encompassing thunder of aircraft directly overhead.

Pamela bolted to her feet, narrowly eluding Xerxes's
frantic grab for her ankle. Let him die here if he wished,
but she wasn't going to. Not now. Not this time. She ran
for the door, snagging her camera bag strap with one hand
as she went. As soon as she hit the door, she cut hard to
the right and started running.

God, no strafing. Not this time. She remembered how
close the deadly rounds from the Hornets had come when
they were clearing the area around Murphy. It was her
fault that the Macedonians had gotten him, her fault alone.
If she hadn't dragged Xerxes down from the observation
point, they'd never have been within range to take him
prisoner.

The feet—Murphy'd left without his boots. For a split
second, she almost thought about running back in to the
shelter to look for them, but dismissed it almost instantly.
There was no time, none at all. She'd be lucky if she made
it out of range before the first—

Her world exploded. The ground under her feet heaved
up as though trying to rid itself of a flea, bucking and
jolting harder than the worst earthquake she'd ever imagined.

The first blow catapulted her forward, and the ground
that rose up to meet her seemed far closer than it had any
right to be. She hit hard, landing on her right shoulder

and rolling immediately over to smash her face into the hard-beaten ground.

Then the second explosion, harder and more violent than the first, but almost inaudible. She shook her head as it tossed her into the air, gravity slamming her back down a second later into the still-reeling earth. It was oddly disorienting, the earth reeling underneath her, dust and flames and debris rising up from the remains of the camp, complete chaos in utter silence.

She lay facedown on the ground, her arms crossed over the back of her head. She waited.

More explosions, or perhaps aftershocks—she couldn't tell exactly which with no sound involved. It seemed as though she were alone in the midst of devastation, cupped in a giant hand that repeatedly picked her up and then threw her at the ground.

She felt something give in her shoulder, and the pain started then. At first it was indistinguishable from the noise and the violence that seemed to have taken root in the earth.

The shaking stopped. She lay on the ground, scarcely able to breathe with the fear pounding through her veins. Finally she tried, drawing in a deep shuddering breath as though her lungs had forgotten how to breathe. She coughed, started hacking hard. The air was almost solid with dust, debris and smoke.

Get away . . . got to get away. The refrain beat steadily in her head. She couldn't understand exactly why—something about a camp was dangerous. All she knew was that she had to move, had to try, regardless of whether she could breathe or not.

She rolled over, still hacking and coughing, then rolled again as she realized she was now on her back, staring up into black smoke and bits of burning wood. She made it to her hands and knees, then tried to push herself upright.

The pain now, hard and demanding, threatening to consume her just as the early fury in the earth had. She felt herself scream but heard no sound—and kept moving. If she couldn't stand, at least she could crawl.

She quickly discovered that her right shoulder would take no weight at all. Even trying to use it to push herself forward brought on waves of agony that threatened to rip her consciousness from her. She still couldn't breathe well, but traces of oxygen were somehow seeping into her lungs. She held on hard to her consciousness and crawled.

Hill 804
1037 local (GMT −2)

The soldier watched as the compound below him exploded. He was far enough away to be well clear of the devastation, positioned just to the east of the path the attacking aircraft would use to clear the area. It was a good position, a fine position, one he'd carefully scouted at General Arkady's request. He'd been particularly careful to select a vantage point that would almost guarantee him a direct hit.

More secondary explosions now, the muffled *whump-whump* of stores of POL—petroleum, oil, and lubricants—catching up fire. The fire below took on the billowing black form characteristic of the ignitable agents involved. The sound reached him as mild overpressures, each one popping his ears and gently buffeting his body as they reached him.

Soon, very soon now. He had seen the aircraft inbound then lost them briefly behind another rise. The increasing smoke and fire was a problem as well, but he'd taken that into account in selecting his position and the prevailing winds were carrying most of it away from him. He'd have five seconds, maybe six. More than enough time to sight the Stinger in on the aircraft, follow it for a moment to make sure he had a lock, then toggle off the missile. A second Stinger canister lay at his feet, just a precaution. He doubted he'd have time to use it, but it was necessary insurance in case something had been damaged in the climb to the hilltop on the first missile.

He could still hear the aircraft engines, even over the explosions, the roar of the fire and the faint screams coming from the camp. The aircraft sounded higher in pitch now, indicating that they'd changed course and were heading back toward him. He shifted the missile slightly on his shoulder and peered through the sighting mechanism, ready for his target.

All of the planning, all of the preparations had been conducted with the utmost secrecy. General Arkady himself had approved the final plans, his site selection, and his chief of staff had personally brought the two Stinger tubes to his house in town. You could tell when professional military men were involved, the patina of expertise applied to the entire mission.

There was only one thing that puzzled him, a question that he hadn't dared to ask. He suspected he knew the answer, but the less he knew, the more likely he was to survive the aftermath of this attack.

Just why did General Arkady want him to shoot down a Greek Tomcat?

Greek Tomcat 107
1038 local (GMT −2)

Sweat rolled down Helios's neck, soaking into the gold Nomex shirt he wore under his flight suit. The damp fire-retardant fabric chaffed again the stubble of beard, creating an almost unbearable itch. Helios took his hand off the throttles long enough to run one finger around the inside of his collar and chase it. Perhaps he'd made it worse by not shaving this morning, but it was a squadron tradition that men went into battle unshaven. Exactly why, he'd never figured out, but such was the case with many traditions.

He dug one nail into the worst spot and scratched, his eyes still keeping up the scan between sky, instruments, and wingman. The scan, the all-important scan—too many aviators died when they let themselves get distracted and failed to keep up their scans. They forgot that the single most important priority, no matter what other hell was breaking loose, was to fly the aircraft.

Finally the itch abated. He placed his hands back on the throttle and tweaked up the volume on the squadron common net. The howls of triumph and exclamations of exhilaration were still crowding the airwaves. He'd give them a few more minutes to glory in the results of the attack before he ordered circuit discipline restored for their approach on the airfield.

He'd just reached for the transmit switch when he noticed the thin tracer of smoke off to his left. His eyes sought it out, and alarms started going off in his head before he'd fully consciously comprehended what he was seeing. His hands were already moving, throwing the lead Greek Tomcat into a hard break to the right.

The circuit went dead as the other pilots saw his maneuver, then the reason for it. The orderly formation disintegrated into a mass of aircraft scrambling for altitude and distance.

Helios's Tomcat had just turned through ninety degrees when the Stinger found it. The RIO had decided that despite the maneuver, they weren't going to outrun the missile. His hand was tight around the ejection handle and yanking down as the missile found him.

Helios couldn't be sure exactly what was happening. One moment he was in his aircraft, riding home on the joyous cries of the rest of his squadron. The next he was hurtling through the air, stripped of the comforting protection of his Tomcat, the wind battering him like sandpaper and howling in his ears. There was a brief moment of silence as he reached the apogee of his ejection arc from the aircraft, a moment when the wind seemed to die down to nothing and he hung motionless in the air. A fleeting sensation of every dream he'd ever had about flying like a bird—then the air around him exploded into fire, sound and fury. The force tumbled him away from the aircraft, sweeping him before it like so much debris. He somersaulted in the air, head over heels with his ejection seat straps still holding him hard in the seat. Just at one of the rare moments when his feet were toward the earth, the parachute deployed. The force jerked him up and away from his tumbling descent toward the earth as though he were a puppet.

He stared up, panicking, wondering if the parachute had caught him at the right angle or whether it would spill open and send him plummeting to the ground without a hope of survival. He held his breath, hanging motionless for a moment until he was sure the chute had taken a solid bite out of the air, then swiveled around to look for his backseater.

There were no other chutes. He could see the other Tomcats splayed across the sky, saw one brave soul break off and head back down toward him. He twisted in his seat pan, trying to look behind him to see if his backseater had somehow made it out, but the parachute held him oriented toward the west.

At least his chute had opened. His mind was racing

now, going through the ejection procedures they'd drill so often in preparation for just this moment. The swaying motion of the parachute was increasing, inducing nausea, although it seemed like the earth was moving rather than him. He caught the risers, pulled around to stabilize the chute and took another look for his wingman.

There, off to the north. A chute, collapsed and streaming behind a dark figure underneath it. He felt a wash of anger that his backseater would die so, coupled with a feeling of relief and gratitude that he'd survived himself.

The ground was racing up toward him now, harder and faster than he remembered from his practice jumps. He drew his knees up and tried to remember how to relax and let his legs take the shock, already mentally walking through the steps.

Something hard slapped against his face. He took his hand off the risers long enough to touch it and saw blood on his hand when he drew it back. Another hard sting on his leg, then a thin streamer of blood coursing out, some of it soaking into the fabric of his shredded flight suit, the rest keeping pace with his body as he fell. He felt a brief sensation of increasing speed and looked up.

Dread flooded through him. The parachute above him was spattered with spots of blue and red—no, not spots. *Holes*. Shrapnel from his aircraft, some of it burning, some of it just brutally razor sharp, was peppering his chute and his body.

One of the risers parted, the upper segment flailing against the canopy while the part he held still clutched in his hand wrapped itself around his wrist.

He was screaming now, damning the gods and the fates that would let him survive the missile, survive the ejection only to be destroyed a mere three hundred feet from the safety of the ground.

The ground. It was rushing up at him now at an incredible rate, each individual feature now distinct and dangerous. He tried to steer the remnants of the parachute toward a patch of cleared ground and grass, but more risers were being severed each second.

He seemed to be level with the ground now, and in a moment of insanity he wondered whether he'd already landed. Landed, and survived.

Then he hit. His feet touched down first, knees bent as he'd been taught, and hope lasted a moment longer. He felt as much as heard an odd, ominous *crack*, then his legs gave way. He twisted to the left, slammed into the ground on his side and bounced back into the air. For a moment he though he'd imagined the initial impact, then he hit the ground again.

The cycle repeated itself endlessly, with time frozen at the first moment that he'd touched the ground. There was no pain, not yet, just the curious and altogether annoying sensation of trying to land on the ground, trying his damndest, and having the earth toss him back up into the sky again. Dirt, grass and sky reeled through his line of sight and he stopped trying to differentiate one from the other beyond the simple fact that blue meant he was being crushed against the green, and green meant he was about to be.

Finally, two hundred feet away from where he'd first hit the ground, the pilot's body made one last slow arc into the air and landed for the last time.

Hornet 202
1039 local (GMT −2)

Thor watched as the Tomcats leaped up into the air and peeled away to the left and the right, suddenly four thousand points lighter without bombs on their wings. Lead punched through the Tomahawk smoke flume and reappeared almost instantly, his aircraft now dulled with a thin film of ash.

Thor counted to three, then pickled off his own load, breaking left just as gravity wrenched the last one off his wings. He felt the Hornet jolt upward, the engine's power now applied just to airframe, fuel load and pilot without the heavy weapons.

Thor came around hard, standing the Hornet on its wingtip until he reached the reciprocal course. The Tomcats were high above him now and still climbing, each one gouting afterburner fire out of its tailpipes. He followed them up, increasing his rate of ascent in order to try to avoid their jet wash. He caught a flash of steel off to his right as his wingman followed.

"How'd it look?" he asked the other Hornet.

"Good hit, good hit," the younger officer said, his enthusiasm patent in his voice. "Man, if I could have pulled a run like that in the pipeline, I'd be a fucking general by now."

"Yeah, felt solid to me," Thor said. They'd have to wait for the BDA but he was willing to stake some mighty stiff drinks on being dead on target.

"Cut the chatter," Tomcat Lead ordered, his voice harsh. "We got some problems."

"You hit?" Thor asked. He hadn't seen any antiair installations except the two the HARMS had taken out, but that didn't mean there hadn't been any. Still, Lead could have called out a warning as soon as he'd—

"No, not that. Button two," Lead ordered.

Thor clicked over to the private circuit in use only between the American aircraft. It was encrypted, ensuring that anyone scanning the frequencies couldn't pick up their conversation. "What gives?" he asked.

"Looks like we got a problem with the Greeks," Lead said. "Look at their disposition. Doesn't look to me like they're wanting to tank and head home."

Thor glanced down at his fuel indicator. Not critical yet, but lower than he liked. He swore silently at himself for pulling the hot dog maneuvers with the steep angle of ascent as they'd left the airfield.

"They're high-low," Lead continued. "And they're not RTB as briefed. They're sitting there in a fighter sponge like they're waiting for someone. One guess as to who that might be."

"What the hell are they doing?" Thor asked. "Surely they're not—" The hard warble of his ESM gear cut him off, the tone indicating that it had detected radar guidance signals from an air-to-air missile.

SIXTEEN

Thursday, 11 May

Greek Tomcat 103
1042 local (GMT −2)

Greek Army Captain Simeon twisted in his cockpit, unable to hold still under the force of the clear, burning rage coursing through his body. He'd known Helios since their earliest days in the Air Force, had gone through all phases up to and including advanced combat fighter tactics together. They'd fought together, drank together, and chased women for the better part of seven years.

All that ended now, Helios's life snuffed out in the most cowardly attack that he'd ever witnessed.

Not that he'd actually *seen* it. Helios had been at the tail end of the Greek wave of aircraft. Just as the base had made the first report of the American's treachery, there'd been a brief, confused sputter from his own ESM gear. His backseater had been howling and he'd slammed his own aircraft up into as steep a climb as he could coax out of the Tomcat. Altitude meant room to maneuver, and while diving for the deck might be an acceptable countermissile technique, no pilot he knew ever wanted to start an engagement so short on elbow room.

Now, with the rest of his aircraft sorting themselves out, their orbit intervals and altitude separation gradually obtaining some semblance of order, Simeon had a few moments to think.

"You saw it?" he asked his backseater over the ICS.

"I think so. Something that looked like a missile any-way. But General Arkady, he said it came from the Amer-ican ship. The bearing was all wrong—it was coming from further inland, not from the sea. Besides, if it had been from the ship, I would have seen it for much longer time."

"Inland? You're certain?"

"Yes. But the detection was so short"—Simeon could hear the mental shrug—"I could be wrong. I probably am. If the generals says . . ."

If the general says it came from the sea, then it did. Neither of us would survive reporting data that contra-dicts his orders. Simeon knew that was exactly what his backseater was thinking.

"A malfunction in your radar," he announced.

"Yes, of course," the backseater said quietly. "But Sim-eon, these orders . . . do we truly want to attack the Amer-icans now? After they've just flown a mission with us?"

More than anything in the world, Simeon did not. Yet caught between the Americans behind him and General Arkady ahead of him, there simply was no choice. Better to die here than to face what would greet him on the ground if he returned without following the general's or-ders.

Or trying to obey them, at least. Simeon had no great illusions about the damage he could do to the men and women in the aircraft behind him. Americans had built the Tomcat, knew its power and capabilities better than any other nation on earth. Their aircraft would be just as potent—even more so, since there were certain capabili-ties built into the American aircraft that were not available on the export models. The Greeks had tried to make up for that by cobbling together some systems they'd bought from Russia, but the results had been far from satisfactory and had resulted in intermittent errors just like the one he'd concocted to explain his backseater's missile detection.

Simeon heard silence on the tactical circuit as the rest of the men orbited and waited for him to decide what to do.

As though he had a choice. He took a deep breath and toggled the microphone on. "You heard the general's orders. Maintain separation and avoid interfering with each other's shots. Weapons free on all American targets."

Someone snorted and did not identify themselves, although Simeon thought he could identify the person. "Weapons free. Which weapons would that be exactly, Lead?" They'd left the airfield with a minimal antiair loadout, configured as Bombcats for this particular mission. Each aircraft carried one Sidewinder and one Sparrow, along with a full magazine of rounds for the gun.

The general hadn't thought of everything, now had he?

At least the American Tomcats were in no better shape. And at least they knew what sort of fight to expect. Except for the Hornets . . . now there was a nasty little addition to the problem. The Tomcat airframes were heavy and powerful, and they'd be forced by wing loading considerations to fight the same fight. The lighter, more maneuverable Hornets were a different problem altogether.

"We use what we've got," Simeon announced. "Call your target."

USS **Jefferson**
TFCC
1045 local (GM −2)

From the intelligence compartment next to TFCC, Lab Rat watched the Greek fighters peel out of their strikes waves. Before they'd even formed up into fighting teams, he tapped the TAO on the shoulder. "Call Admiral Wayne. Tell him it's urgent."

Tavista Air Base
Command Center
1050 local (GM −2)

Tombstone Magruder was flanked by six guards as he entered the command post. The look on his face would have caused most officers to break out into a cold sweat and start planning their civilian careers. Yet General Arkady merely waved a congenial greeting and beckoned him over to stand before the radar screen.

"What is the meaning of this?" Tombstone demanded, his voice even colder than the expression on his face.

Arkady glanced up, then surveyed the guards as though slightly surprised to see them there. "I wanted you to see this. Under the circumstances, I thought you might need some persuasion."

"Persuasion? You mean like placing the rest of my officers and troops in custody and assigning guards to keep them in one room? You've got the wrong idea about how allies behave toward one another, General." Tombstone stalked into the room as though it were his own squadron spaces. "Unless my people are released within the next ninety seconds, I'm withdrawing all American forces from participation in UNFORGREECE. And just in case you think I don't have the power to do that, you just try considering exactly who those men and women will obey if it comes right down to it."

"Which is exactly why I've put them all together for safekeeping," Arkady said, his pleasant expression broadening into a smile. "Yes, I understand your American forces far better than you think I do."

"You understand nothing," Tombstone spat. "Nothing at all. Not about fighting this war, not about the UN, much less about any of us."

Arkady's face froze for a moment, then the smile faded into an expression far more menacing. "Don't make the mistake of underestimating me."

"Like you've done us?"

Arkady shook his head, the menace fading away as he did so. "Look at your disposition of forces first. Then tell me I don't understand your people."

Tombstone could see the tactical picture as clearly as though he'd charted it out himself. The American aircraft, both Tomcats and Hornets by their symbology numbers, were arrayed in an orderly formation leaving the area of their last strike. Ahead of them, a disorderly gaggle of Greek aircraft were breaking away from a fighter sponge and forming up into pairs of twos, one taking high station and the other taking low. The loose-deuce fighting formation, a two-on-one combo that rarely failed to give the Americans a distinct advantage over other nations more accustomed to fighting under the direction of a ground controller.

"Why?" Tombstone asked finally as he watched the two waves of aircraft approach each other. Two even lines, sets of twos—at least the lead American pilot had gotten the idea and was reconfiguring his forces into fighting pairs. "Why any of this?" The six guards crowded in closer to him as his fingers curled into fists.

"Because this is an internal problem." Arkady paused for a moment to let Tombstone consider his words. "As we've said from the very beginning, there is no place for the rest of the world in resolving this matter. But you Americans have become accustomed to simply barging in anywhere in the world that your misguided sense of knighthood seems to tell you that your presence is needed." Arkady's calm facade was cracking now, revealing the insanity underneath it. "My people were making sophisticated battle plans, inventing the very sciences that you use today when your ancestors were still worshipping trees. We don't need the world to solve our problem for us any more than we needed the friendship of the Romans all those centuries ago."

The Greek general turned to stare at the screen again, and watched with satisfaction as the two waves of aircraft merged into a fur ball. "And now we'll teach the world one more lesson—to stay out of our country."

Devil Dog 202
1051 local (GMT −2)

Thor put the Hornet in as steep a climb as he could manage without going into afterburner. Even before the engagement began, fuel was already his limiting factor. A bad thing anytime, but particularly so when your opponent was a Greek Tomcat carrying more pounds of fuel after a bombing run than you could at max load.

The thin whine of the ESM gear filled the cockpit. A lock. Thor glanced at his HUD. A Sidewinder probably— the IR guided antiair missile was the weapon of choice with the Hornet's tail pointed almost directly at the oncoming Tomcat.

Why had the Tomcat picked him? The question beat in the back of his head as he flew upward, gauging the exact moment when he'd have to take evasive action.

"I'm on him, Thor," his wingman said. Cassidy "Hopalong" Kramer, a nugget still less than one year out of the Fleet Replacement squadron but one of the best natural pilots Thor had ever run across. "Break right when I say."

One the HUD, Thor could see Cassidy's Hornet streaking in from above, diving and pivoting in midair to cut back in behind the Greek Tomcat in perfect killing position. It had better be quick—Thor could feel his airspeed bleeding off, the knots clicking down as the altitude crept up. The hair on the back of his neck started to prickle, and his hand reached for the throttle. Low fuel or not, in a few seconds he was going to need that extra power to keep him out of the stall envelope.

The ESM warning shifted upward in tone, indicated a solid lock. Then it broke into an excited chatter. Thor reached for the controls—missile launch—no way he was waiting, he had to get the hell out of Dodge *now*.

"Now!" Hopalong sang out as though echoing his thoughts and Thor broke hard right.

"Where's the missile?" Thor demanded as he let gravity take hold, bolstering his airspeed and preparing for evasive action. "Where is it, dammit?" He tapped the afterburners, accelerating the Hornet well into a comfortable flying attitude.

"Fireball caught it," Hopalong crowed. "Got that bastard on guns! Man, splash one Tomcat!"

"Where's his wingman?"

"He's just . . . wait, he's . . . shit, Thor, he's on me! Cut back around me and nail him. I'm going rolling scissors." Hopalong spun his Hornet onto his back and went into a hard, spiraling horizontal roll. The wingman started to follow, then evidently recognized the trap. If the Hornet could trap the less-maneuverable bird into a horizontal game, the Hornet won. Sooner or later, Cassidy would have cut inside the Tomcat's turning radius and either stitched a line down its side with gunfire, hoping to hit a fuel tank, or pickled off a heat-seeking missile locked hard on the Tomcat's tailpipe.

But this Tomcat pilot wasn't that stupid. He exploited the Tomcat's greater thrust to wing ratio and grabbed for altitude, clearly intended to pace the Hornet from above and force the game into the vertical.

Thor pulled up his own dive for the deck when his airspeed was well within the envelope again. He still had five thousand feet on the climbing Tomcat, but the range . . . could he make it in time to slip in behind him? He considered it for just a second, then slammed into afterburner and closed the horizontal distance between them.

The Tomcat pilot caught on just as his vertical ascent passed through the horizontal plane of Thor's airspace. The massive fighter twisted in midair, fighting against inertia and gravity to slew the glaring tailpipes away from Thor and to bring the Vulcan Phalynx cannon mounted under the left wing root to bear on the smaller aircraft.

But the Greek pilot was fighting more than two pissed off Hornet pilots—he was up against the laws of momentum and mass, and he didn't stand a chance. Thor saw it before the Greek did and waited as the Tomcat started pulling out of the vertical climb and turning to face Thor.

Just as the clear canopy of the other fighter swung into view, but before the Tomcat could bring its own guns to bear, Thor toggled off a short burst from his gun. So maybe he couldn't shoot the Macedonians on either side of Murphy when he'd wanted to, not that time, but guns and rounds were something that every Marine aviator schooled in the tenets of close air support understood very, very well.

The rounds, every tenth one a tracer, spat out across the front of the Tomcat. The canopy shattered, large chunks of plastic and metal supports streaming back from the cockpit along with a fog as the cockpit depressurized.

Thor continued the stream of gunfire to the right, taking a few precious microseconds to do it, then slammed into afterburner while simultaneously turning hard to the left. His last few rounds caught the engine intake and the right engine exploded into flames.

Get out! You've got time! Against all sense, Thor screamed at the doomed aviator in the crippled plane, shouting at him to eject before the flames raced up the fuel lines and detonated the rest of the fuel.

The pilot in the cockpit was motionless. As Thor flashed by, he caught a glimpse of the shattered helmet, the spreading redness coating the inside of the cockpit.

Just as he cleared the other aircraft, it erupted into flames. The force of the explosion buffeted him as he swept by, tilting the tail of his Hornet up slightly.

"Two of them," Hopalong shouted, victory plain in his voice. "Ain't nothing can mess with a Marine Hornet, *nothing*. Specially not no Tomcat."

Despite the jubilation in his wingman's voice and the sheer relief of being free of the fighter on his tail, Thor felt a creepy sensation. Splash a Tomcat—not something he'd ever thought he'd hear a Hornet pilot say. Tomcats were American aircraft, or owned by America's allies across the world. You fought side-by-side with them, not against them.

"Where's everybody else?" Thor asked, scanning his own HUD and answering the question even as he asked it.

"To the west," Hopalong answered. "Hot Rocks and Lobo are taking on the one that's left in their pair, and the rest of them are out of action."

"Maybe. So where the hell did they go?" Thor asked. He looked down at the fuel gauge and groaned. The two short spurts on afterburner had been critically necessary, but he'd expended over half of his remaining fuel. "And

more importantly—where the hell are *we* going to go?
For some reason, I find myself awful reluctant to head
back to the airbase we just left."

"Not to worry, Thor." Lobo's cool, sardonic voice came
over the circuit just as the final enemy Tomcat burst into
flames. "That's the good thing about carrier aviation. You
take your airfield with you. *Jefferson*'s putting gas in the
air and they've got a green deck. Let's go home, boys—
now follow mama."

"What about the rest of our people?" Thor asked. "We
can't just leave them back there."

"We can and we will," Lobo snapped. "What exactly
did you plan to do, strafe the airfield then dive bomb on
your empty fuel tanks?"

"Marines don't leave Marines behind," Thor countered.

"They do when there's no other way. Now get your ass
into formation and let's plug and suck. We'll pick up
some reinforcments and be back. And this time, we'll be
ready for them."

Thor clicked his mike twice in acknowledgment. Cassidy moaned softly and said, "Man, I love it when she
talks dirty."

Hill 802
1052 local (GMT −2)

By the time the air was crowded with aircraft overhead,
Pamela had covered another one hundred yards. The wall
of trees loomed up at her another forty feet away, dark
and alluring as the waves of noise and destruction washed
over her. The pain in her shoulder, the same one she'd
injured before, was gnawing at her consciousness now,
insisting that life would be so much easier if she'd just

stop moving for a few moments—maybe a minute, no longer, just enough time to let it ease up some. A short rest, that's what she needed. Very short. And then she'd go back to crawling on gouged and bloody hands and knees toward the forest so far away.

She'd just started to let herself sink down to the ground when two arms clamped down around her waist. They lifted her, taking the weight off her screaming shoulder, and just for a moment she thought she was flying through the air again, experiencing those pain-free moments she'd had before hitting the ground.

Then the bottoms of her feet found the ground underneath them and the arms slid up higher, rucking her blouse high around her armpits. "Come on, lady, you can walk. Get moving."

Through a blur of pain and disorientation, she stared at the face. Familiar, she knew him . . . where had she . . . ?

Murphy. The last few minutes and hours came crashing back down on her, sending her reeling in his arms. "Come on," he said, and swore quietly. "We got to get out of here."

She stumbled along, regaining her balance as she went, with one of Murphy's arms still around her waist. It went faster now, and she could see that the tree line was just in front of them. She wiggled in his arms, twisting back around for a look at the aircraft in the sky. Two were just breaking to either side of the camp, low enough that she could see the markings on the tail assemblies as they climbed away from their targets.

Greek. She squinted back toward their course and saw the second wave. More Tomcats—Greek? No, the lighter aircraft just behind them were Hornets, so the Tomcats were probably American. And probably off *Jefferson*.

"Damn you, can't you stop for a single moment?" With a vicious jerk on her injured shoulder, Murphy dragged her into the stand of trees. "You still don't get it, do you?"

She pulled free of him, cutting off the low moan that rose involuntarily in her throat as pain shot through her shoulder. "Yes, I get it. If I didn't, I'd still be back in the camp."

With Xerxes. The unspoken thought cut through her like a knife, blocking out the pain for a few moments. She felt the sickness start deep in her stomach and vault up to the back of her throat. She turned away from him retching, and fell to her knees.

"Easy," he said, and forced a canteen up to her lips when she'd emptied her stomach. "You're safe now." The ground shuddered under them as secondary explosions from the first wave of bombs tore through the structure she'd just been in. Panic reeled through her. A thin laugh broke out from her lips. Safe—as if she'd ever be safe again, as if the term had any meaning whatsoever with five hundred pound bombs pulverizing the ground so close by.

As if reading her thoughts, Murphy said, "We've got to keep moving. They get off course a little, we're toast."

Pamela drew in a deep, shuddering breath and fought for her self-control, reaching deep for reservoirs of strength she wasn't certain she had. Somewhere inside, she found an iron core of determination founded on the realizations she'd had on her role in the world. "I'm okay now." She looked up into his battered face, then down as his bare feet. "Thanks. I wouldn't have made it without you."

He looked away. "It's okay. Just don't do anything stupid and get me killed, all right?"

She nodded. "Can you walk?" she asked, pointing at his bleeding and battered feet.

"Do I have a choice?"

"Let's go, then. Which way?"

He pointed deeper into the woods, and said, "We'll break out before long, but right now the only thing I care about is getting away from ground zero, you know? We'll worry about making our way back into Greek territory after the bombing stops."

"Okay." She looked back toward where she'd come from and saw that she'd managed to drag her camera all the way along with her. "I need that." Without waiting for his agreement, she covered the forty feet separating her from her gear, snatched it up with her good hand, then ran back into cover with him. "We can go now."

He shook his head in disgust. "Like I said—you never stop, do you?"

She started to explain, then settled for, "You're right. I don't."

The stand of trees proved to be far too small to even be called a copse. Instead, it was a narrow strip running between two cultivated fields and the larger stretch that held what had been the Macedonian's camp. They broke out on the other side of it only four minutes after they started walking.

"Which way?" Pamela asked.

He pointed back in the direction the fighters had come from. "That way. We can stay in cover for a while longer and at least we know we're traveling in the right direction. I'll recognize some of the landmarks as we go, although they're going to look different from ground level than they did from the air."

They moved more slowly now, conserving their strength. The sound of the explosions gradually grew fainter, not as much due to any great distance that they covered but simply from the screening effect of the trees. Within a few minutes it started to sound like distant thunder again.

One wave of aircraft stormed by, ascending and clean winged just as the second wave rolled in, still low to the ground and moving more slowly with their wings laden with bombs. They stopped for a moment and watched, felt the power echoing down in their bones at the sound and fury so close by overhead.

The two waves of aircraft passed each other by, the Greek Tomcats climbing harder now when all at once the orderly formation broke into shards as aircraft peeled off in every direction save the one they'd originally been headed.

"What the hell?" Murphy stormed forward to the edge of the tree line and stared up at the disorder. "They're in combat spread, or at least trying to get there." The separate aircraft were reforming into recognizable pairs, one high, one low, and starting hard climbs to higher altitudes. "What the hell spooked them? They've got to have cleared the area before they started in."

Just then Pamela saw it. At first she thought it was a cloud in the distance, but the odd spiraled shape to it grew steadily longer, arcing up across the brilliant blue sky so clear that it hurt her eyes. She pointed up at it. "Missile."

"Stingers," Murphy said, then swore.

She watched as it corkscrewed its way across the sky now, moving impossibly fast toward the closest Tomcat. The pilot dodged and jinked, desperately trying to shake it. At the very last second, she saw the canopy pop up and wretch back behind the Tomcat in its slipstream. The two ejection seats, the back one first by only a millisecond, shot out at angles intended to rocket their occupants clear of the airframe. Just as they cleared the Tomcat, the missile found its target and the aircraft exploded in a brilliant flash.

The first chute opened, then twisted around the tumbling ejection seat, wrapping the risers into a tangled mass. The silk streamed out above the aviator, fluttering impotently, following him down to the ground.

The second chute bloomed then, at first looking precariously lopsided in the sky, then catching the air and filling. The aviator started his gentle descent to the ground when a chunk of flaming debris from the aircraft cut through one riser on its way to the ground. Then a second fragment tore through the fragile fabric itself.

"They'll be after our people next," Murphy said, his voice hard with anger. He traced back the path of the missile to a hillside less than a mile away. "I'm not going to let that happen." He started off at a broken trot, limping badly.

"Wait," Pamela said. "Just hold up a minute, would you?"

He kept going, and threw the words back over his shoulder at her. "I thought you didn't choose sides, Drake."

"I don't. I just have to reload." She slid the pistol out of her camera pack and a clip out of a side pocket configured to hold film canisters.

He was back by her side almost instantly. "I'll take that." His hands closed around the gun, easily prying hers off. She let go and stepped back.

Murphy popped the clip in and chambered a round. "Got any more?" She pulled out two more clips from her bag and held them out to him.

"No sides doesn't mean being stupid," she said. She hoisted the still camera. "Now—lead on."

Anyone watching them would have immediately dismissed the floundering pair as posing any possible threat unless the watcher was close enough to see the nine millimeter tucked into Murphy's waistband or the ugly expression on his face. They were moving slowly, awkwardly trying to keep to cover when they could, stumbling across open patches of field when they had to. It took them almost twenty minutes to make their way to the base of the hill. It was grassy and gently sloping along the sides, but the summit was a rugged crag of weathered rock and gnarled trees.

"How are we getting up there?" she asked. "Can we make it?"

He led her around the base, studying the slopes and the summit. "We have to go up this side. He's got the other side covered."

"How do you know?"

"That's the direction facing the flight path. And no one's shot us yet. You stay down here—I'm going up."

"No way."

"Listen, you'll just slow me down. You're not trained in this—you'll make noise, give our location away, and he'll pop us both before we get within range. You want that, risking those guys lives just so you can play soldier?"

She pointed at his waistband. "I'm doing my part already. Besides, you're not going to shoot me to keep me from going. It'd make to much noise."

"How about if I just tie you up?"

"I'll scream the second you touch me."

Murphy sighed and seemed to give into the inevitable. "Okay. Come on up here, then. You stay to my right and slightly behind. You got that?"

Pamela scrambled up the lower slope, her balance more sure than his had been. "Got it."

"One other thing. You see that tree over there? That'll be our emergency rendezvous spot." He pointed at a gnarled oak at the edge of the last strip of trees. She turned to make sure she had the landmark fixed in her mind.

Just as she looked away, she caught an impossibly fast

flicker of movement. There was a second of pain as his
fist found the side of her head, a flash of light, and then
she slid to the ground unconscious.

The first one hundred yards was easy going. Lush grass
clung to the sides of the slope, interspersed with boulders
jutting up ancient gray and weathered. Murphy's American mind came to an immediate conclusion—difficult to
mow. No way you'd get a riding mower up here, either.
This would be strictly a hand job, probably with a rope
belayed off the boulders just the way you weren't supposed to do it.

Further up the hill, with his injury now draining his
strength and the soil increasingly rocky under his bare
feet, he saw why the Greeks used the field as grazing for
goats. The incline was steeper now, and he had to use the
boulders to steady himself on occasion. Be rough going
if you were trying to get up here with a pack and a couple
of weapons, but certainly not impossible. If you had
boots. If you weren't hurt.

He paced himself, keeping one eye on the summit for
any sign of movement or activity. Nothing so far. Bad
field craft, not having a roving lookout to cover your six.
Two possibilities—it was either one man alone, or two
damned sloppy ones. He patted the pistol. Either way, the
odds looked pretty good to him.

By the time he reached the smooth rocks capping the
hill, he was feeling pretty bad. Not so bad that he couldn't
carry on, of course, but pretty bad. He paused for a moment with his back to a boulder, looking downhill and
shielded from sight from the top of the hill. He let his
lungs build back up the oxygen reserve in his tissue,
sweep away the fatigue and lactic acid that had been
building up, making sure that he was where he needed to
be for the final push. He pulled the pistol out, checked to

make sure a round was chambered and reviewed the plan:
sneak up on the guy and shoot him. No explanations, not
even if the guy spoke English. No second thoughts, no
listening to pleas for mercy. After all, this Stinger guy
hadn't shown any mercy to the pilot he'd downed, had
he? It'd probably been a buddy of his that had forced
Murphy himself to punch out of his aircraft. Besides that,
there wasn't any point in taking chances. Kill them all
and let God sort them out, that was the Marine Corps
theory.

He was feeling better by the minute, now that he'd had
a little rest. Took more than a banged-up leg to slow down
a Marine, a hell of a lot more. He flexed his muscles,
trying to keep from tightening up, and edged around the
boulder to start his last move up the hill. This last bit was
tricky, steep and mostly rock. He tucked the pistol back
in his pocket for easy access and to free up both hands.
No sounds of anyone moving, no indication that his approach had been detected. He slipped around the ancient
rock, moving quietly on bare feet.

The muzzle of an AK-47 stared directly at him.

Pamela rolled over on the ground and vomited. Her head
throbbed as though she'd punched it through a wall of
rock. Her hand went up to the side of her head, touched
swollen pulsating flesh, and pain seared through her. She
groaned, rolled over on her side, and willed her vision to
clear.

What the hell had happened? She remembered the
bombing, getting clear of the building, then . . . Murphy.
Situational awareness came flooding back. He had her gun
and he'd gone up to take out the Stinger jockey.

Her head was starting to clear, although it still hurt
fiercely. Her vision was a bit blurry—concussion, she decided, and swore that Murphy would pay for that when

she caught up with him. She rolled over on her stomach, fighting down another wave of nausea, and shoved herself with her good arm up to her knees. The world spun around her for a moment, then settled down.

Where the hell was he? How long had she been out? She stared up the hill and squinted, trying to make out moving figures among the shadows and rocks there, but it was no use. Her vision was still too blurred.

She struggled up into a standing position and stretched experimentally. Nothing else seemed to be broken, and apart from the pounding in her head, there were no new injuries to catalogue. She reached for her camera and slung the strap around her neck. She'd need her good hand to steady herself on the way up.

Murphy's mind was calling up every synonym he'd ever heard for stupid. Most of them were obscene, and not a few involved his mother. Still, none of the phrases really seemed sufficient to cover this particular situation.

"You are noisy," the man said finally in clear English. "Like a goat."

"And you're lucky," Murphy said.

Pamela paused just below the summit. A sheer rock wall made it almost a vertical climb to the relatively flat summit. She couldn't make it. Murphy would have managed it with no problem, even injured. On most days, she could have kept up.

But today was not most days. "You'll never get away with this," she heard Murphy say.

It figured. Whenever he had planned had gone badly wrong. Had they been working together, he might have had a chance. But now . . . she swore silently at the stupid bullheadedness of the man.

She gazed up at the rock wall above her and ruled out

trying to climb it. Even if she could find the strength to pull herself up, she would make so much noise that all she would accomplish would be getting them both shot. For now, for whatever reason, at least they were both alive.

And why hadn't the Macedonian already killed Murphy? He had had no compunctions about shooting down American aircraft, had he? So why keep the Marine alive for one second longer than necessary?

More importantly, what could she do about it?

She squatted down next to the rock and leaned up against it. The heat-soaked rock felt good against her sore muscles. She opened her camera bag and dug through it just on the off chance that there would be something in it she could use as a weapon.

Normally the truth is my weapon. Or at least the truth as she saw it, she silently admitted. More and more it was becoming clear to her that there was more than one way to look at the truth.

Her fingers brushed against a cold plastic shape that her mind recognized immediately. She closed her hand around it then pulled it out of the pack, careful to avoid making any noise. At this angle from the other two, it was unlikely they would be able to hear her, but there was no use taking the chance.

Finally, she had it out of the bag. It laid bare in her palm like a small, black lifeline. She punched the power button and waited for a dial tone. Ever since the Black Sea conflict, she'd known the private number to CVIC on-board *Jefferson.* Known it, and had been saving it for some very special occasion. This looked like it qualified.

Five bars appeared on the LED screen, indicating that she had a good signal. She wedged herself in between two rocks, hoping that she was right about the other two not being able to hear her, and punched out the numbers.

USS **Jefferson**
1100 local (GMT −2)

The intelligence specialist who answered the phone had been in the Navy for ten years. During his time working CVIC, he'd come to know and appreciate the arcane pathways through which information traveled. Aircraft carriers now had instant access to the Internet, email, and a highly classified Web on which sensitive intelligence data was distributed. He himself was the designated Webmaster for USS *Jefferson.*

So when the voice on the other end of the telephone line announced itself in a breathless, hurried tone as "Pamela Drake—ACN News. I have to speak to Commander Busby immediately," he was only mildly surprised. He debated for an instant hanging up on her, and even reached out to the cradle to cut the connection when caution stopped him. He doubted Commander Busby wanted to talk to this woman, not after what she had put this ship through so many times. Still, it was not a decision he wanted to make for his boss. Besides, Commander Busby had been looking glum recently. Maybe yelling at a reporter and filing some sort of complaint against her network would cheer him up.

So, instead of hanging up on her, he said, "Wait one minute." Then he put her on hold.

He ambled back to Commander Busby's office himself, which took another ten seconds. Maybe the commander would let him listen in as he blasted the reporter they'd all come to despise.

The technician had heard that Admiral Magruder used to be involved with Drake, and he shook his head over that. How a squared-away pilot like Tombstone could see anything in a woman like that was beyond him. But then, a lot of what admirals and pilots did didn't make sense.

"Commander?" he asked from the doorway to Lab Rat's office. "Pamela Drake on line one for you, sir." He smirked.

An annoyed expression flitted across Lab Rat's face, to be replaced by resignation. He sighed. "Fine, I'll take it. Thank you." Lab Rat lifted up the receiver then turned to look at the intelligence specialist. "Thanks."

The technician got the hint. He turned and left, and heard Lab Rat shut the door behind him.

"Busby," he said into the phone. A faint hiss of static and occasional burble of noise indicated that the connection was far from solid. "Miss Drake?"

"I can't talk very loud. They'll hear me. Write this down—Hill 802. There's a Macedonian terrorist on top of it who just shot the down a couple of American Tomcats. A Marine went up after him—Murphy, the Marine they got the first round. Something's wrong . . . I think Murphy screwed up. Is there anything you can do?"

Lab Rat's blood ran cold. "Captain Murphy? Are you sure of that?"

"Of course I'm sure," the voice on the phone snapped back. If he had had any doubts about the identity of the caller, that convinced him. "He's been held as a POW by the Macedonians. Listen, you have to get somebody out here right away. That Macedonian is going to shoot him."

"Hill 802? And what's your cell number?" Lab Rat asked, scribbling the numbers down on the sheet of paper. "Okay, thanks. I'll see what I can do." He started to hang up, then thought better of it. "Stay on the line—we'll keep this connection open. I may need you for a spotter."

Silence, then she said, "I'm a reporter." For the first time, he heard a note of uncertainty in her voice.

"You chose sides when you called in this report, Miss Drake," he said coldly, tired of her equivocations over the years. "Now make up your mind—are you going to let

Murphy die to preserve your precious neutrality? Or are you going to finish what you started?"

"Fuck you. Fuck you all."

Busby waited for the click to indicate that she'd hung up. The line remained open. Finally, he said, "I'll be right back."

Hill 802
1105 local (GMT −2)

For a moment, Pamela was tempted to pitch the telephone down the hill. Only two things prevented her. First, the possibility that the noise might alert the two above her. And second, the very faint possibility that Lab Rat might be able to do something. At least he had taken her call—she hadn't been sure he'd do that.

Angel 301
South of Hill 802
1106 local (GMT −2)

The pilot of the SAR helo listened to the transmission from USS *Jefferson* and then turned to his copilot. "Did we even bring it?"

"Yep. Seemed like a good idea, being over land and all."

"And I suppose Chief Rodgers knows how to work that thing."

The copilot smiled. "Oh, he knows. He's always wanted to be a combat gunner instead of an air-sea rescue guy."

Hill 802
1107 local (GMT −2)

Pamela heard a buzz behind her, and swiped at it with her hand. The damn mosquitoes—that's all she needed on top of everything else. She turned around, intending to catch it and crush it. So maybe she couldn't get her hands on the Macedonians, at least she could kill their insects.

There was nothing there. Puzzled, she checked around her, then realized what she was hearing. A smile broke out on her face. It was still a long way off, and her hearing was still dulled from the bombing, but she could recognize it now. The helicopter.

Murphy was quicker to recognize the sound than Pamela had been, trained as he was as an aviator to recognize the sound of help on the way. But he kept his eyes fixed on the Macedonian face, willing his own expression not to give anything away. He studied the man's features for a moment, wondering why he had let him live this long.

The realization, when it came, struck him like a thunderbolt. Something about the man's features, something a beard had covered earlier. Realization dawned. "I know you," Murphy said wonderingly. "I've seen you before."

The man shifted the gun slightly, dropping from Murphy's face to his midsection. "I was waiting to see if you would realize that," he said calmly. "When you didn't recognize me immediately, I knew we were still safe."

"Oh, I certainly do," Murphy said, now completely convinced. "You're not a Macedonian at all. I've seen you, but not at the POW camp. You're on General Arkady's staff."

Fifteen feet below, Pamela heard Murphy's voice, the anger hard and cold. The words were almost indistinguishable—almost. She lifted the phone to her mouth. "Are you still there?" she whispered."

"Commander Busby is arranging for some assistance, ma'am," a new voice said. "I am Petty Officer Barker.

"Find Busby right now," Pamela said. "Tell him the terrorist that shot those Tomcats was Greek, not Macedonian. You got that?"

"But the Greeks are—" he began.

"Don't waste my time," she snapped. "Just go tell him. And do it now."

Angel 301
Location
1118 local (GMT -2)

The pilot pointed to the hill looming before them. "Hell of a spot, but that's got to be it." Beside him, the copilot studied the chart. "Yeah, that's it. They're on the east side."

"Fine. We'll come up behind them from the west. It doesn't look like they'll be able to get a line of sight on us until we're right in front of them."

Line of sight—that was the issue. Stingers wouldn't go chasing them around the terrain.

The pilot put the bird into a gentle bank around the hill, staying low and keeping the massive rock formation between the helo and the people he was looking for. When they were fifty feet from the formation, hovering unsteadily, he glanced back at the crewman. "You ready?"

Hill 802
1119 local (GMT −2)

Pamela stared at the helicopter hovering so close, joy leaping in her heart. Never had she been so delighted to see an aircraft with the American flag painted on its fuselage. She pointed up, then made a broad sweeping motion, indicating that they should go around the rock. By now, there was no chance that the two men at the summit did not know the helicopter was here. But she hadn't heard any shots yet, so Murphy might still be alive. The helicopter pivoted smoothly in midair, wobbled for a moment, then moved slowly around hill. As it turned, Pamela saw the open hatch on the right side of the helicopter. Safety-strapped to one side of the hatch, a young man in a flight suit was holding a weapon. He raised his hand in greeting, then dropped it down to the stock and pulled the weapon tight against his shoulder.

A machine gun. Pamela felt the sick dread invade her chest. Just how were they going to distinguish between Murphy and the Greek with a weapon like that?

Maybe they didn't intend to. And if anyone could understand, it would be a Marine. Sometimes the life of one had to be sacrificed for the lives of many.

She had always known the military had to make those sorts of choices, had agreed in a way. But that had been when it was an abstraction, just a principle.

Not when it was someone she knew. She wasn't even sure she liked Murphy all that much, but she did know him. And that made all the difference in the world.

The noise decreased slightly as the helicopter disappeared from view around the ancient hill. Well, maybe she couldn't go straight up, but she certainly could go sideways. As it was, if Murphy were going to die, she bore partial responsibility for making the call to Lab Rat.

The least she could do would be to be there to witness it and take pictures.

As the helicopter swung into view, the Greek soldier lunged for Murphy. He grabbed him, tried to hook his arm around Murphy's neck while still holding on to his weapon. "This is why I kept alive," he said. "They can't hit me without hitting you. And I do not think they are willing to take that chance."

As the Greek moved around his left side and his arm settled around the Marine's neck, Murphy saw his chance. He stepped back with his left leg, way back around behind the Greek. He bent over slightly, transferred his weight to his back knee, and straightened up abruptly. At the same time, he slammed his left elbow into the Greek's gut, then followed up with a hammer smash to the groin.

The elbow found its target. The Greek grunted loudly and folded over. The groin shot missed, and Murphy felt his hand hammer into the man's upper thigh. While not incapacitating, the blow was enough to further distract the Greek. Murphy followed up by pivoting to his left, grabbing the man's long hair with both hands, and smashing his face down into Murphy's knee. He felt the nose give way, then teeth scrabbled to take a bite out of his leg.

The weapon—where is the weapon? Murphy nailed the Greek with two more solid shots to the gut, then a hook into the jaw. The man stumbled back, not yet unconscious, but clearly not able to follow all that had happened in a few short moments. He held the weapon loosely in his right hand, the barrel pointing well away from Murphy.

With a roar, Murphy leaped for him, letting his weight do the work to carry the man to the ground. The Greek rolled, still surprisingly agile. Murphy's pounce hit the Greek's midsection and all at once they were rolling across the rocky summit. Stones slashed at Murphy's back as he rolled, and sudden pain slashed through his shoulder.

Murphy kept his grip on the Greek, trying to clamp one arm down around his neck as his free hand fumbled for the weapon. He felt the Greek's knee rise up between his legs, and turned at the last moment to avoid the blow.

"Both of you cease immediately," a voice boomed out from the helicopter. "Stop now, or I'll shoot."

Murphy was on his back now, with the Greek over him. "You'll pay for this. Pay, and pay again," the Greek shouted, aiming a punch at his face. Murphy shoved and turned, barely avoiding the blow, and countered with his own assault.

Gunfire stitched the ground just three feet from them, spraying loose rock shards and dirt all over both of them. Something hard and sharp dug into Murphy's thigh, but he could barely feel the pain. They were close to the edge now, too close. Murphy backpedaled, trying to get away from the edge of the cliff, but the Greek still had hold of his shoulder. Murphy brought his forearm down in a smashing blow across the other's arm, and just succeeded in pulling the Greek closer. The iron grip remained unshaken.

"Shut your eyes," a higher voice ordered them imperiously. "Murphy, shut your eyes now!"

The Greek turn slightly to snarl at the intruder. Murphy, on the other hand, did what any good Marine would do. He shut his eyes.

Even behind his closed eyelids he could see the brilliant flash that lit up the area. The Greek howled, and Murphy felt the iron grip on his shirt loosen. He kicked hard at the Greek's kneecap, grabbing for the weapon with both hands. For a moment, they played tug-of-war, and Murphy kicked again. Finally, his strength and training made the difference. The weapon came free.

He snugged it up to his shoulder in one motion, a reflex borne of years of training. His hand slid automatically over the well-worn stock, down the trigger guard, and applied exactly the right amount of squeeze to the trigger. Squeeze, don't pull—they'd taught him that for years.

The gunfire, when it came, seemed almost anticlimactic. It spattered the rocks, filling the air with a mass of flying fragments. Pamela hunkered down in a crevice to avoid the deadly hail of bullets, ricochets and stone shards. She heard tiny metal pings as the helo slid sideways into its own field of fire.

Between the noise of the helicopter, the howling from the Greek whose dark-adapted eyes were in pain from the brilliant flash of Pamela's camera, and the beating he'd taken from Murphy, he didn't have a chance. He cried out one last time more, clasped his hands to his chest, and fell back.

Murphy stood for moment, frozen in firing position. Another round? He waited to see if there were any signs of life.

"You want to help me up?" Pamela demanded from down below. Still Murphy did not move.

"Come on, Murphy. Get me up there. Haven't I earned it?" Still Murphy watched the Greek's body, waiting for any signs of life.

Gradually, it began to seep into his mind that it was all over. He was alone with the dead Greek terrorist and a SAR helo hovering nearby. Still holding the weapon pointed at the body, he walked slowly up to the body and kicked it. Blood was pouring out of three holes, soaking into the deteriorated rock and pooling in nooks and crannies. The man's eyes were open, lifeless, and slightly rolled back.

Angel 301
Hill 802
1125 local (GMT −2)

Even with earphones and a headset on, the noise inside
the helicopter was deafening. The aircrew was plugged
into the interior communications set, but there were no
spare jacks for their passengers. Pamela could see the
flight engineer's lips moving and knew he was talking to
the pilots up front. From the expression on his face, the
news wasn't pleasant. She saw him mouth something
about hydraulics but couldn't make out the rest of the
sentence.

His injuries and the final battle had finally taken their
toll on Murphy. He was slumped down across two seats,
his eyes shut. Whether he was unconscious or had simply
fallen asleep, Pamela couldn't tell. But she saw the air
crewman check him several times, and she knew that they
were trained in first aid. Evidently whatever he found satisfied the air crewman, because he let Murphy sleep un-
disturbed.

Her own injuries and exhaustion were starting to make
themselves known. It was getting harder and harder to
concentrate, and she could feel her own eyes drifting
closed. After a cursory exam, the crewman had patted her
on the shoulder—the good one—and gently assured her
she'd be fine. "Nothing that the docs back on the carrier
can't fix," he shouted, just before they had taken off.

The extraction—the most remarkable display of airmanship she'd ever seen, the pilot edging the helicopter
over to the rocks, gently hovering right at the edge of the
cliff and holding the aircraft steady. Unbelievable. They'd
used safety lines, of course, but it had been almost as easy
as stepping onto the helicopter from solid ground. Any
closer, and rotors would have scraped the rock outcrop-
pings that loomed over them.

She glanced at the body of the Greek soldier, now secured in the aft of the helicopter with nylon straps to the deck. He lay sprawled lifeless on the steel deck, his head thumping occasionally as the helicopter maneuvered.

"We have to take him," Murphy had insisted. "He's our only proof."

"Won't they take your word for it?" she had asked.

Murphy shook his head. "They might. But there's a lot on the line here. We're talking about an act of war by an ally. That's going to upset more apple carts than I even want to think about. No, I want hard proof. Something I can show them."

Even though she understood the necessity for it, there was something unsettling about having the dead body in the helicopter with them. The way the head lolled, the arms loose and floppy, even the stink as his bodily functions had let loose at the moment of death. Yes, she'd seen men dead before, but it had usually been in the heat of battle when she'd been hot on the trail of her story.

Then, her priority had been to stay alive. There had not been time to watch the dead and wounded. It was only later, during those moments when the medical and treatment units had already taken charge, that she actually saw them.

And not like this. Not freshly killed. She shuddered, unable to take her eyes off the dead body.

Murphy's eyes popped open. He fumbled with his blouse pocket for a moment, then withdrew a green wheel book and a stub of pencil. He scribbled, tore the sheet out of the booklet and passed it across the aisle to her.

She looked down at it and read, "That could have been me. Thank you."

She shook her head, unable to comprehend. Murphy had been the one who saved himself.

She shivered, knowing that if the picture turned out the

way she thought it would, the two men silhouetted against the dark sky with the light from the helicopter playing over them, that there would be an award in it for her.

But you told him to close his eyes, one part of her mind insisted.

Yeah, stupid move, that. Better to have him looking straight at the camera, capture the entire expression on his face. Now *that* would've been worthwhile.

You told him to close his eyes.

And just why had she done that? It had been instinctive, with everything happening so fast she couldn't really break the time apart into discrete moments. The helicopter, the climb around the edge of the cliff, the mad, driving passion to get the photo, to finish the story. That had been what was on her mind. Not Murphy.

You told him to close his eyes.

Murphy passed her the pencil. She thought for a moment, and scribbled "You're welcome."

Somewhere over the horizon was safety, safety in the middle of the ocean where none existed on land. USS *Jefferson*, the world's most powerful nuclear aircraft carrier, lay waiting. As many times as she had schemed to get on board, done everything in her power to force the Navy to admit her to their innermost sanctums, had sworn and cursed at the massive ship, had damned the Navy for taking Tombstone Magruder away from her, it was to the *Jefferson* she was forced to turn for safety.

Pamela Drake leaned forward in the helicopter and strained her neck to see out the scratched and blurred window. Was that it out there, on the horizon? She squinted, trying to make the shape out, but what she had thought was *Jefferson* remained simply a ragged patch on the horizon. She turned to the air crewman. "How far out is she?"

He smiled and laid a reassuring hand on her shoulder. "Forty miles, maybe a little further. We'll be on board in about twenty minutes. Don't worry, you're safe now."

Pamela started to shoot back a harsh reply, angered that he could think she was concerned about her own safety. She bit off the words before they formed in her mouth, suddenly uncertain. If truth be known, she was afraid— more so than she had ever been in her life before.

"Peacock, get everyone strapped in." The pilot's voice over the ICS carried that hard, laconic note that Pamela had learned to associate with a pilot under pressure. She'd heard it too often in Tombstone's voice to be mistaken.

"What's going on?" she asked, even as the air crewman pressed her back in her chair and double-checked and tightened the seat harness. "What's happening?"

"Seems we got a little company out here," the pilot's voice came back, calm and casual. "Nothing to worry about yet. Listen to Peacock—he's going to review ditching procedures with few. You've been on a helicopter before, haven't you, Miss Drake?"

"Ditching procedures?" She repeated his words in a stunned tone of voice. "Who is this company you're talking about?"

There was a long pause, then the pilot said, "There are three groups of fighters inbound on our location. From the IFF and link picture, they're Greek, Macedonian, and American. Right now, I suspect they're more interested in each other than they are in us. But when elephants dance, helicopters get out of the way."

Peacock knelt down before her and began reviewing ditching procedures. "Find a handhold, know where it is in relationship to the nearest exit." He pointed to the hatch at the side. "That will be yours. Stay in your seat until all motion ceases. We may sink quickly, but just because there's water in the cabin, don't try to leave it. You have to stay until the water slows the rotor blades down or they'll cut you to pieces as you leave. Got that?" Pamela nodded, remembering previous helicopter safety briefs.

"Once all motion ceases," Peacock continued, "unstrap yourself and pull yourself toward the exit. We may turtle—flip upside down. We usually do. Don't let that disorient you. Keep one hand holding on to something at all times." He held up the small air canister with a face mask attached. "I will be right here in case you get in trouble. Don't worry, I'll get you out." He flashed her a cocky grin. "Haven't lost a passenger yet."

"Do you have comms with the carrier?" Pamela asked.

Peacock nodded. "Yes, this close we should be fine. But we'll be there in—"

"This can't wait." She pointed at the man lying motionless on the helicopter deck. "There's something they have to know immediately."

USS Jefferson
TFCC
1128 local (GMT −2)

Batman stared at the small symbols converging on each other just off the coast. "I don't like this, not one little bit. Tell that helicopter to get the hell out of the way. Where are his fighters, anyway?"

"They were running out of fuel, Admiral," the TAO said. "Should be finished with the tanker in just a moment. Bad news on the helo, too. He's got a hydraulics leak. Can't tell how bad yet. He's still got all controls, but pressure to the system is slowly dropping."

Batman stood and began pacing in the small compartment. "Why the hell are the Macedonians doing this, anyway? It's not like they have a chance." He pointed at the screen. "Are they completely insane? Between the Greeks and our own forces, they're so badly outnumbered that there's not a chance in hell that—"

"Home plate, Angel 103," a voice came over tactical.

Batman brushed aside the TAO and picked up the microphone. "I'll tell him myself." He keyed the mike. "This is Admiral Wayne. You need to be at wave top getting the hell out of there because—"

"Admiral, with all due respect, sir, this can't wait. There's something you need to know immediately." The pilot's voice was calm and unbothered by the fact that he had just interrupted the admiral in command of the battle group. There was a strange rustle over the speaker, then the pilot's voice, sounding distant now, said "Go ahead, Miss Drake."

Every face in TFCC turned up to stare at the speaker. Batman's jaw dropped, and he felt the blood rush to his face. Just as he started to speak, Pamela cut him off.

"Admiral Wayne, we found the sniper who was taking shots at your Tomcats. Both of us recognize him. He's on Admiral Arkady's staff."

"What sort of nonsense is this?" Batman snapped. "He's not Greek—he's Macedonian. I realize that they may all look alike to you, Miss Drake, but mistaking our allies for the enemy is understandable under the circumstances."

"Give me that," a new voice said in the background. Another rustling noise, then a new voice on tactical. "Admiral, this is Captain Buddy Murphy, Marine Corps. Drake is right. I recognize him. The Greeks are shooting at our aircraft, Admiral. They're probably the ones who shot me down as well." There was no mistaking the anger in the Hornet pilot's voice.

"Greek?" Batman turned to air at the tactical display.

The three waves of aircraft were now only fifty miles apart. His mind raced furiously. With aircraft spoiling for a fight and wings loaded with weapons closing in on one another, there remained one critical, all important question left unanswered: Just who the hell were the bad guys?

SEVENTEEN
Thursday, 11 May

Angel 103
Forty miles west of USS Jefferson
1129 local (GMT −2)

"Divert? No way, Jefferson. We're inbound with casualties." The SAR pilot's voice was firm. "We'll take a vector around the big boys, but—"

"Not an option," Jefferson's TAO replied. "Air's clobbered with fighters for a hundred miles in every direction. You don't have enough fuel."

"I don't have enough airfield, is what I don't have," the SAR pilot muttered, but Pamela could tell from the sound of his voice that he wasn't transmitting. There was silence for a moment, then the circuit crackled back to life. "Roger, so do we have a bingo field?"

"We did. Until they started shooting at us."

"Peachy. Just fucking peachy."

"Can it, Angel 103," a new voice said over tactical, one that Pamela recognized immediately. "It's not like you've never landed anywhere except a carrier. Find a quiet spot, hole up for a while, and we'll get you back onboard as soon as we can."

"Roger, sir." The surliness was gone from the helicopter's voice. "Wilco."

"Fine. Advise us of your LZ coordinates. Guard this circuit—you'll know soon enough when we'll want you airborne again. And stand by for additional tasking. I may

want you to disembark your current stick and be available
for SAR in the area."

"Aye-aye, Admiral. We'll guard this circuit and military air distress."

"Roger. Out."

Silence on the circuit again. Finally, the pilot said over
ICS, "Everybody copy that?" A chorus of yes answers
followed. "Good. I've got a local map, but I need some
intell. Any input would be welcome, especially from you
locals. And you, Miss Drake. Not that you'd need any
encouragement."

"Now that you mention it," Pamela said, "I know where
we could go. Refuel, too."

"Fuel is good. You're talking about the Macedonians,
I take it?"

Pamela nodded, then realized he couldn't see the gesture. Listening too long on the circuit had given her the
feeling of being inside the middle of the battle, as though
she were sitting right between the pilot and the copilot.
"Yes. They'll be monitoring military air distress, right?"

"Should be. They've got assets airborne, they're going
to be listening."

"So we call them on MAD, make the arrangements."

"You think they'll go for it? Might be that the last they
heard, the Americans were shooting at them."

"I'm not going back to that camp," Murphy said. "No
way. I went to enough trouble just getting out of it."

Pamela turned to him. "That was then, this is now. It's
the only place we can land, refuel, and be available for
other SAR missions."

"I say again for possible penetration," Murphy said sarcastically. "You do realize that we're talking about the
same people that had me trussed up like a pig a few hours
back?"

"Get it through your thick Marine head," she snapped,

losing all patience with him. "They're not the enemy. You got it?"

Murphy nodded. "Oh, I've got it. I'm just wondering if they do."

USS **Jefferson**
1132 local (GMT −2)

"You're going where?" Batman roared. "I told you to hole up somewhere, not defect."

"Sir, what Miss Drake says makes sense," the helo pilot answered. "We owe the Greeks bad for what they've done. And if the Macedonians aren't our allies, at least they're the next best thing—the enemy of an enemy."

"So you're assuming the enemy of an enemy is a friend," Batman answered.

"Beats the alternative. I'm losing hydraulic pressure every minute, sir. If I set this bird down somewhere, there's every chance I can't get her back up. Then you've got a SAR mission on a SAR crew and pax, and I have to tell you, I'd feel pretty foolish about that."

"It wouldn't be the first time."

"It would for me."

"That's it," Pamela said over ICS only, "keep him talking. He'll calm down. Tell him I'll blast his name over every hourly broadcast if he doesn't."

"Thank you, Miss Drake. Appreciate the advice, but I believe I can probably deal with Admiral Wayne on my own terms," the pilot said.

"Fine." Pamela slumped down against the hard cushion of the pax seat. Just like the military—you offer your help and they shit on you. After all she'd tried to do for them . . . after Tombstone . . . after . . .

They don't have a lot of reason to trust you, do they?
One small part of her mind interjected. *Cuba, the Black
Sea, Vietnam . . . there've been enough times.*

That was then, she argued, infuriated. Bad enough that
she had to deal with the military without having to confront her own transgressions once again.

Batman knows you.

He knows who I used to be. Back before . . . before I
understood.

Ah, a reformed woman. Changed your ways, have you?

They didn't *need* changing. I've always been on their
side.

And were you before?

Not always, she admitted reluctantly. At least, although
she'd always thought of herself as a patriotic American,
perhaps a jaded, cynical—call it realistic—one, but an
American nonetheless.

But on the ground, watching the reality of combat, challenged by Xerxes to reexamine her own choices and beliefs, she'd come to a new understanding of what it meant
to be an American.

*And what we're required to do because of who we are.
Tombstone's starting to make more sense to you than he
ever did before, isn't he?*

In that second, she understood what she'd never fully
grasped before. No matter that she could recite the intri-
cacies of foreign conflicts and the history that predated
them, pronounce the names of every foreign leader and
his coterie, identify the most obscure geographic regions
on a map—she'd been ignorant. Even after years as a war
correspondent, even after all the awards, the hoopla, the
public recognition, she'd never really crawled inside the
military mind. Known what it was to go out on a mission
with the probability that you'd never return. Known what

it was to plan those missions, knowing you were condemning the crews and ground forces almost as surely as
if you'd put a gun to their heads yourself. But you sent
them out anyway and learned to live with the results. Because not so long before, your superiors had faced the
same hard choices, made the same agonizing decision.
And in a way, executing the mission was sometimes easier
than ordering others to.

"Yes, Admiral," the pilot said, and Pamela realized she
hadn't been paying attention. "We'll try it right now. Out.
Miss Drake, were you listening?"

"Not closely—could you fill me in?" Pamela heard a
new trace of humility in her voice, one she wasn't entirely
sure that she liked.

"Sure thing. Admiral wants me to try to put you in
contact with the Macedonians. Tell them he's going to
come up on a frequency—hold on, I'll write it down for
you—and wants to talk. Tell them that the U.S. is withdrawing its forces from support of any Greek aggression,
and that we're standing by to enforce the no-fly zone.
Against both sides. We're going to want some time to
clear this whole thing with Washington. Basically, it's
stop the problem, stop the clock. Just like in a trainer.
You got that?"

"I got it. Tell me when we go to live feed. That is,
when the circuit's on. Whatever you call it."

She heard a quiet chuckle over the ICS. "Roger.
Standby—*now*."

Pamela took a deep breath, and started perhaps the most
important broadcast of her life with the words she'd used
on so many other occasions. "Good afternoon. This is
Pamela Drake, ACN correspondent, speaking to you live
from . . ."

USS Jefferson
1133 local (GMT −2)

Batman listened to Pamela's words echoing on the speaker. His eyes sought out Lab Rat, who was leaning against the far bulkhead with his eyes shut. Anyone who didn't know him might have thought that he wasn't paying attention, but Batman knew what he was doing. Lab Rat was filtering out all the distractions, focusing the entire power of his intellect on the words coming over the speaker. It was this capability for concentration, this ability to bring single-minded intensity to bear on a particular problem that made him so valuable as an intelligence officer.

And would have been deadly in an aircraft, Batman thought. As powerful as Lab Rat was as an intelligence officer, he thought that the other man might have lacked the ability to maintain his scan, to avoid being fixated on any one aspect of the problem while maintaining the overall picture and executing the mission. In the air, too much concentration was almost as deadly as too little.

But as an intelligence officer, Lab Rat was in his natural element. Deception, obfuscation, the fog of war—he sliced through them as easily as Batman could peel out of a formation and do a barrel roll. And now, he was worrying at the problem of shifting alliances, listening to Pamela's words to detect any false notes—for if truth be known, Batman was not entirely sure he was doing the right thing, taking her up on her offer to contact the Macedonians.

But what choices did he have? With the SAR helo leaking hydraulic fluid and the shifting alliances being sorted out in the air, Batman was out of options.

Finally, Pamela finished her broadcast. There was a moment of silence, then, clearly prompted by the military men in the helicopter, she added, "Over."

More silence. Lab Rat was motionless, his chest barely moving as he took shallow breaths. Outside the compartment, someone laughed, the noise oddly alien as it seeped into the secured compartment. Inside TFCC, no one moved.

Macedonian camp
1133 local (GMT −2)

Xerxes stared up at the speaker, a puzzled expression on his face. He turned to the radio operator. "Where is the signal coming from?"

The radio operator leaned across the room and tapped on the blip on the radar screen. "I am not certain, sir, but it appears to be correlated with this airborne contact. The American helicopter."

"SAR, they say."

"Yes, sir."

"Hmm." Xerxes felt the tension begin to drain out of his face. Was it possible she was telling the truth? And just how far did he dare to trust her? "What are the American fighters doing now?"

"They're flying CAP stations, sir. In between us and the Greeks. Nice, tight orbits, unless one of the Greeks tries to break through. They've used their guns a couple of times, mostly as a warning it looks like. No missiles in the air yet."

Xerxes picked up the microphone. "Miss Drake. This is not an encrypted circuit, so I'm not going to pass any sensitive information over it. Do you remember where I took you the first time?"

"Yes."

"Could you find it again? From the air, I mean—things

often look different when you're airborne instead of on the ground."

"I'm pretty sure I can."

"Good. Land your aircraft there. I can't have you flying directly into the camp, not just yet. They'll track you by your transponder. Have you told them where it is?"

"No, I haven't. Not yet."

"Don't. Go to—that place—and I'll have aircraft technicians and someone from my staff meet you."

Silence for a moment, then, "If I can, I won't tell them. Unless it endangers the safety of this crew or any American forces."

Xerxes heard new steel in her voice, and in a flash, he knew what it meant. *She's chosen sides. Finally. Now maybe she can understand.*

USS Jefferson
1135 local (GMT −2)

Lab Rat opened his eyes. The pale blue irises shone in the dim light. He looked across the room and into Batman's eyes. The intelligence officer nodded once, then appeared to break the spell that had held him motionless for the last fifteen minutes.

"You think it's legit?" Batman asked, already knowing what Lab Rat would say but having to ask the question anyway.

"Yes, Admiral, I do. I suggest we get that helo vectored in ASAP. They're going to need some time for that hydraulics line. There's no telling when we may need her back in the air." A flurry of increasingly frantic calls over tactical provided an unintentional emphasis to his words.

Batman grimaced. "Okay." He turned to the TAO. "Send her in."

"One other thing, Admiral," Lab Rat continued. "The Macedonians—we may not be able to choose up sides in this fight just yet." He paused for a moment, and Batman understood what he was asking.

"I'm going to enforce status quo for now. Nobody dies, not if I can help it. No Greeks, no Macedonians, and most of all, none of our people. And if that means shooting down Greek aircraft while we're waiting for word from Washington, I'll do it."

Lab Rat nodded, an almost cursory motion as though he'd already known what his admiral would decide.

And of course, Batman thought, he did.

EIGHTEEN
Thursday, 11 May

The White House
0700 local (GMT −2)

Sarah Wexler gazed across the desk at the man she'd come to regard as a friend and mentor over the years. She could see the tension in his eyes, the toll this was taking on him. For a moment, she felt the surge of sympathy.

But hadn't it been that way for them all? The waiting, knowing something was terribly terribly wrong, the eternal waiting—it seemed to her at that moment that waiting was at the crux of any career in politics.

The president was leaning back, his hand interlaced in front of him and resting on his stomach. He had gained weight since the college days, not much, but it showed in his midsection. The middle finger of his right hand was tapping out a rhythm against the knuckles of his left hand, and she tried to discern the order to it. The president was a particular fan of jazz music, and on occasions that she caught him humming in time to the tapping, she was generally able to recognize the song.

He caught her staring at his hands, and smiled sheepishly. The index finger stopped its tapping.

"What was it?" she asked. Because of their long friendship, the president knew exactly what she meant.

"Rhapsody in Blue," he answered. "I can hum a few bars to help pass the time."

Sarah shook her head. "No, it won't be much longer

now." She was certain of that, although she could not have explained how she knew it. Perhaps it was from years of keeping her finger on the pulse of the communications between nations, of weaving these webs of intrigue and competing interests that made up the body politic. Whatever it was—call it intuition if you had to— she could feel things moving to a head. And so could the president. She could see it in his eyes, in the slight tensing of his muscles as he steeled himself for the decisions he must make.

"They're all airborne," she said softly, repeating the fact that they both knew. "It is just a matter of time."

"Time for us. Fuel for them." Suddenly, he seemed to reach a decision. He reached for the telephone on his desk, paused for moment, and looked across at her. "There will be hell to pay for this, you know."

She nodded. "There always is."

The president drew in a deep, slow breath, and punched in a two digit number. "Mr. President," he said without preliminaries. "You have two minutes to order your forces to return to base. Otherwise, it is weapons free." He listened for moment at the angry babble of words spewing out of the receiver. Then he moved the telephone away from his ear and replaced it gently in the cradle without further comment.

"When was the last time you hung up on anyone?" the president asked. "It's been years for me." He leaned back in his chair again, looking suddenly years younger. "I'll have to try that more often."

Devil Dog 202
1136 local (GMT −2)

Thor kept the Hornet in a tight spiral, heading up to assigned CAP altitude. To the south, clusters of radar re-
turns merged, split apart, and then circled about each
other. Gradually, out of what looked to be a massive circle
jerk, the Greek aircraft were splitting off into pairs, tran-
sitioning from a bombing run formation into combat
spread high-low fighting sets.

They had the right idea, he supposed. But they were
damned slow about it. The possibility had been briefed,
he knew, and the Greek formation ought to have been
ready for it. After all, they had guys on the ground that
knew what the hell was going on, that had to have known
that this friendly joining of forces with the Americans was
all for show.

And they'd shot down his buddy. That, more than anything else, made it personal.

"Hey, Thor, you're going to screw yourself into the
stars, you make that orbit any smaller." It was Hot Rocks,
riding wing on Lobo. "Pay attention, swabbie. I'll show
you how to maintain a CAP station." Thor heard the double click of the microphone, signifying Hot Rocks had
copied his last. For a moment, he wondered about Hot
Rocks, then shrugged. Whatever problems Golden Boy
had had during his first cruise, he'd worked them out. Or
Lobo had beat them out of him—frankly, he wouldn't put
it past her to smack him around a little bit, if only to get
his attention.

No matter. Kid was one hell of a decent aviator now,
and that was all that mattered.

"Blue Flight, interrogative status?" Thor asked. One by
one, in flight order, the Hornets checked. Each one was
on station, had adequate fuel reserves, and was copying
the LINK loud and clear. "Roger, Lead's on station.

Weapons tight for now—but don't take the first shot."

"Blue Lead, Green Lead," Lobo's voice said over tactical. "They'd be a fool to try anything right now, with everything we've got in the air."

"Roger. I ain't relying on their smarts, though," Thor answered. "I seen men die for dumber reasons."

Just then, the milling Greek aircraft formed into two waves of strike aircraft. Just for a moment, the lines of blips ran straight and true across the screen, then the pairs broke off and vectored off in all directions, but primarily heading north."

"Like I said," Thor said. "Blue Flight, take the western flank. Green Leader, you got the east?"

"Roger," Lobo replied, and Thor thought he could hear the adrenaline beating in her voice. "We'll clean up our set them come bail you out."

"In your dreams, sweetheart." Thor punched the Hornet into afterburner, let the sweet howl of the engines seep into his bones. It was time for some payback.

Macedonian Tomcat
1137 local (GMT −2)

"What are they doing?" the pilot snapped. "Ground, I need answers now."

"Stand by—wait, out."

"Wait, out, hell. What the hell are the Americans doing?"

"Weapons tight on American forces," a new voice replied, and the pilot realized it was Xerxes. "All Greek forces are declared hostile, weapons free. But don't target the Americans, not now."

"They're working with the Greeks," the pilot howled. "They bombed us!"

"The rules just changed," Xerxes replied, and his tone of voice indicated that the discussion was concluded. "I say again, weapons tight on American forces. Weapons free on Greek forces. God be with you, my men."

Devil Dog 202
1138 local (GMT −2)

"I'm taking the lead."
"Got it—I got the next one, over."
"I'll back you up on that."
"Ready—Fox two, Fox two."

Thor listened to the other aircraft in his flight announcing their targets and watched their decisions reflected in the symbology on his HUD LINK display. As each pilot designated a radar blip as a target and assigned a missile to it, the LINK reflected it.

Thor noticed a couple of leakers, an inbound pair of fighters veering off further to the west than most of the others. He thumb-clicked a target designation and waited for a split second for the screen to reflect his decision. As soon as it did, he peeled off toward it with his wingman in the high slot.

"Two, you got them?" Thor asked his wingman. "Sixty miles out, just over 600 knots. Looks like they're going high-low."

"That's affirmative," his wingman answered. "I'll take the high, of course, then, give you a hand."

"In your dreams." And why the hell did everyone seems so convinced he needed any help, anyway? First Lobo, now his wingman. Thor had been killing MiGs long before either of them had strapped into their first ejection seats.

The sharp warning buzz of his ESM gear cut off the strain of thought. *Lock, got a lock—not a chance at that range, he's just trying to throw me off. Well, two can play that game.* Thor designated the target and selected an AM-RAAM missile. He waited until his fire control system beeped a cheery acknowledgment, then toggled off the AMRAAM. The light aircraft jolted upward as the missile left the hard point, then arrowed away as its own propulsion system kicked in.

Well, that will at least keep him busy. The AIM—120 (advanced medium range air-to-air missile) was a follow-on to the Sparrow. It was capable of turning on an active seeker head after launch, at either a given time or distance, and guiding independently onto the designated target. It had a blast fragmentation warhead with a smart fuse, and could receive midcourse guidance updates to refine terminal honing track. It was capable of speeds of up to Mach 4, with a range of forty miles. The 345-pound missile carried a fifty-pound warhead.

For just a moment, Thor wished that his beloved Hornet was capable of carrying the Phoenix missile. With its longer range of over one hundred miles, the Phoenix might not always find its target, but it certainly forced the enemy into a defensive mode.

Thor waited until the missile began its approach on him, then he initiated countermeasures. Chaff and flares kicked out of the underbelly of the aircraft, rotating wildly in the air and doing their damnedest to present an attractive target to the incoming missile. Seconds after deploying countermeasures, Thor cut the Hornet into a hard breaking turn. He watched the radar screen, and saw the missile waiver for moment, then settle on the massive cloud of metallic strips and heat sources.

Nothing to it, he thought. The day they come up with a smart long-range missile is the day I'll worry.

The make was now barely forty miles out, just at the outer edge of his AMRAAM engagement envelope. Take the shot now? Or wait a few minutes, give time to close to a distance with increased probability of kill.

But now the enemy Tomcat was climbing, and turning slightly away from him. He could see it in the distance now, fire spouting out of the tailpipes as it streaked straight up in the sky.

Not going to get me that way, asshole. You grab enough altitude, then try to sneak in behind me. Well, two can play that game.

Thor debated for a moment swapping targets with his wingman, and taking the other aircraft, which was now at a lower altitude than his original one. It made sense, since his wingman would have to expend less energy to match the other Tomcat altitude.

But dammit, this was personal. The bastard had *fired* on him, just like he fired on Murphy. And he was going to make them pay for it.

The heavier Tomcat he'd targeted was now below him, turning nimbly for an aircraft of its size. But while the Tomcat might be able to outlast the Hornet in the sky, there was no way the Greek pilot could put his aircraft through the same paces that Thor could with the Hornet. No way at all.

His prey cut hard to the south, sacrificing some altitude for additional speed and tightening the turn. Thor was on him in an instant, barreling down from on high to slip in behind in perfect targeting position. The Tomcat knew he was there—had to know—and started a desperate series of jinks and turns through the aerial killing ground, pumping out flares and chaff like there was no tomorrow.

And indeed there would be no tomorrow for this particular traitor, Thor thought, as he slid the weapons selector switch from AMRAAM to Sidewinder. Not at this range. Not with this weapon.

The nine-foot Mach-two missile exploded off the Hornet's wing, streaking out for the Macedonian. The rollerons stabilized it in the air as the guidance system detected the irresistible lure of the Tomcat's engines pumping heat out its ass. Thor pickled off another missile, wary of the first Sidewinder falling for the alluring flares now gyrating in the air in front of it, but there was no need for it. At this range, the first Sidewinder barely had time to clear Thor's wing before it was trying to climb up inside the Tomcat's tailpipe. Thor broke hard right, barely clearing the massive fireball of detonating warhead, unexpended aviation fuel and metal shards from the Tomcat. The second missile exploded inside the fireball itself, throwing the metal debris out at an even faster speed.

"Scratch one Greek," Thor howled, breaking circuit discipline as well as Marine Corp cool to announce his victory. It was payback, and it felt good. Real good.

The harsh warning of his ESM gear broke off his Rebel yell in midcry. A radio call from his wingman confirmed the danger—"Thor, on your ass! Get the hell out of my line of fire."

Thor dropped the nose of the Hornet down and headed for the deck. In his pursuit to wreak vengeance on the Tomcat, he'd forgotten the primary rule that every aviator learned early on, or paid for with his life—the scan. Even with the HUD, it was possible to get so fixated on a particular target that the pilot forgot to watch the rest of the battle or neglected to fly his aircraft. And Thor had done exactly that. While he'd been stalking the lead Tomcat, the other one had managed to slip by his wingman and turn into Thor, waiting until the right moment to slip in behind him.

"Get him off me, get him off me. He's got a lock!"

"Thor on my mark—break right. *Mark!*" his wingman shouted over tactical.

Thor slammed the Hornet into the hardest turn he'd ever experienced, standing the Hornet on wingtip and continuing his downward path toward the ground. His HUD showed two missiles clobbering the air above him, their tracks marked with elongated speed leaders pointing directly at the Tomcat on Thor's six.

Thor continued the turn through one hundred and eighty degrees, knowing there was no way the Greek Tomcat could keep up. As he reached the reciprocal of his previous course, he pulled the aircraft up. The ground was coming up far too fast, craggy and foreboding in this part of the country. Not that Marines minded flying nap of the earth—hell, they lived for close air support to the guys on the ground!—but doing it at damned near max speed on a steep angle of descent bordered on suicidal. He had to have some altitude, and had to have it now.

"Goddamn it, Thor, you're right back—left, break left! You can't shake him, but you can get the fuck out of the way!"

Suddenly, Thor was fed up. Allies that turned into enemies, allies shooting down Marine fighters, the ribbing from Lobo and his wingman—enough was enough. Yes, by gaining altitude, he'd put himself squarely back in the path of the oncoming Tomcat, right. His wingman should have taken the shot—Thor would find out later why he hadn't. But since he hadn't, it was time for a little on the job training.

"Back off, asshole," Thor snarled. "Let me show you how this is done."

"Thor, you can't—he's almost on you!"

"I said, back off!" Thor nailed the Hornet into the afterburner zone, then cut hard back to the right. The Tomcat—the HUD said it was right behind him, closing hard and fast. The ESM warning buzzer confirmed it.

Joint Chiefs of Staff
The Pentagon
Washington, DC
1005 local (GMT +5)

The chairman of the Joint Chiefs of Staff stared down the folder on his desk. One last problem to wrap up with Greece and Macedonia—and one that should be fairly simple to solve. He turned to the chief of naval operations, who was sitting off to the side on a long, low leather couch that graced one wall. "You know what you have to do."

"Dammit, I don't like it," the CNO said. "It sends the wrong message. We can't have sailors disobeying orders whenever they feel like it."

"Nor can we afford to look like complete and utter idiots to the rest of the world," the chairman observed. He flipped quickly to the pages, searching for anything that would make him change his mind.

In theory at least, he agreed with the chief of naval operations. In theory. But when it came to getting things done in Washington, to managing the health and well-being of the armed services, to representing their interest to congress, to molding the forces into groups that could try to fight the wide range of missions they were given these days, all the while juggling the current perceptions of the American public—well, sometimes theories just didn't cut it.

He knew the chief of Naval operations understood that. He had to, or he would not have risen to his current position. The CNO was right—it did send a wrong message, both to the American public and to the military in general.

But the alternative was even worse.

"This youngster—Airman Smith—he's come up absolutely clean on the extended background investigation I ordered. There's no political agenda, nobody behind him. Not as far as we can tell."

"I know. I saw the same report."

"Then you understand why it has to be this way?"

"Of course I do. It's just that I don't like it. I don't like it one damned little bit."

"A good thing that's not the requisite for this job. Liking everything we have to do, I mean."

The CNO stood, sighed, and headed for the door. He paused, turned back to the chairman, and said, "One day this will come back to bite us in the ass, you know." The chairman nodded. "Better an ass biting in the future than a castration at present, don't you think?"

USS **Jefferson**
1500 local (GMT −2)

Airman Smith stood at attention in the flag passageway. He flexed his knees, trying to ignore the aching starting in his feet. His hands were down by his side, his thumbs along the seams of his dress white uniform. He stared straight ahead, in best boot camp tradition, holding his eyes locked on some point far off in the distance. He had been standing there for thirty minutes, studiously ignoring and being ignored by everyone that walked by.

They probably all knew who he was. They had to, didn't they? He got mail from everywhere around the world, had seen his own face on CNN and ACN, and had read the carefully filtered reports that were allowed on-board USS *Jefferson*.

A hot sense of shame coupled with righteous indignation swept through him. Some letters bothered him more than most, and oddly enough, they were from people who were on his side. For the most part, they congratulated him on standing up to the evil empire that was the United States Navy.

They didn't get it. They just didn't get it. There was nothing wrong with the Navy, nothing at all. Given a choice—a choice he might not have now—he'd stand a Navy for at least twenty years. Hell, maybe even go for thirty. For one fleeting moment a few months back, he even entertained the idea of commission. Being an officer in United States Navy—now that was something to be proud of.

It wasn't going to happen that way now. He tried to do the right thing, follow orders, obey the Greek officer under whose command he'd been placed. But didn't they see how wrong this was for America? Nobody, not one single person, not even the fancy defense attorney they'd appointed to represent him had appeared to understand that.

It was wrong—pure and simply wrong.

The door to the admiral's quarters opened, and a navy captain stepped out. Staring into the officer's stern, impassive face, Airman Smith realized how ludicrous the idea that he could ever have been an officer was.

The master-at-arms standing behind him poked him lightly in the back. "Remember what I told you. Keep your cover on. I want to see you marching smartly up to stand in front of the admiral's desk. Hand salute and sound off. You got that?"

"Yes, Chief."

"Then get going."

Smith's muscles protested at first, but it was a relief to be able to take the weight of one foot at a time, anyway. The navy captain was holding the door open now, and Smith paused for a moment, instinctively uncomfortable at the idea of preceding a senior officer into the admiral's quarters.

"Go on, son. I'm not going to bite you."

Smith's rigid concentration broke. He actually turned his head and stared into the captain's face. Stern, yes, but he saw a trace of something else there. Not friendship, no—just a warmth that didn't make sense. No, the captain wouldn't bite him, but the captain's boss was about to send Smith to a court-martial, and that was close enough.

"Go on," the captain urged, his voice gentle. The master-at-arms poked him in the back again.

Stunned beyond belief, Smith operated on reflex. He stepped into the room, saw the admiral's desk, and made his way forward at a brisk pace, squaring his corners. He stopped two paces in front of the desk, and snapped into a salute position. He waited until the admiral looked up, then said "Airman Smith, reporting as ordered, Admiral."

A single sheet of paper lay on the desk in front of the admiral. Smith was too scared to try reading it upside down. Admiral Magruder gazed at the him for a moment, and pointed at the chair. "Sit down, Smith."

There was dead silence in the room. Of all the things Smith had been expecting, starting with an ass-chewing then working its way up to a physical beating, an invitation to sit down was not among them.

"Go on, it's all right. You and I need to talk." Admiral Magruder looked up at the navy captain and the master-at-arms. "Thank you, gentlemen. That will be all."

Gentlemen. He called the chief a gentleman. Anywhere except here, coming from someone more junior, that would have earned the speaker the traditional, "Don't call me a gentlemen, I know who my parents are," from the chief.

Smith heard them walking away behind him, and the *snick* of a door shutting. He sat rigidly at attention, one hand resting lightly on each leg.

The admiral tapped the paper on the desk in front of him. "You've heard what's happening in the world, haven't you? That our allies the Greeks turned out to be not such good allies?"

"Yes, sir."

"Well, what do you think of that?"

What did he think? Was the admiral actually asking the opinion of a very junior airman? Smith tried to find his voice, tried to think of something that didn't sound stupid to say. "That was bad, Admiral," he finally said, aware as he spoke how lame that sounded. "They shouldn't have done that."

The admiral nodded. "But they did. And it's made a lot of people look very foolish. Powerful people, ones that really hate looking stupid. You can understand that?"

By now Smith's throat was so dry that he could hardly speak. His hands were sweating profusely, and he could feel the moisture bleeding through the cotton pants to his legs. "I guess so, Admiral."

The Admiral nodded once again. "What I'm going to tell you stays between the two of us, you understand. No talking about it with anyone else. Because you're getting a very, very good deal, and it wouldn't take much to screw it up."

Smith couldn't force words out of his throat, so he simply nodded. It was rude, yes, but it was all he could manage.

The admiral leaned forward and fixed him with a stare. "A lot of people probably think you did the right thing," he said. "What do you think?"

"I . . . I . . ." Smith tried to speak, but his voice simply wouldn't work. The admiral stood. Smith jumped to his feet as well. The admiral waved him back into the chair then walked over to a credenza and poured a glass of water. He crossed the room again to stand in front of Smith, towering over the airman like a dark god. "Here. Drink."

Smith's hands were shaking so badly he almost dropped the foam cup. He tried to sip on the cold water, coughed as it went down the wrong pipe, then tried again.

The admiral waited until he'd finished, then asked, "Want more?"

"No, thank you, Admiral." Smith found his voice was working again.

"As I was saying—do you still think you did the right thing?"

Smith thought for a moment, then said, "It seemed like the only thing I could do, Admiral. Things were going wrong, real wrong. I thought about it a lot before, and even more afterward. I guess there might have been ways—maybe request Captain's Mast or something like that. The lawyer said I should have tried that."

Magruder nodded. "But it's always easier to think of alternatives afterward, isn't it?"

"Yes, sir. I guess it is."

"Which brings us to my point," Admiral Magruder continued. "The charges against you are being dismissed. You understand why?"

Dismissed? How in the world could that happen? He had disobeyed a direct order, hadn't he?

"It all goes back to people looking stupid," the admiral said. "If they court-martial you now, your defense attorney is going to thrash this out in every newspaper and on every television station in the world. Bad enough that we made the wrong call on the Greek forces. Even worse to be seen persecuting some young sailor over it. People will think that you knew this would happen and that we're trying to cover it up. So you see, there's not much else they can do to make this go away."

"Yes, Admiral."

"But I don't want you thinking that it was the right thing to do," Magruder continued. "I keep wondering, what if you were on the flight deck while I was getting ready to launch? What if you decided you didn't want to obey an order from the catapult officer? Would you simply walk away? Because that's the heart of the problem, Airman Smith. There are times it is correct to disobey orders, but those times are damned few. If the order's illegal, unlawful, something like that. But what you did was make a judgment call. And I'm not sure that's something we want our airman doing until they get a little bit more senior, you understand?"

From somewhere deep inside, courage trickled back into Airman Smith's heart. "But what if you're on the cat and something was wrong, sir? But everyone else said it was okay, you should launch anyway. What if I was the only one who saw something bad, wrong, something that might kill you?" He hesitated for a moment, searching for an example. "Like I think the steam pressure on the catapult is wrong, that somebody's made a mistake. You would want me to speak up then, wouldn't you, sir?"

A thin look of amusement crossed Tombstone's face. "Indeed I would. So, as you see, sometimes there aren't any simple answers. For what it's worth, I think you were wrong this time. And I also think it took a hell of a lot of courage to take the stand you did. The wrong stand, but a stand nonetheless. So the question is not really what we're going to do with these charges—that's already decided. The question is what the Navy does with you now. What do you want?"

As Tombstone watched the young sailor leave, he tried to decide how he himself felt about the entire matter. Allied missions were nothing new to him, and he wasn't bothered at all by the possibility of working with the Greeks again someday. Indeed, shifting political alliances so often proved that today's enemy was tomorrow's friend. That's why it was always better to plan out the desired end state in any conflict.

But this business about placing U.S. forces under UN command—well, that was another matter entirely. Even a young airman had been able to see that, and had done what he could to stop it.

There was a rap on the door, and Batman poked his head in. "All done?"

Tombstone nodded. "And guess what the kid wants?"

"A medal?" Batman asked sarcastically. He walked into the admiral's cabin, and slumped down in the seat that Smith had just vacated. "I tell you, we lost too many men and women out there. I'm going to be signing too many posthumous recommendations for awards as it is."

"I know. I wonder if we had all followed Airman Smith's path if we could have saved any lives?"

The two admirals were silent for a moment, each considering the possibilities. Each examined his own soul, trying to decide whether or not a young airman had had the courage to do something he wanted to do and hadn't.

Finally, Batman spoke. "For what it's worth, he was right . . . and wrong."

Tombstone nodded. "That's exactly what I told him."

"So what does he want?" Batman asked, returning to Tombstone's original question. "A meritorious promotion?"

"Nope. You'll never guess. He wants to go back to his division and forget about this. That's all."

Batman beyond. "It figures. That's what the good ones always want, isn't it?" And what about you, old friend? What do you want?" Batman's voice was suddenly serious.

"A tougher question, that." Tombstone leaned back in his chair and shut his eyes, letting the tension flow out of his body. "You don't get asked that very often in this business, you know? What it is that you want, I mean."

"I know. If someone asked me the same question, I'd be hard put to think of anything that. Well, maybe the CNO's job. Or the chairman's."

Tombstone opened his eyes. "Is that what you really want, Batman? Or is that just what you're supposed to want? Can you even tell the difference anymore? I wasn't sure I could, not until recently."

"I don't know." Batman sounded honestly puzzled. He spread his hands in a gesture of resignation. "I mean, it's what you're supposed to want, right?"

"But you know what it is that we both really want, don't you?" Tombstone pressed. "We want to be back in the cockpit, lieutenant commanders, maybe even lieutenants. Flying missions, just worried about getting the missiles on target. All the rest of this, the political stuff— none of it mattered back then, did it?"

"You're right about that. But you get promoted, things change. But, sure . . . if I had my choice, I'd be back in the cockpit. Just like you would."

"Well, then. That's not going to happen, we both know that. And as for CNO, that's not in my future anymore. My uncle laid it out for me. But this new job he's given me, sort of troubleshooter admiral—it might turn out to be interesting, you know? I mean, if I can't fly."

"You're getting in more stick time than I am lately," Batman said. "So what's your next mission, Admiral Troubleshooter? Going to solve the energy crisis? Bring about world peace?"

Tombstone laughed. "No, the interesting thing about this is I don't know what I'll be doing next. That's what's good about it, you know? It feels like a weight off my shoulders. No staff, no aircraft. Sure, I miss the flying, but I don't miss the tons of paperwork. And it sounds like I'll be going to some interesting places fixing problems. Batman, I think it's a chance to make a difference, just like I did back then."

Batman stared at him for a long moment. "You always did make a difference, Tombstone. Whether you knew it or not, you made a difference. And in the end, that's all any of us really want, isn't it?"

"I told him no," Tombstone said suddenly. "Airman Smith, I mean. No way he was going back to his division after that. I have something different in mind for him."

Macedonian camp
1800 local (GMT −2)

Pamela scanned the crowd, looking for Xerxes. The last time she'd seen him, he'd been covered with grime and filth, wearing a field uniform he had had on for days. In the days that had passed since her evacuation to *Jefferson*, she'd thought of him often. About maybe going back, exploring what had never really had a chance to grow between them. But there had been interminable briefings, then the wrap-up report to make, not to mention demands

for interviews from every other network in the world. To
her aggravation, she'd been pulled off the story. She was
now part of it, not reporting it.

But wasn't that true about any conflict? Wasn't the media as much a part of it as the forces fighting on the
ground and in the air? Look at the role that CNN had
played in Desert Storm and Desert Shield—today, every
world leader monitored their transmissions continuously.
The international news networks were often the first to
report breaking stories and the initial stages of any conflict.

So how to maintain objectivity if she was by default
part of the story? It was a question she had yet to resolve
in her own mind.

Pamela spotted him then, standing apart from the rest.
He looked oddly uncomfortable in a full dress uniform,
shoes shined and softly gleaming, and new rank insignia
on his collar. A promotion—two grades, she knew, automatically filing the information away.

He was staring at her, a warm smile of welcome curling
around corners of his lips. Freshly shaven, spotlessly at-
tired and rejuvenated by sleep, he looked like a different
man.

She shoved through a throng of competing network reporters, snapping out a harsh, "no comment," and made
her way over to him. A phalanx of security guards kept
the reporters at bay, but the cameras still tracked her, the
hard spotlights blurring her vision.

"It all worked out, didn't it?" she said.

Xerxes's dark eyes burned into her. "It did. Thank you
for your assistance."

She brushed aside his gratitude. "It was Murphy who
made the difference. He was the one who recognized the
man as a member of Arkady's staff. I was just along for
the ride."

Xerxes's stare grew more intense. "Something more than that, I believe," he murmured. He took a small step toward her. "But we have several matters left to resolve, don't we?"

"Such as?"

"You know what I mean."

And she did. Sure, he'd forced her to face the toughest ethical question she'd run across, had challenged her to take sides. In the end, she had, and there was no turning back from that fateful decision.

Could there be something more between them? She found herself hoping desperately that there could be. "Is there somewhere quietly could talk?" she asked. And maybe more than talk, one part of her mind suggested.

"Certainly." His hand closed gently over her elbow. "Come with me." The longing she heard in his voice set every nerve in her body aflame. She let him lead her toward a waiting staff car.

"Pamela!" One voice broke out over the fervor of reporters behind her. "Dammit, Pamela, listen to me."

She turned to see Mike Johnson, the regional news desk supervisor, waving at her. There was a look of urgency on his face.

She turned to Xerxes and saw his face clouding over. "I'll be back in just a second—I've got to see what he wants. He's one of my bosses." Not entirely true, and she could see that Xerxes realized that. Pamela Drake of ACN answered to damned few people, and Mike wasn't one of them.

Still, as regional news desk supervisor, he knew what was going on. And if ACN HQ wanted to track her down, he'd be the person they'd send. "One second." She summoned up her most convincing smile, pulled lightly away from his grasp, and headed toward the cordon of security guards that were holding him back.

"What is it? Make it quick, I'm due for some down-time," she snapped.

"You may not want any—not with this going one." He thrust a message form at her. "Chechnya and the Russians. It's exploding again. And the chemical weapons thing—they've got proof this time. Maybe a thousand dead so far."

Chechnya. She stared down at the message, not opening it. If she started reading it, she would have made her decision. She looked back at Xerxes. He was already in the car, door open, waiting for her.

"We can have you there in four hours," Mike continued. "You're the closest one—you could beat everyone else to the story."

That went without saying, didn't it? She was always first—always.

Still, she hesitated, utterly tempted by the possibility of life without broadcast news. Not without it, maybe, just not taking first place every time. This one would blow over, as they always did. Then there'd be another hot spot, another story. Would it hurt this once to sit it out?

She opened the message. The details were there. She looked up at Mike, her eyes gleaming, already planning on how she'd spin it. Mike started rattling off her itinerary, drawing her away from the crowd and toward a waiting ACN aircraft. He reached out and rested his hand on the spot that had so recently felt Xerxes touch.

Xerxes! She turned back to look at the staff car and saw it was already pulling away. A tidal wave of regret washed over her, replaced almost immediately by a mental list of resources she'd need, contacts, accommodations, the normal preparations for conducting a long siege in a foreign country.

"Bottled water, lots of it." She started listing off her other requirements, including a request for her favorite cameraman, all the while staring at the car disappearing across the tarmac.

TWENTY

Thursday, 1 June

U.S. Naval Academy
Annapolis, Maryland

The Marine staff sergeant stood in front of the ragged formation, surveying the men and women lined up. Supposed to be the cream of the crop, they were, but you sure couldn't tell it from the way they looked now. Long hair, ragged jeans, and smart-ass smirks on most of the faces. Talking, playing grab ass, checking out the chicks, all the normal things that a group of forty teenagers might do when they were strangers.

Mostly teenagers, he amended. Not all of them. Ten of them were coming from the Fleet or the Corps, maybe had some idea of what to expect. They'd have been through boot camp at least. Knew how to march. Must have done something right or they wouldn't have earned one of the few slots at the Naval Academy reserved for fleet sailors and marines.

He'd check their records out first, try them out in some leadership positions and see how they shaped up. Not every enlisted man was cut out to be an officer—but then, not every college grad or senate nominee was, either. At least the priors knew what an officer did.

And there he was, the one he'd been looking for. Hanging back on the last rank, quietly at attention, watching everything without seeming to look at it directly. The staff sergeant let his eyes linger on the young sailor, wondering how much of what he'd heard was true. No matter—he'd find out soon enough for himself. But there was one thing this particular plebe was going to learn right off, and that was that Staff Sergeant Carter was his god for the next two weeks.

Smith felt the staff sergeant looking at him, but kept his eyes caged, staring straight ahead as though they were encased in iron bars. It was a lesson from boot camp that had come back immediately in the first moments that the Marine had barked at them.

He still couldn't believe he was here. Not after . . . not after Greece. Just to have survived without being court-martialed, not losing a stripe, no punishment at all unless you counted the flack he'd had to take from some of the guys on the boat. Especially after they found out about Annapolis.

Admiral Magruder's words came back to him. It was just before they shipped him off, maybe two weeks after everything had been resolved.

"You ask questions. That's good. You're not afraid to make a tough call. Also good. I'm going to make sure you know how to ask the right ones from now on—and how to live with the answers," the admiral had said.

Annapolis.

"You got something on your mind, slimeball?" a voice shouted in his right ear. Smith barely repressed a flinch.

"No, Staff Sergeant Carter."

"Then wipe that shit-eating grin off your face. Now, asshole."

Smith's inadequate attempt earned him five laps around the field. He loved every single one of them.

Glossary

0–3 level: The third deck above the main deck. Designations for decks above the main deck (also known as the damage control deck) begin with zero, e.g. 0–3. The zero is pronounced as "oh" in conversation. Decks below the main deck do not have the initial zero, and are numbered down from the main deck, e.g. deck 11 is below deck 3. Deck 0–7 is above deck 0–3.

1MC: The general announcing system on a ship or submarine. Every ship has many different interior communications systems, most of them linking parts of the ship for a specific purpose. Most operate off sound-powered phones. The circuit designators consist of a number followed by two letters that indicate the specific purpose of the circuit. 2AS, for instance, might be an antisubmarine warfare circuit that connects the sonar supervisor, the USW watch officer, and the sailor at the torpedo launched.

C-2 Greyhound: Also known as the COD, Carrier Onboard Delivery. The COD carries cargo and passengers from shore to ship. It is capable of carrier landings. Sometimes assigned directly to the air wing, it also operates in coordination with CVBGs from a shore squadron.

Air Boss: A senior commander or captain assigned to

the aircraft carrier, in charge of flight operations. The "Boss" is assisted by the Mini-Boss in Pri-Fly, located in the tower onboard the carrier. The Air Boss is always in the tower during flight operations, overseeing the launch and recovery cycles, declaring a green deck, and monitoring the safe approach of aircraft to the carrier.

Air Wing: Composed of the aircraft squadrons assigned to the battle group. The individual squadron commanding officers report to the Air Wing Commander, who reports to the admiral.

airdale: Slang for an officer or enlisted person in the aviation fields. Includes pilots, NFOs, aviation intelligence officers and maintenance officers and the enlisted technicians who support aviation. The antithesis of an airdale is a "shoe."

Akula: Late model Russian-built attack nuclear submarine, an SSN. Fast, deadly, and deep diving.

ALR-67: Detects, analyzes and evaluates electromagnetic signals, emits a warning signal if the parameters are compatible with an immediate threat to the aircraft, e.g. seeker head on an anti-air missile. Can also detect an enemy radar in either a search or a targeting mode.

altitude: Is safety. With enough airspace under the wings, a pilot can solve any problem.

AMRAAM: Advanced Medium Range Antiair Missile.

angels: Thousands of feet over ground. Angels twenty is 20,000 feet. Cherubs indicates hundreds of feet, e.g. cherubs five = five hundred feet.

ASW: Antisubmarine Warfare, recently renamed Undersea Warfare. For some reason.

avionics: Black boxes and systems that comprise an aircraft's combat systems.

AW: Aviation antisubmarine warfare technician, the enlisted specialist flying in an S-3, P-3 or helo USW aircraft. As this book goes to press, there is discussion of renaming the specialty.

AWACS: An aircraft entirely too good for the Air Force, the Advanced Warning Aviation Control System. Long-range command and control and electronic intercept bird with superb capabilities.

AWG-9: Pronounced "awg nine," the primary search and fire control radar on a Tomcat.

backseater: Also known as the GIB, the guy in back. Nonpilot aviator available in several flavors: BN (bombardier/navigator), RIO (radar intercept operator), and TACCO (Tactical Control Officer) among others. Usually wear glasses and are smart.

Bear: Russian maritime patrol aircraft, the equivalent in rough terms of a US P-3. Variants have primary missions in command and control, submarine hunting, and electronic intercepts. Big, slow, good targets.

bitch box: One interior communications system on a ship. So named because it's normally used to bitch at another watch station.

blue on blue: Fratricide. U.S. forces are normally indicated in blue on tactical displays, and this term refers to an attack on a friendly by another friendly.

blue water navy: Outside the unrefueled range of the air wing. When a carrier enters blue water ops, aircraft must get on board, e.g. land, and cannot divert to land if the pilot gets the shakes.

boomer: Slang for a ballistic missile submarine.

BOQ: Bachelor Officer Quarters—a Motel Six for single officers or those traveling without family. The Air Force also has VOQ, Visiting Officer Quarters.

buster: As fast as you can, i.e., bust yer ass getting here.

CAG: Carrier Air Group Commander, normally a senior navy captain aviator. Technically, an obsolete term, since the air wing rather than an air group is now deployed on the carrier. However, everyone thought CAW sounded stupid, so CAG was retained as slang for the Carrier Air Wing Commander.

CAP: Combat Air Patrol, a mission executed by fighters to protect the carrier and battle group from enemy air and missiles.

Carrier Battle Group: a combination of ships, airwing, and submarines assigned under the command of a one-star admiral.

Carrier Battle Group 14: The battle group normally embarked on *Jefferson*.

CBG: *See* Carrier Battle Group.

CDC: Combat Direction Center—modernly replaced CIC, or Combat Information Center, as the heart of a ship. All sensor information is fed into CDC and the battle is coordinated by a Tactical Action Officer on watch there.

CG: Abbreviation for a cruiser.

Chief: The backbone of the Navy. E-7, 8, and 9 enlisted paygrades, known as chief, senior chief, and master chief. The transition from petty officer ranks to the chief's mess is a major event in a sailor's career. Onboard ship, the chiefs have separate eating and berthing facilities. Chiefs wear khakis, as opposed to dungarees for the less senior enlisted ratings.

Chief of Staff: Not to be confused with a chief, the COS in a battle group staff is normally a senior navy captain who acts as the admiral's XO and deputy.

CIA: Christians in Action. The civilian agency charged with intelligence operations outside the continental United States.

CIWS: Close In Weapons System, pronounced "see-whiz." Gatling gun with built-in radar that tracks and fires on inbound missiles. If you have to use it, you're dead.

COD: *See* C-2 Greyhound.

collar count: Traditional method of determining the

winner of a disagreement. A survey is taken of the opponents' collar devices. The senior person wins. Always.

Commodore: Formerly the junior-most admiral rank, now used to designate a senior navy captain in charge of a bunch of like units. A destroyer commodore commands several destroyers, a sea control commodore the S-3 squadrons on that coast. Contrast with CAG, who owns a number of dissimilar units, e.g., a couple of Tomcat squadrons, some Hornets, and some E-2s and helos.

compartment: Navy talk for a room on a ship.

Condition Two: One step down from General Quarters, which is Condition One. Condition Five is tied up at the pier in a friendly country.

crypto: Short for some variation of cryptological, the magic set of codes that makes a circuit impossible for anyone else to understand.

CV, CVN: Abbreviation for an aircraft carrier, conventional and nuclear.

CVIC: Carrier Intelligence Center. Located down the passageway (the hall) from the flag spaces.

data link, the LINK: The secure circuit that links all units in a battle group or in an area. Targets and contacts are transmitted over the LINK to all ships. The data is processed by the ship designated as Net Control, and common contacts are correlated. The system also transmits data from each ship and aircraft's weapons systems, e.g., a missile firing. All services use the LINK.

desk jockey: Nonflyer, one who drives a computer instead of an aircraft.

DESRON: Destroyer Commander.

DICASS: An active sonobuoy.

dick stepping: Something to be avoided. While anatomically impossible in today's gender-integrated services, in an amazing display of good sense, it has been decided that women do this as well.

DDG: Guided missile destroyer.

Doppler: Acoustic phenomena caused by relative motion between a sound source and a receiver that results in an apparent change in frequency of the sound. The classic example is a train going past and the decrease in pitch of its whistle. When a submarine changes its course or speed in relation to a sonobuoy, the event shows up as a change in the frequency of the sound source.

Double nuts: Zero zero on the tail of an aircraft.

E-2 Hawkeye: Command and control and surveillance aircraft. Turboprop rather than jet, and unarmed. Smaller version of an AWACS, in practical terms, but carrier-based.

ELF: Extremely Low Frequency, a method of communicating with submarines at sea. Signals are transmitted via a miles-long antenna and are the only way of reaching a deeply submerged submarine.

Envelope: What you're supposed to fly inside of if you want to take all the fun out of naval aviation.

EW: Electronic warfare technician, the enlisted sailors that man the gear that detects, analyzes and displays electromagnetic signals. Highly classified stuff.

F/A-18 Hornets: The inadequate, fuel-hungry intended replacement for the aging but still kick-your-ass potent Tomcat. Flown by Marines and Navy.

Familygram: Short messages from submarine sailors' families to their deployed sailors. Often the only contact with the outside world that a submarine sailor on deployment has.

FF/FFG: Abbreviation for a fast frigate (no, there aren't slow frigates) and a guided missile fast frigate.

Flag officer: In the Navy and Coast Guard, an admiral. In the other services, a general.

Flag passageway: The portion of the aircraft carrier which houses the admiral's staff working spaces. Includes the flag mess and the admiral's cabin. Normally separated from the rest of the ship by heavy plastic curtains, and designated by blue tile on the deck instead of white.

Flight quarters: A condition set onboard a ship preparing to launch or recover aircraft. All unnecessary person are required to stay inside the skin of the ship and remain clear of the flight deck area.

Flight suit: The highest form of navy couture. The perfect choice of apparel for any occasion—indeed, the only uniform an aviator ought to be required to own.

FOD: Stands for Foreign Object Damage, but the term is used to indicate any loose gear that could cause damage to an aircraft. During flight operations, aircraft generate a tremendous amount of air flowing across the deck. Loose objects—including people and nuts and bolts—can be sucked into the intake and discharged through the outlet from the jet engine. FOD damages the jet's impellers and doesn't do much for the people sucked in, either. FOD walkdown is conducted at least once a day onboard an aircraft carrier. Everyone not otherwise engaged stands shoulder to shoulder on the flight deck and slowly walks from one end of the flight deck to the other, searching for FOD.

Fox: Tactical shorthand for a missile firing. Fox one indicates a heat-seeking missile, Fox two an infrared missile, and Fox three a radar guided missile.

GCI: Ground Control Intercept, a procedure used in the Soviet air forces. Primary control for vectoring the aircraft in on enemy targets and other fighters is vested in a guy on the ground, rather than in the cockpit where it belongs.

GIB: *See* backseater.

GMT: Greenwich Mean Time.

green shirts: *See* shirts.

Handler: Officer located on the flight deck level responsible for ensuring that aircraft are correctly positioned, "spotted," on the flight deck. Coordinates the movements of aircraft with yellow gear (small tractors that tow aircraft and other related gear) from maintenance areas to catapults and from the flight deck to the hangar bar via the elevators. Speaks frequently with the Air Boss. *See* bitch box.

HARMS: Anti-radiation missiles that home in on radar sites.

Home plate: Tactical call sign for *Jefferson*.

Hot: In reference to a sonobuoy, holding enemy contact.

Huffer: Yellow gear located on the flight deck that generates compressed air to start jet engines. Most navy aircraft do not need a huffer to start engines, but it can be used in emergencies or for maintenance.

Hunter: Call sign for the S-3 squadron embarked on the *Jefferson.*

ICS: Interior Communications System. The private link between a pilot and a RIO, or the telephone system internal to a ship.

Inchopped: Navy talk for a ship entering a defined area of water, e.g., inchopped the Med.

IR: Infrared, a method of missile homing.

isothermal: A layer of water that has a constant temperature with increasing depth. Located below the thermocline, where increase in depth correlates to decrease in temperature. In the isothermal layer, the primary factor affecting the speed of sound in water is the increase in pressure with depth.

JBD: Jet Blast Deflector. Panels that pop up from the flight deck to block the exhaust emitted by aircraft.

USS *Jefferson*: The star nuclear aircraft carrier in the U.S. Navy.

leading petty officer: The senior petty officer in a work center, division, or department, responsible to the leading chief petty officer for the performance of the rest of the group.

LINK: *See* data link.

lofargram: Low Frequency Analyzing and Recording display. Consists of lines arrayed by frequency on the horizontal axis and time on the vertical axis. Displays sound signals in the water in a graphic fashion for analysis by ASW technicians.

long green table: A formal inquiry board. It's better to be judged by six than carried by six.

machinists mate: Enlisted technician that runs and repairs most engineering equipment onboard a ship. Abbreviated as "MM" e.g., MM1 Sailor is a Petty Officer First Class Machinists Mate.

MDI: Mess Decks Intelligence. The heartbeat of the rumor mill onboard a ship and the definitive source for all information.

MEZ: Missile Engagement Zone. Any hostile contacts that make it into the MEZ are engaged only with missiles. Friendly aircraft must stay clear in order to avoid a blue on blue engagement, i.e., fratricide.

MiG: A production line of aircraft manufactured by Mikoyan in Russia. MiG fighters are owned by many nations around the world.

Murphy, law of: The factor most often not considered sufficiently in military planning. If something can go wrong, it will. Naval corollary: shit happens.

national assets: Surveillance and reconnaissance resources of the most sensitive nature, e.g., satellites.

NATOPS: The bible for operating a particular aircraft. *See* Envelope.

NFO: Naval Flight Officer.

nobrainer: Contrary to what copy editors believe, this is one word. Used to signify an evolution or decision that should require absolutely no significant intellectual capabilities beyond that of a paramecium.

Nomex: Fire-resistant fabric used to make "shirts." *See* shirts.

NSA: National Security Agency. Primarily responsible for evaluating electronic intercepts and sensitive intelligence.

OOD: Officer of the Day, in charge of the safe handling and maneuvering of the ship. Supervises the conning officer and other underway watchstanders. Ashore, the OOD may be responsible for a shore station after normal working hours.

Operations specialist: Formerly radar operators, back in the old days. Enlisted technicians who operate combat detection, tracking, and engagement systems, except for sonar. Abbreviated OS.

OTH: Over the horizon, usually used to refer to shooting something you can't see.

P-3's: Shore-based anti-submarine warfare and surface surveillance long range aircraft. The closest you can get to being in the Air Force while still being in the Navy.

Phoenix: Long-range anti-air missile carried by U.S. fighters.

Pipeline: Navy term used to describe a series of training commands, schools, or necessary education for a particular specialty. The fighter pipeline, for example, includes Basic Flight then fighter training at the RAG (Replacement Air Group), a training squadron.

Punching out: Ejecting from an aircraft.

purple shirts: *See* shirts.

PXO: Prospective Executive Officer—the officer ordered into a command as the relief for the current XO. In most squadrons, the XO eventually "fleets up" to become the commanding officer of the squadron, an excellent system that maintains continuity within an operational command—and a system the surface Navy does not use.

rack: A bed. A rack-monster is a sailor who sports pillow burns and spends entirely too much time asleep while his or her shipmates are working.

red shirts: *See* shirts.

RHIP: Rank Hath Its Privileges. *See* collar count.

RIO: Radar Intercept Officer. *See* NFO.

RTB: Return to base.

S-3: Command and control aircraft sold to the Navy as an anti-submarine aircraft. Good at that, too. Within the last several years, redesignated as "sea control" aircraft, with individual squadrons referred to as torpedo-bombers. Ah, the search for a mission goes on. But still a damned fine aircraft.

SAM: Surface-to-air missile, e.g., the standard missile fired by most cruisers. Also indicates a land-based site.

SAR: Sea-Air Rescue.

SCIF: Specially Compartmented Information. Onboard a carrier, used to designated the highly classified compartment immediately next to TFCC.

Seawolf: Newest version of navy fast-attack submarine.

SERE: Survival, Evasion, Rescue, Escape; required school in pipeline for aviators.

shirts: Color-coded Nomex pullovers used by flight deck and aviation personnel for rapid identification of a sailor's job. Green: maintenance technicians. Brown: plane captains. White: safety and medical. Red: ordnance. Purple: Fuel. Yellow: flight deck supervisors and handlers.

shoe: A black shoe, slang for a surface sailor or officer. Modernly, hard to say since the day that brown shoes were authorized for wear by black shoes. No one knows why. Wing envy is the best guess.

Sidewinder: Anti-air missile carried by U.S. fighters.

Sierra: A subsurface contact.

sonobuoys: Acoustic listening devices dropped in the water by ASW or USW aircraft.

Sparrow: Anti-air missile carried by U.S. fighters.

Spetznaz: The Russian version of SEALS, although the term encompasses a number of different specialties.

spooks: Slang for intelligence officers and enlisted sailors working in highly classified areas.

SUBLANT: Administrative command of all Atlantic submarine forces. On the west coast, SUBPAC.

sweet: When used in reference to a sonobuoy, indicates that the buoy is functioning properly, although not necessarily holding any contacts.

TACCO: Tactical Control Officer: the NFO in an S-3.

Tactical circuit: A term used in these books that encompasses a wide range of actual circuits used in onboard a carrier. There are a variety of C&R circuits (coordination and reporting) and occasionally for simplicity sake and to avoid classified material, I just use the word tactical.

tanked, tanker: Navy aircraft have the ability to refuel from a tanker, either Air Force or Navy, while airborne. One of the most terrifying routine evolutions a pilot performs.

TFCC: Tactical Flag Command Center. A compartment in flag spaces from which the CVBG admiral controls the battle. Located immediately forward of the carrier's CDC.

Tombstone: Nickname given to Magruder.

Top Gun: Advanced fighter training command.

Undersea Warfare Commander: In a CVBG, normally the DESRON embarked on the carrier. Formerly called the ASW commander.

VDL: Video Downlink. Transmission of targeting data from an aircraft to a submarine with OTH capabilities.

VF-95: Fighter squadron assigned to Airwing 14, normally embarked on USS *Jefferson*. The first two letters of a squadron designation reflect the type of aircraft flown. VF = fighters. VFA = Hornets. VS = S-3, etc.

Victor: Aging Russian fast-attack submarines, still a potent threat.

VS-29: S-3 squadron assigned to Airwing 14, embarked on USS *Jefferson*.

VX-1: Test pilot squadron that develops envelopes after Pax River evaluates aerodynamic characteristics of new aircraft. *See* Envelope.

white shirt: *See* shirts.

Wilco: Short for Will Comply. Used only by the aviator in command of the mission.

Winchester: In aviation, it means out of weapons. A Winchester aircraft must normally RTB.

XO: Executive officer, the second in command.

yellow shirt: *See* shirts.

"Fasten your seatbelt! Carrier is a stimulating, fast-paced novel brimming with action and high drama." —Joe Weber

CARRIER

Keith Douglass

U.S. MARINES. PILOTS. NAVY SEALS.
THE ULTIMATE MILITARY POWER PLAY.

In the bestselling tradition of Tom Clancy, Larry Bond, and Charles D. Taylor, this electrifying novel captures the vivid reality of international combat. The Carrier Battle Group Fourteen—a force including a supercarrier, amphibious unit, guided missile cruiser, and destroyer—is brought to life with stunning authenticity and action in a high-tech thriller as explosive as today's headlines.

_CARRIER	0-515-10593-7/$6.50
_CARRIER 6: COUNTDOWN	0-515-11309-3/$5.99
_CARRIER 7: AFTERBURN	0-515-11914-8/$6.99
_CARRIER 8: ALPHA STRIKE	0-515-12018-9/$6.99
_CARRIER 9: ARCTIC FIRE	0-515-12084-7/$5.99

Prices slightly higher in Canada

Payable by Visa, MC or AMEX only ($10.00 min.), No cash, checks or COD. Shipping & handling: US/Can. $2.75 for one book, $1.00 for each add'l book; Int'l $5.00 for one book, $1.00 for each add'l. Call (800) 788-6262 or (201) 933-9292, fax (201) 896-8569 or mail your orders to:

Penguin Putnam Inc.
P.O. Box 12289, Dept. B
Newark, NJ 07101-5289
Please allow 4-6 weeks for delivery.
Foreign and Canadian delivery 6-8 weeks.

Bill my: ☐ Visa ☐ MasterCard ☐ Amex _____ (expires)
Card# _____
Signature _____

Bill to:
Name _____
Address _____ City _____
State/ZIP _____ Daytime Phone # _____
Ship to:
Name _____ Book Total $ _____
Address _____ Applicable Sales Tax $ _____
City _____ Postage & Handling $ _____
State/ZIP _____ Total Amount Due $ _____

This offer subject to change without notice.   Ad # 384 (3/00)

New York Times Bestselling Author

JOE
WEBER

"One of America's new thriller stars."
—Tom Clancy

❑ **PRIMARY TARGET**
0-425-17255-4/$6.99

❑ **DEFCON ONE**
0-515-10419-1/$6.50

❑ **HONORABLE ENEMIES**
0-515-11522-3/$5.99

❑ **TARGETS OF OPPORTUNITY**
0-515-11246-1/$6.50

Prices slightly higher in Canada

Payable by Visa, MC or AMEX only ($10.00 min.), No cash, checks or COD. Shipping & handling:
US/Can. $2.75 for one book, $1.00 for each add'l book; Int'l $5.00 for one book, $1.00 for each
add'l. Call (800) 788-6262 or (201) 933-9292, fax (201) 896-8569 or mail your orders to:

Penguin Putnam Inc.
P.O. Box 12289, Dept. B
Newark, NJ 07101-5289
Please allow 4-6 weeks for delivery.
Foreign and Canadian delivery 6-8 weeks.

Bill my: ❑ Visa ❑ MasterCard ❑ Amex _____ (expires)

Card# _____

Signature _____

Bill to:
Name _____
Address _____ City _____
State/ZIP _____ Daytime Phone # _____

Ship to:
Name _____ Book Total $ _____
Address _____ Applicable Sales Tax $ _____
City _____ Postage & Handling $ _____
State/ZIP _____ Total Amount Due $ _____

This offer subject to change without notice.   Ad # 861 (5/00)

Think: *The Hunt for Red October*
Think: "The X-Files"
Think: The most original
techno-thrillers of the year.

Greg Donegan

__ATLANTIS   0-425-16936-7/$6.99

Three areas on the Earth's surface defy explanation: The
Bermuda Triangle, the Devil's Sea of Japan, and a small
region of Cambodia. Now, the destructive force behind these
mysteries has been revealed. They invaded before...when they
destroyed Atlantis. *And now they're back.*

__ATLANTIS: BERMUDA TRIANGLE

0-425-17429-8/$6.99

When a nuclear missile is launched from the waters of the
Bermuda Triangle, ex-Green Beret Eric Dane must lead a
team into the depths to confront an enemy which has but one
objective: The total annihilation of all life on Earth.

Prices slightly higher in Canada

Payable by Visa, MC or AMEX only ($10.00 min.), No cash, checks or COD. Shipping & handling:
US/Can. $2.75 for one book, $1.00 for each add'l book; Int'l $5.00 for one book, $1.00 for each
add'l. Call (800) 788-6262 or (201) 933-9292, fax (201) 896-8569 or mail your orders to:

Penguin Putnam Inc.	Bill my: ❏ Visa ❏ MasterCard ❏ Amex _____(expires)
P.O. Box 12289, Dept. B	Card# _____
Newark, NJ 07101-5289	Signature _____
Please allow 4-6 weeks for delivery.	
Foreign and Canadian delivery 6-8 weeks.	

Bill to:
Name _____
Address _____ City _____
State/ZIP _____ Daytime Phone # _____
Ship to:
Name _____ Book Total $ _____
Address _____ Applicable Sales Tax $ _____
City _____ Postage & Handling $ _____
State/ZIP _____ Total Amount Due $ _____

This offer subject to change without notice.   Ad # 891 (3/00)